Little
BLACK
Book

TABATHA VARGO
& MELISSA ANDREA

ALSO BY TABATHA VARGO

THE CHUBBY GIRL CHRONICLES

On the Plus Side
Hot and Heavy—Coming Soon!

THE BLOW HOLE BOYS

Playing Patience (Zeke)
Perfecting Patience 1.5 (Zeke)
Finding Faith (Finn)
Convincing Constance (Tiny)
Having Hope (Chet)—Coming Soon!

WICKED TRINITY

Wicked Fate
Wicked Hope –Coming Soon!

ALSO BY MELISSA ANDREA

DARKNESS DUET SERIES

The Edge of Darkness
The Grace in Darkness
A Darkness Wedding, Novella – Coming Soon
The Beauty in Darkness – Coming Soon

THE DISCOVER SERIES

Flutter
Shatter – Coming Soon

BY TABATHA & MELISSA

A Mortal Sin Novel
The Wrath of Sin
Exposed: Volume 1—Coming soon

Dayna —
Sebastian
says be
naughty?!
— Nargo

—To the sexiest men we know

My name's **SEBASTIAN BLACK**, and I want to buy you. I could have any woman I want, but I choose you.

NO RELATIONSHIP,
JUST SEX.

Here's my offer…
I'll put your name in my **LITTLE BLACK BOOK**, and when I want you, I'll call you. When I call, you're going to come, in more ways than one. It will be mutually pleasurable for both of us.

THERE ARE ONLY TWO RULES:
DON'T EVER DENY ME.
DON'T FALL IN LOVE.

If you do either, I'll remove you from my book and payment stops.

Do we have an understanding?

ONE

SEBASTIAN BLACK

WILMA AND BETTY FUCK LIKE porn stars. I knew from experience, I'd been fucking them for the last four months.

I dug my fingers into chocolate hair and pressed down, until the back of her throat massaged my slippery tip. A flat tongue added pressure underneath my shaft as a dainty hand massaged my sack. A moan pressed against the back of my teeth and Betty giggled on the head of my cock. The loud slurping filled the hotel room, as she sucked me like my come was the answer for world peace.

Strawberry blonde hair moved up and down between Betty's thighs. She moaned over and over again, as Wilma licked and sucked her sweet, pink folds. The wet smacking noises were an aphrodisiac, pushing me faster toward release. It was a beautiful thing to hear and watch—nerve candy for the five senses.

I couldn't hold back any longer—especially not with two sexy women fucking and sucking everything in the room. I let go, coming hard and fast with a string of curse words. Both ladies captured my spray, lapping it up like a fine wine, licking their lips as my personal flavor coated their tongues. It was truly a thing of beauty.

Later, with both women asleep beside me, I peeled back the sheet and crept from the bed. Wilma muttered something in her sleep as I slipped on my pants and buttoned my shirt. My expensive jacket covered my arms and the tie around my neck was perfectly tied. When I left the hotel room, I was thoroughly sated and ready to take on the chaos of New York City at night.

By the time I made it back to the club, Vick was waiting in my office.

"You look like you've been thoroughly fucked and sucked into oblivion," she said, pouring me a glass of my favorite scotch.

"Wilma and Betty..." I hummed. My fingers wrapped around the glass of Johnnie Walker, as I melted into the leather of my favorite chair.

I'd spent many nights with the redhead and brunette. They were my favorite threesome go-to girls. Wilma ate pussy like a starved woman, and Betty sucked dick like she was going for a gold medal in blow jobs.

"I'm surprised you're not bored with them yet," Vick snorted.

She pulled off her jacket and threw it across the back of the black leather couch in my office.

"Not yet." A grin stretched my face and I swished my scotch around, making the ice clink against the sides of the glass.

Victoria, a.k.a. Vick, was my assistant, and had been for the last six years. We grew up in foster care together, and she was my right-hand man. We covered each other's asses when shit got out of control, which it tended to do when we were younger. She was the only person in the world who knew every detail of my life—the biggest hard-ass I knew—and the only woman in my life I hadn't fucked.

It wasn't that Vick wasn't attractive, she was sexy in a *Laura Croft: Tomb Raider* kind of way; it's just she was more like a sister to me. I didn't have any siblings. Hell, I didn't have *any* family, so our relationship was special, even if I never told her so.

Men found her attractive. Her long, dark hair was always pulled into a tight ponytail and her wardrobe consisted of black. She had pouty lips that were formed into a permanent frown, and big cerulean eyes. Vick made her resting bitch face look sexy—like she was minutes away from slinging a whip and fucking you senseless.

I kicked lots of ass over her growing up. Then, I ran away from the system, leaving her to fend for herself. It killed me when I found out she'd earned money selling her ass during the years we were apart. Needless to say, when I became the rich fuck I am today, I pulled her along for the ride. I made sure she'd never have to lie on her back for money again.

"Any luck finding your Jessica Rabbit?" she asked, fingering the night's paperwork, putting together figures.

Tilting the glass to my lips, the smooth liquid slid down my throat, igniting a burn in my chest. I set the glass on a table and stood. "Jessica Rabbit is a myth. There are no Jessica's in the world, but if I find one, you'll be the first to know," I winked. "What's it looking like?"

She held up a paper with a smile. "Tonight was good. Ten grand more than last night. Looks like the article in the *New York Times* paid off. Of course, the fact they named Clive's the 'hottest new nightclub in New York' didn't hurt."

I took the paper from her and looked down at the percentages. She was right. Clive's had brought in almost double the revenue from the night before. The fact I was banking so much on a weeknight meant I had single-handedly built Clive's into a success.

I'd come a long way from the seventeen-year-old punk I used to be. I owed it all to Clive... the nightclub, and the man himself.

When I was nineteen, I came face to face with the end of Clive's shotgun. What could I say? I was into some crazy shit. He could have turned me in. Hell, he could have killed me, but instead he gave me a job at his hole-in-the-wall bar and taught me everything he knew about the business. He became like a father to me. The only father I knew, since mine had dropped me off on a set of church steps with a shitty diaper wrapped around my ass.

Sadly, Clive died when I was twenty-two, leaving me the bar and some old stock and bond certificates. I sat on those certificates as I worked the bar and lived in the tiny apartment above it. It wasn't until years later, I found out those certificates were worth millions.

I took that money, opened my own place, naming it after the man who gave me everything, and became the twenty-nine-year-old success I was today. I rubbed elbows with celebrities, and some of the wealthiest men I knew became rich due to my advice.

Women threw themselves at my cock, like it was made of pure gold. I didn't turn anyone away. Until eventually, I got bored with the same tedious women and their dull positions. Taking matters into my own hands, I started a little black book.

Inside my book was a buffet of women who were willing and ready for my call. Each one specialized in something different, and each one was named after a cartoon character of my choosing.

"Okay. Good work, Vick. Go home and get some sleep. It's almost three in the morning. If we're doing this well on a Thursday, you'll need tons of rest for the weekend." I set the papers on my desk and turned toward the door. "Also, hire a new waitress. When I was coming through earlier, I saw a few tables waiting for service."

"I'm on it," she said, turning the desk lamp off and heading my way.

Locking the office door behind us, I walked her to the black Chevy Camaro I bought for her birthday two years before. It wasn't the most expensive car, but it was what she chose.

"See you tomorrow," I said, shutting her car door.

Going back into the club, two bartenders were still inside closing up. The lush crimson and black décor made the place look dark and sexy. Once the lights went out, you could barely see your hand in front of your face. The walls were wrapped in blood-red swag and black chandeliers hung from the ceiling like sinister diamonds of light. The twenties-style pieces placed throughout the room, topped it off. It was designed exactly as I requested.

"Goodnight, Mr. Black." The petite blonde bartender said when I walked by the bar.

"Lock it up tight," I instructed.

Taking two stairs at a time, I moved quickly toward my apartment above the club. Not many people knew I lived and worked in the same building, but the paranoia that came with teenage years full of drug slinging, kept me from leaving the club unattended.

Once inside, I stripped down and went for a hot shower. Eight, strategically placed, shower heads beat my body with steaming water. It felt good to wash away my earlier encounter with Wilma and Betty. Sighing out loud, I knew this would be the most relaxing part of my night, as the ability to have a good night's sleep had eluded me for years. My history took away all the peaceful moments in my life. Sleeping through the night like a normal person wasn't going to happen anytime soon. A couple hours here and there was all I needed.

Before going to bed, I flipped through my book and examined the names—ranging anywhere from Disney and Looney Tunes, all the way to Hanna-Barbera. My eyes landed on the B's and then bounced around until the name Bambi caught my attention. Losing myself in a wet and ready woman always kept the past from rushing up on me... and it had been weeks since I'd lost myself between Bambi's thighs. Maybe a change of pace was what I needed. It was time to give her a call tomorrow.

I STOOD AND ZIPPED UP my slacks. Shoving my arms into my shirt, I pulled the collar close and buttoned each button quickly.

"What's the rush?" The seductive voice came from behind me.

Turning around, my eyes devoured a pair of long, shapely legs. The perfectly shaved V between her thighs glistened and reminded me that not five minutes before, it had milked me dry. She sat up and put on the purple, silk panties I'd bought her a few months before.

"This will be our final visit," I muttered dismissively, tying my tie.

She was developing feelings and I wasn't down for that shit, at all. Touchy feely non-sense was something I wanted nothing to do with. Also, I was bored with her, which I remembered was the main reason I hadn't contacted her for weeks.

She was a bad investment, who had taken an obscene amount of time getting me off. That was all the proof I needed. Because of her I was going to have to get a quick lunch, verses my usual at Red's Lounge.

"Excuse me. May I ask why?" she questioned, slipping silk bra straps over her shoulders.

Her name wasn't actually Bambi, but I never asked for their names. They were irrelevant. I only needed to know their bodies, and they only needed to know mine. I gave my women a name that suited them. For this chick, Bambi was a perfect fit. Every time she wanted something she'd look up at me with big, pleading, doe eyes. It was annoying.

When I told her Bambi was her new name, she smiled like it was a compliment. Little did she know, she was just a fill-in until something better came along—my myth, my Jessica Rabbit. She didn't even get full payment, and thought the grand I paid her each week was worth what I made her do in bed.

I plucked my jacket from the back of the chair and stepped around the bed.

"Wait a minute. Let's talk about this." She whined, hopping on one foot, attempting to put on her sex kitten heels.

The hotel room door slammed in her face before she could stop me. I adjusted my tie and pressed the button on the elevator. An aggravated sigh pushed past my lips and I shook my head when the door opened behind me.

Thankfully, the elevator opened at the same time. She gawked at me with those big doe eyes, clad in only a bra, skirt, and heels. As the elevator doors closed, I could see a mascara-filled tear sliding down her cheek. It disgusted me.

Reaching into my pocket, I pulled out my book and opened it. Licking my thumb, I shuffled through the pages until I came to Bambi's. I drew a thick black line through her name and number, and then called to have the payments to her account stopped.

STANDING IN FRONT OF THE two-way mirror in my office, my eyes admired the crowd of dancers below. This was mine. The building, the club, everything was mine. It was the only thing I truly loved. The only thing I would never get tired of.

The beat of the music shook the glass and I pressed my palms against it to feel the vibrations.

The door to my office opened, allowing the music to come in and blend with the sensations running through my fingers. I didn't bother turning around, I knew who it was. She shut the door behind her, making the room silent again.

"So I tried to pay my monthly mortgage today, but the lady told me I no longer *had* a mortgage. Apparently, my condo has been paid in full. Know anything about that?" Vick inquired, accusation dripping from her tone.

I was hoping she'd never bring it up. With my back to her, a knowing grin tugged at the side of my mouth. "Nope." I quickly changed the subject. "Any deep pockets out tonight?"

She didn't push the whole money situation and I was glad. I never wanted to be put on a pedestal as some financial hero, and I could always count on Vick to keep me grounded.

"Definitely some deep pockets." I heard the smile in her voice. "You coming down? There's a few red-carpet walkers asking for you."

Spending the night in a VIP room full of celebs used to be exciting, but not so much anymore. I'd slept for shit the night before—nightmares waking me every time I closed my eyes. I wasn't feeling it. But like any other good businessman, I knew I had to make an appearance—act the part of the rich club owner. It was total bullshit. I knew it, and Vick knew it, too.

"Yeah. Let them know I'll be down in a bit."

Vick didn't respond, but the door opened and closed again.

Turning away from the mirror, I grabbed my coat and buttoned it up as I took to the steps. I was instantly hit with loud music and red lights when I stepped onto the main floor.

I moved along the outside wall toward the bar for a drink. I'd need the good shit, if I wanted to make it through the night. With my back to the bar, I had a front row view of the sweaty bodies grinding against each other. The distinct smell of alcohol and sexual desire floated around the room.

Once I got the attention of one of my bartenders, I nodded at him, signaling I was ready for my first drink. I didn't have to wait long before a glass was sliding in my direction. Turning, I leaned against the bar and took in the room, sipping my drink. My eyes bounced from one half-naked woman to the next.

And then I saw her.

Long waves of crimson fire shimmered in the lights, as she worked her way across the room. She turned and smiled at a table full of guys who were talking to her and making obscene gestures. Her thick-lipped smile kindled something deep in my groin—a tiny spark ignited and made my balls ache. Long lashes skimmed her cheeks, amplified by the eye-batting she gave the guys before walking away.

When she turned my way, I saw the name *Clive's* stretched across her full chest. The yellow T-shirt material clung to her breasts and I could see the white lines of a simple bra underneath. She was oblivious to her seductiveness, which made her all the more appealing.

Maneuvering around the room, she turned from one side to the next, giving me different views of her curves. She obviously worked for me, but had no business in a place like this. Her face full of makeup wasn't fooling anyone. Her inner beauty shone through in the way she moved. Even with the tight shirt and short shorts, she stood out. She was a bright, white beacon of beautiful innocence amongst all the sin swimming around the club.

She was pure perfection, with flawless, ivory skin and round hips that begged for my touch. She was exquisite, she was timeless, and little did she know, she was as good as mine.

TWO

ROSSLYN HARRIS

"I 'M SORRY FOR YOUR LOSS."** Ms. Ellen took my hand. Her skin was paper-thin, allowing me to see a grid work of purple and blue veins. "She's in a better place now, my dear."

I stared at her age spots in a daze, nodding, but unable to speak.

Ms. Ellen sang in the choir at my grandma's church. I'd met her when I was ten, and my one-year-old brother, Kyle, and I had gone to live with my grandma. That was twelve years ago—right after the world had come crumbling down around me.

My world was once again falling apart. Gran had gone to be with the Lord. She'd put up a good fight, but in the end, her body was just too old to hang on anymore. I'd taken care of her for most of my life, and she always provided for me and Kyle. But now she was gone, and I was left with a thirteen-year-old to support, with no job in sight.

After the funeral, and once everyone left the house, it was just me and Kyle.

"Are we going to be okay, Roz?" Kyle was helping me pack large amounts of food into the refrigerator.

Bringing food to the house after a funeral was what people did. I didn't understand it, and I wasn't sure what I was going to do with three big bowls of potato salad, but the people kept coming with their arms full of covered dishes. I mean, how many people did they think lived here, exactly?

"We'll be fine. We meet with the attorney tomorrow. I'm sure Gran left us a little something to keep us afloat until I get a job." I wiped at the counter with a wet cloth and sighed. "Why don't you go upstairs and get ready for bed? I'll be up in a bit."

I could barely look at him. I knew what I'd see if I did. Brown hair that he insisted on keeping in his face, and green eyes full of worry. No matter how many times I'd assured him we'd be okay, the truth was, I wasn't so sure.

"Okay." He moved toward the stairs and turned around. "Hey, Roz?"

"Yeah?"

"Can I sleep in your room tonight? It's going to be weird with her gone."

My heart shattered. I'd gone the entire day without crying, to be strong for Kyle, but I could slowly feel my façade fading. I nodded my head and held the tears back, knowing they would fall the minute he was gone. "Sure, kid."

As soon as I heard him hit the top of the stairs, I let the tears go. The lump sitting in my throat cleared as the tears continued to fall and the weight on my chest lifted a bit.

"MISS HARRIS, I HATE TO tell you this, but there's nothing left in your grandmother's estate," Ms. Brighton said.

In my opinion she was too young to be a lawyer. Yet for such a young woman, she was dressed like a sixty-year-old. Her gray suit was outdated and her pants were too high. When she sat, the bottoms rose up, showing off hose with runs in them and scuffed heels.

She clicked the top of her pen over and over again, making me want to pull my hair out.

"Excuse me?" I was sure I'd heard her wrong.

"As per your grandmother's will, all monies remaining will go to paying off her debts. Anything after that was to go to you and your brother. However, there wasn't even enough to pay everything off." Again, she continued with the incessant pen clicking. "You are getting the Oldsmobile, though. So that's good, right?"

The Oldsmobile, which was almost as old as my grandma, was all mine. *Joy.* I got to keep the rust bucket that sucked up too much gas and threw out white smoke when pressure was applied to the gas pedal.

My eyes were locked on Ms. Brighton's pen. The clicking ran through my brain and pushed away all the thoughts coming to consume me.

"What about the house?" My voice was a broken whisper. My legs were trembling with nerves, letting me know I was going to have a hard time leaving. If I could even stand.

Ms. Brighton's expression spoke volumes. "Unfortunately, the bank will take possession of the house in thirty days. I'm so sorry." Finally she set the pen down and crossed her fingers. "Is there a family member you can stay with until you get your affairs in order?"

I shook my head in shock. "No."

Looking through the small window on Ms. Brighton's door, I saw Kyle. He was sitting in the chair where I'd left him. His pencil was moving lazily over the pages of the notebook he'd brought with him. "Our parents died twelve years ago. We have no one."

"Oh..." her eyes dropped toward her desk and she shifted uncomfortably in her chair. The pen clicking started once more. Only this time it was in fast nervous clicks. "I'm sorry, Ms. Harris it... *sounds like you're shit out of luck.*"

Okay, so she didn't *actually* say that, but I knew that's what she was thinking. She was quick to end the meeting and usher me and my homeless brother out of her office, which was fine by me. After her crushing news, I felt like the drab décor was slowly suffocating me.

When Kyle and I stepped out of the building, the New York air wasn't any less smothering, but I welcomed the soothing breeze anyway. Digging into my pocket for the last of my change, I gave it to Kyle and watched as he ran off to buy a soda and a pretzel from a little food cart.

Sitting down on the concrete steps, I dropped my head in my hands and breathed in the strong exhaust-filled air and let the New York sounds drown away my despair. I wouldn't fall apart right now. I couldn't. Kyle didn't need to know how bad things were.

"So did Gran leave us a fortune?" Kyle joked when he found me face down on the steps.

I looked up at his innocent face and smiled, squinting against the afternoon sun. In that moment, I vowed to do whatever I had to do to make sure Kyle didn't have to grow up before his time. He'd already lost so much, I wouldn't let him lose his childhood like I had.

"Define fortune," I stood and ruffled his hair.

He made a low growling sound, pushing at my hand and proceeded to fix his hair.

Looking up at me he became serious. "Everything's going to be alright, Roz. You always take care of everything."

I smiled through tears threatening to fall. "We'll get through this, kid. We always do."

As much as I wanted to tell him everything was going to be fine, I didn't know how bad things we're going to get and I wouldn't lie to him.

I HELD KYLE'S HAND ON the ride back to Gran's house. I'm not sure what I was thinking, his hand was almost as large as mine now. And even though I was sure he hated holding my hand, he didn't let go.

In fact, he said nothing, even though I knew there were a million questions swimming around in his head. After his comment at the attorney's office, I wasn't sure I could speak to him without breaking down, so I was grateful he stayed silent.

Once we got home, I made my famous mac n' cheese and hotdogs. We'd eaten this so many times over the last few years I couldn't stand the smell anymore, but it was Kyle's favorite, so I endured it. I'd been almost depressed when we'd run out of funeral food.

He helped with the dishes before running up to his room to slip on his headphones and doodle in his notebook. He was too old to be tucked in and he didn't need my help getting things ready for school anymore.

After a quick clean up around the house, I checked on Kyle and then spent the night in my room, trying to figure out what the hell I was going to do.

No way could I afford to keep the house, even if I did find a job. It was a huge, five-bedroom home, and Kyle and I didn't need all that space. A small two-bedroom would suffice. Luckily, I got to keep everything in the house, which meant I wouldn't need money to furnish the new place.

Once my eyes began to get heavy, I knew the day's events were to blame for my exhaustion and I was all too happy to end the day. I turned toward the lamp beside my bed and saw the college pamphlets on the end table.

The sight of them made me want to cry, but I picked them up anyway. A couple of months ago when Gran started to look like she was healthy enough for me to not be around all the time, I'd looked into going to a community college.

After our parents' deaths went unsolved, I felt denied the justice Kyle and I deserved. I hated that feeling. I hated the unknown and didn't want another family to suffer the way Kyle and I had. I needed the closure that was rightfully mine.

I wanted to dedicate my time to criminal law and try to make a difference. It sounded naïve and cliché to think I could change anything when it came to the criminal system, but I could try.

I sighed. It didn't matter either way now. College was definitely out of the question and having these forms was only going to depress me further. I dumped the forms into the trash and hit the light. Ten minutes later, I fell into a fitful sleep.

I SAT STRAIGHT UP IN bed, gasping for air. Same nightmare, different night. Sweat trickled down my neck and into my nightgown. I pulled the fabric from my skin and tried to catch my breath.

It'd been a while since I'd had a nightmare about the night my parents died, but with everything going on around me, it wasn't a big surprise.

"You okay, Roz?" Kyle's voice came from behind my bedroom door.

His voice was changing. Every now and again it would crack or squeak and he would sound older for a few brief seconds. He was slowly becoming a man, and I silently wished Dad could be there to teach him the ways of all things manly.

"Yeah. Just a nightmare. You can come in," I waited for the door to open. "What are you doing up?" I checked the clock by my bed for the time.

"I heard you making noises in your sleep." He came across the room and sat on the end of my bed.

"I'm sorry I woke you. You have school tomorrow and I have job hunting to do. We both need our sleep."

"It's okay. I wasn't sleeping all that great anyway."

I patted the bed beside me and Kyle climbed under the covers. Turning on my side, I wrapped my arm around him. "Goodnight."

"Night."

"**YOU KNOW, I COULD GET** you a job at Clive's. It pays well and you'd be home all day since you wouldn't have to be at work until six." Trish said.

She was my only friend. Growing up, I never had time to go out and meet people because I was always taking care of Gran. Trish was the only person in school who made time for me and understood I couldn't go out partying on the weekends.

We'd been friends since tenth grade and she still looked exactly the same. Same blonde hair, same blue eyes, and same perfect body. My own body had started to grow since high school. My butt was a little wider and my boobs, a little heavier. I still had my tiny waist, which was good, but I hated having to go up a size in my jeans just because my hips were so curvy.

"I'm not working at a bar. Plus, who would watch Kyle at night?"

"Kyle's thirteen, he can watch himself, Roz. I was staying home alone much earlier than that. You'll be there when he gets home, and you can make sure he gets dinner, or help him with his homework, or whatever. Then he can get ready for bed and go to sleep. Buy him one of those little pre-paid phones so he can call if something happens, and tell him to lock the doors."

Trish talked as she flipped through a magazine. It was obvious she never had to worry about another person besides herself. I couldn't just leave Kyle at home all alone. Especially not now. He was already having a hard time sleeping at night, no way could he stay home alone.

"I can't even afford a cell for myself. How would I be able to afford one for Kyle? It's out of the question. Keep thinking. There has to be some places hiring around here."

She sighed. "Fine. We'll keep looking."

I knew she was annoyed, but she'd just have to deal with my decision. I wasn't going to budge.

Every day, after dropping Kyle off at middle school, I'd spend the day putting in applications everywhere. I didn't have a cell, so I'd checked the answering machine every afternoon with hopes of someone calling me back. I'd already gotten the phone bill, which I couldn't afford to pay, so I needed a job like yesterday.

Two weeks later, there had been no calls, and our house phone had been disconnected. I was desperately trying not to spiral into despair, but the water and electricity were the next to go—not to mention, we only had two more weeks before we had to be out. I was at the end of my rope, and desperate.

Kyle and I searched for boxes at all the local stores and packed the belongings we wanted to keep. Everything else, we sold. By the time the bank was taking the house, we managed to move our belongings into Trish's parent's garage.

We each packed a suitcase for everything we'd need until a place was found. As sad as it was, and as bad as it broke my heart, we moved into the Oldsmobile.

I was sure Trish would have given us a place to stay had I told her about our predicament, but I was too proud. She was my age, and worked and lived on her own. I was ashamed I couldn't do the same.

The little bit of money we had from everything we sold would get us through. It paid for gas and food and really, that was all we needed until I could get us into an apartment.

As we pulled into the parking lot of his school, I grabbed his arm before he could make his hasty exit.

I turned worried eyes on him and gave him a warning. "Remember, Kyle, don't tell anyone about our living arrangements. It won't be like this for long, I promise. Just bear with me, okay?"

"I'm not going to say anything. I'm not an idiot, Roz." He smiled sweetly at me. "We'll find something. I told you, I'm not worried."

I smiled at him as he got out of the car, but I felt low— lower than low—and I knew what needed to be done. I had to put Kyle first, and that meant I was going to Trish to beg for a job.

I got out the car and tripped over the sidewalk going to Trish's front door. She lived in a nice apartment complex. It was nothing I could afford as of yet, but with her help, I was hoping to. I knocked on the door ten times before she finally answered it. Her eyes were thick with sleep, and her hair was wildly sticking up in odd directions.

"Someone better be dead," she rasped.

"No one's dead, but I need your help." I stepped around her and sat on the couch.

She sighed, closed the door, and turned to me with her hands on her hips. "You do realize I just went to bed like an hour ago, right?" She dramatically fell onto the couch beside me and pulled a throw blanket over her legs.

"I'm sorry, but I need that job at Clive's. I know you've already done a lot for us. And I really appreciate you and your parents giving me a storage space and helping me and Kyle load it all up, but I need one more favor and I promise I'll never ask for anything again."

"Fine. Vick is looking for another waitress. I told her about you. Just show up this afternoon around five. I'm pretty sure she'll give you the job," Trish slurred. Her eyes slowly began to close.

"Just like that? I don't have to interview or anything?"

"Wear a pair of the shortest shorts you can find. That should get you right in."

I walked out of Trish's apartment with a pair of the shortest shorts I'd ever seen and a sinking feeling in my stomach. It wasn't ideal, but it was money. At that point, I would have done whatever I had to do to make sure Kyle had a roof over his head and food in his stomach.

"CAN YOU START IMMEDIATELY?"

Vick was nice, but to the point. There was no sugar coating, and she obviously didn't believe in small talk or getting to know you. She was pretty, but didn't flaunt it. I got the impression she'd rather you fear her.

"Yes." I tried to sound self-assured, but I couldn't have felt more out of place if I tried. "I can start this weekend if..."

"Good," she interrupted as if I hadn't been talking. "I could use someone tonight."

She slipped off the barstool to the cocktail table we'd been sitting at and left me behind. I frowned before I realized she wanted me to follow her. Like a good little lap dog, I hoped off my stool and caught up to her with quick steps.

"Tonight?" There was no keeping the slight tremor from my voice this time. "But don't I need some kind of training? I've never..."

Vick stopped and turned abruptly, causing me to skid to a halt. She crossed her arms and stared me down like she was an alpha and wanted me to submit. I almost did.

"You need training to carry drinks around?"

Well when she put it like that. "No," I said firmly, but I felt my cheeks heat up.

"You said you could start immediately and I need someone tonight. Do you want the job or not?"

"Yes."

The word flew out of my mouth, even though I knew starting right at that moment was a bad idea. I still didn't know what I was going to do with Kyle. We were living in a car for God's sake. And Clive's was in the middle of the city. Not the best place to leave a thirteen-year-old, in the car... alone.

But we'd make do. We always did.

"Okay then." She dropped her arms and gave me a once over. "I'll get you an outfit and I'll have one of the girls show you around after you're done changing."

I panicked when I thought of Kyle. "But..." Her impatient sigh stopped me and I bit my tongue. "I just have to make a phone call."

"Make your call and I'll have one of the girls bring you an outfit. Find me when you're dressed."

I nodded and she turned to leave.

Before she got too far, she turned around again. "Tell Mike, the bartender, to let you use the phone."

"Thank you," I said to her retreating back. Turning around I saw a muscular guy behind the bar. "Are you Mike?"

When he looked at me, he flipped his head to the side to move the blond hair hanging in his eyes. Leaning onto the bar, face inches from mine, he smiled big enough to show teeth.

He'd obviously been going nuts with the steroids. His arms were easily the size of my head and his shirt could barely contain the muscles trying to pop free from his chest. He reminded me of the Hulk just before he turned green.

"Lucky for me, I am," he winked.

I wanted to roll my eyes at his corny one-liner, but instead I forced a smile. "Great. Vick told me to find you so I could use the phone?"

He didn't say anything as he pulled the cordless phone from beneath the bar and handed it to me.

"You work here?" he asked, when I took the phone.

"Started... right now, actually."

"Glad to hear it."

I dialed Trish's number and gave him another forced smile.

When she answered, I gave her a quick rundown of my conversation with Vick and while I hated to ask her for another favor, I had no choice.

"Will you chill, Roz?" she snapped. "Kyle and I are practically BFF's." I could hear Kyle's laughter in the back and suddenly wondered if leaving him with Trish had been a good idea.

She was easily every teenage boy's wet dream and no matter how much I didn't want to think about it, I'm sure she had some kind of effect on Kyle.

"Just don't teach him any bad habits," I warned.

"Never. Look, I'll get him some McDonald's and he can stay here tonight while we work. He'll be fine, Roz."

In the background I heard Kyle echo Trish's words and knew I had no other choice. I sighed and agreed to her plan.

I hated to do it, even though I was assured he would be fine. Not to mention, Trish was nice enough to leave her cell with him, since it was his first night alone.

I was saved from having to engage in anymore conversation with Mike when one of the Clive's girls brought me a uniform—at least I think it was supposed to be an outfit. When I unfolded the new shirt and shorts they were more like underwear.

Ten minutes later, I found Vick and stood there while she stared me down like I was a piece of meat.

"Turn around," She ordered, and I did a full turn. "Let me..."

She took a step closer and grabbed the material of the shirt at my ribs. Then she adjusted it to show more of my breasts. It was the most uncomfortable thing I'd ever been through, but it got me the job.

"Perfect. Now find Mike again and he'll give you the run down. Have fun," she taunted before turning away.

The first night was brutal. I dropped multiple drinks and bumped into customers. I almost slipped and broke my leg, and a few times I got the order wrong. Vick didn't believe in training, she believed in learning by experience, which meant I was thrown straight into a busy Friday night. I failed miserably.

Two hours in, I was sure I owed Clive's more money than they owed me, but I wasn't going to give up. I needed this job, and I wasn't about to let it slip through my fingers—like half of the drinks I attempted to serve.

"Just keep smiling, Roz. The guys like you. You have that innocent thing working in your favor," Trish said, as she slid beside me with a full tray.

"What innocent thing?" I asked loudly over the music.

She turned and winked at me before disappearing into the crowed.

Was I missing something completely obvious? I thought about this while I waited for the bartender to load me down with my order. The lights above were too bright—the music, too loud. I reached up and swiped at the sweat coating my forehead. I was exhausted.

The work shirt Vick had given me was two sizes too small and squished my boobs together. It didn't help that I'd spilled several drinks down my front, giving everyone a view of my bra.

"She's right. Your innocence works for you." A deep voice sounded from beside me, startling the crap out of me. He was so close, he didn't have to scream over the music.

I could feel his body heat against my bare skin, and it sent chills down my body. Peeking over at him, I caught a glimpse of a stylish black suit, before turning away and waiting for the bartender. I didn't see his face, but it didn't matter what he looked like. I needed to focus on my new job, not the men in the club.

It was obvious I was ignoring him and I heard his deep chuckle when the music paused before the next song started.

"You're holding your tray wrong. That's why you keep spilling your drinks." This time I felt his warm breath against my neck. "Don't use your palm, use your fingertips."

Without him knowing, I adjusted my fingers beneath the tray and instantly felt the extra control my fingertips provided. I turned to look at him and was met with the most gorgeous man I'd ever laid eyes on.

His soft blue eyes were a deep contrast to his tanned skin and dark hair, which was styled in a strategic mess. He ran his fingers through it, pushing some strands out of his eyes. If that wasn't enough, he grinned at me, showing off an adorable set of dimples. Perfect white teeth shined back at me, as he bit his bottom lip.

I almost swore out loud. Quickly, I turned my eyes away from him, before I embarrassed myself. "Thanks," I said out of the corner of my mouth.

He was already gone. I didn't see him leave, but I felt it. The side of my body cooled and the ear-splitting sounds of the music came back in full force.

Mike swept by and set the drinks I needed on my tray. He winked at me like he was sure I was interested in him. His cockiness was in vain because he couldn't have been more wrong.

I didn't spill another drink that night. By the time I was cashing out my tips, I was exhausted and in desperate need of a shower.

"So what do you think?" Trish asked. She was picking up old beer bottles and empty glasses from one of her tables.

The room was empty, except for a few workers who were cleaning up. No one was looking at me, but I couldn't help but feel eyes all of over me. Something about being in Clive's after it closed was unsettling.

"Earth to Roz... What. Do. You. Think?" she asked louder, signing to me like I was deaf.

I wanted to say I'd never come back, but after counting all the cash I had from tips that night, I knew I couldn't turn the job down.

"I'll be back tomorrow night."

THREE

SEBASTIAN

I STOOD AT THE TWO-WAY mirror, looking down into the empty club. A few of the workers, including the new girl, cleaned and chatted.

She bent over a table with a wet cloth and wiped it down. Her shorts rode up and the bottom of her ass cheeks popped out. My cock grew hard just looking at her. I hadn't reacted that way over a woman in a long time, and I wasn't sure I could be the patient man I needed to be, in order to claim her as mine.

She was different. I knew propositioning her right off the bat was going to be a bad idea, but I didn't care. I didn't want to get to know her and I didn't want her to get to know me.

First things first, I had to fire her. I never mixed business with pleasure, and being between her creamy thighs was much more important to me than an extra waitress.

"The new girl worked out nicely, don't you think?" Vick asked while sorting paperwork.

"She did. Too bad I'm firing her," I said, tilting my glass to my lips.

"What? Why?" Vick spun to face me and papers flew from the desk. "She just started."

I turned and found her bent over, picking up her mess from the floor. "She's my Jessica."

Vick stopped and stared at me. "Are you sure? You just said the other night that Jessica Rabbit was a myth. What makes you think this girl has it?"

I was glad she had the smarts to not tell me the girl's name. If I found out her name, all bets were off.

"I just *know.*"

She batted a piece of sweaty hair from her face and rolled her eyes with a hefty sigh. "I guess I'll fire her tomorrow then. I'll start searching for her replacement."

She was pissed off, but she knew me well. When I wanted something, I went after it. I didn't care how I got it.

"Don't bother. I want to fire her."

"Fine," she said tightly, but I ignored it.

"You can fire Mike for me, though." I didn't like the way the little bastard was looking at *my* Jessica, and since I was never one to share, he had to go.

"Mike, the bartender?" Vick asked confused. "Why?"

"Because he doesn't know how to keep his eyes to himself."

I didn't need to say more. She didn't need to know anything other than the fact I wanted him fired as soon as possible.

I could feel Vick staring at me, before she finally headed for the door.

"I'll look for his replacement as well."

It wasn't like she had to look very far. We had, literally, hundreds of applicants who wanted to work at Clive's. I sat behind my desk and thought about Jessica. Her image alone was enough to make my dick throb painfully.

I undid my belt and unbuttoned my pants. Easing back into my chair, I slipped my hand in my pants and palmed my cock, squeezing hard. I could have easily called on one of my girls to take care of my needs, but it was easier to imagine a certain redhead's lips wrapped tightly around the head of my shaft.

Firing her was the only way to go. I needed her desperate. A good girl like her wouldn't be working at a place like Clive's, unless she absolutely needed the money. Money was something I had in spades, so money would be what brought her to me. I wanted her to *need* me. I needed to feel it in her touch—in the way her body rocked against mine. I wanted it more than my next breath.

THE FOLLOWING NIGHT, SHE WAS late to work. I could have fired her on the spot, but I wanted to spend the night watching her move. I sat tucked away at the bar, letting my eyes roam over her curvy body. The sway of her hips, as she slid through the room with her newfound tray holding skills, was almost too much to take. I thought about all the things I wanted to do to her—the noises she would make.

The bar hid my raging hard-on, while I sat and sipped my drinks. A few times our eyes locked and I was sure she was blushing. She was starting to sweat and the back of her tight shirt was clinging to her body. The strands of red hair close to her face, stuck to her cheeks. She looked incredibly sexy, exactly the way I imagined she would when I was done fucking her.

Once the doors were locked, I downed the last of my drink and waited to make my move. Firing someone had never been hard for me, but knowing she needed the job made it a little difficult.

I didn't want to hurt her, and I knew when she walked out of my club, she'd have no idea how much money I was going to start paying her. She would probably be upset, until I made my proposition.

One minute she was there next to her friend, cleaning tables, and the next she was gone. I stood from the bar and moved around the room, pretending I wasn't searching for someone. Finally, I gave up and moved outside. I made my way into the alley beside the club and that's where I found her.

She was leaning into the window of an Oldsmobile. It wasn't the smartest place for a girl to be out alone, and I was about to walk over and bring her back inside when I heard her speak.

"I'm sorry, Kyle. I know it's boring, but we don't have any other choice until I make enough to get into an apartment." She swiped at her cheek and I was sure she was crying. "I'm almost done. I just needed to come out here and check on you. Let me run in, finish cleaning my tables, and grab my tips. Don't unlock these doors for anyone and stay low."

And then she was coming toward me. I stepped into the shadows and watched as she passed on her way back into the bar. When the door shut behind her, I crept into the alley and peeked into the back window.

A boy. A young one at that, was curled up on the backseat reading a book with a tiny flash light. My Jessica looked too young to have a son his age, but then again, what did I know about how women aged. I'd once slept with a forty-year-old I was sure was younger than me.

Going back inside, I went straight upstairs to my office. "Vick, I have a job for you."

She looked up from the night's paperwork and frowned at me. "Right now? Can't it wait? I have work to do here."

I knew she was still pissed off about losing two people, but she could get the fuck over it. "Leave the paperwork, I'll do it. There's a car in the alley beside the bar. Follow it." I didn't give her time to answer, before I turned and left my office.

Taking the stairs two at a time, I went straight to Jessica and prepared myself to fire her. I wasn't about to let the fact that she possibly had a son get in the way of what I wanted. More mouths to feed meant she needed money. It was the perfect scenario.

"I need to speak with you," I said from behind her.

She turned around and gasped like she was surprised I was still inside the club. Obviously, she hadn't figured out who I was yet.

"Excuse me?" she replied, looking around for help. "The club is closed. You're not supposed to be..."

I laughed. "Sweetheart, I own the fucking place. I assure you, I have every right to be here."

I turned and walked toward the bar, without waiting for her to follow.

FOUR

ROSSLYN

SATURDAY NIGHTS WERE EVEN BUSIER than Friday nights. By the time we closed, my feet were aching and so was my lower back.

I'd been too busy to even go out and check on Kyle during the night. He refused to stay at Trish's house, and honestly, I knew I couldn't keep depending on her. Instead, I parked our car in the abandoned alley beside the club, with plans to sneak out and check on him every thirty minutes.

He had books and a flashlight and I made sure he knew not to open the door for anyone, but still, I was a nervous wreck all night. As soon as I could, I left the bar and snuck out to the alley to check on him. I found him sitting there reading with an annoyed look on his face. He obviously felt too old to be checked on.

When I got back inside to finish up, I was met with the gorgeous guy from before. I'd noticed him staring at me earlier in the night. He was always staring, and a couple of times I thought he was going to approach me, but he never did.

Most of the men in the club had no problems with expressing their interest. It wasn't like I was surprised by their groping hands or fuck-me eyes. We were practically wearing nothing, so it was to be expected. That didn't mean I liked it, in fact I *hated* it. It made me feel sleazy and dirty.

That wasn't the case when tall, dark, blue eyes looked at me though. There was something dangerous about him. He encouraged the extra sway in my hips when I moved through the room, and as much as I wanted to be embarrassed by it, he was the reason I pulled my shirt down a few extra inches.

The way he watched me made me think he was interested in me, but apparently it was because he was the owner and I was obviously doing something wrong.

I followed him over to the bar and he motioned for me to sit down on one of the stools. I sat and he moved to stand in front of me. He turned his baby blues on me and reached up to tuck a stray hair behind my ear.

His simple touch heated my skin and my breathing got harder. I felt embarrassed by my reaction to him. Experienced girls didn't fall apart at such an innocent gesture. Out of the corner of my eye I could see the motionless bodies of the staff and if I strained, I could hear their whispers.

It wasn't normal for the owner of a club to tuck the wait staff's hair behind their ears.

"Jessica," he said with a seductive grin.

I almost didn't realize he called me by the wrong name. His voice was so dark and deep—hypnotic. I shook my head, my correction on the tip of my tongue. "No. My name is—"

He stopped me with a rough finger over my lips.

Sparks tickled my lips, making me roll them together.

"No. When you're with me, you're Jessica."

And then it all made sense. The owner of Clive's was certifiable. It was a shame for such an attractive man to be totally crazy, but there you go.

"Sir, I'm not really sure what this is about, but..."

"My name's Sebastian." His words were rough and clipped.

"I'm sorry, Sebastian..." I said slowly, not wanting to make any sudden movements. "Is there something I can do for you? I really need to get back to work so I can get out of here as soon as possible." My eyes flew toward the club doors and I was ready to flee any minute. But *Sebastian*, a.k.a. my crazy boss, obviously had other plans.

He put his head down and chuckled softly to himself. It was a deep, erotic sound that punctured all the right places.

"As a matter of fact, there is something you can do for me. A lot of things actually, but we'll get back to that later."

The bartender slid him a drink across the bar, and he watched me over the rim of his glass as he took a quick sip.

"I hate to do this, but I have to let you go. We at Clive's appreciate you applying for the job, but I don't think this is the right position for you."

He said the word *position* like it was the name of a dirty movie. Listening to his smooth voice and staring into his never-ending pools of blue, I almost missed the point behind his words.

And then, his words sank in and gutted me.

This couldn't be happening.

Not with my brother, outside parked in our home, waiting for me. I had to do something. I wasn't certain I could find another job quick enough. Things were already sitting at rock bottom. I wasn't sure I was going to come back after this hit.

"Sir..." the word slipped from my lips. It sounded broken and afraid.

"Sebastian," he corrected.

"Sebastian, I—"

He cut me off again. "I love how you say my name." He appeared to be thinking to himself.

"You're actually the first one to know my name. It's inconvenient, somewhat forbidden, but I kind of like it."

I had no idea what he was talking about. Of course people knew his name. Before I knew who he was, I distinctively remember Trish talking about the owner who was named Sebastian Black.

I didn't know how to respond to him, so instead I chose to ignore what he said. "I can't lose this job. Please, let me try again tomorrow night. I know I'm not perfect, but I didn't drop anything tonight. I'll be even better next time. *Please,* give me—"

Again, he silenced me with a single finger. What was with this guy?

"I have something else in mind for you, my beautiful, perfect myth."

I didn't hate that he was flirting with me, and I already gave up trying to understand what the hell he was blathering about, but I sensed if I wanted to keep my job, it was best to not respond.

"A proposition of sorts." He grinned before turning on his drink again.

I watched his smooth lips close around the edge of the glass and a strange tingle ran down the length of my spine.

I wondered what it would feel like to feel his lips against my skin.

My thoughts surprised me and I shifted them back to his last comment. "Anything's better than nothing. Tell me what it is, and I'll do it."

He made a soft noise resembling a growl. "I love the sound of that, especially from those lips."

I swallowed hard.

"Stay behind once everyone's gone. We'll talk about this privately. Understood?"

I nodded, even though I knew leaving Kyle in the car any longer than needed was a bad idea. Still, I couldn't lose my job, and if that meant staying an extra five or ten minutes, I was doing it.

"Okay," I agreed.

I stood to go back to work, and he stopped me with a hand on my arm. My flesh prickled and that same, strange sensation from earlier worked its way up my arm.

"No, sit until everyone's gone," he said before casually strolling away. His confidence filled the room like water.

I ended up sitting at the bar, while the other waitresses stared holes into the back of my head. I couldn't imagine what it looked like. The new girl, sitting on her butt, flirting with the owner in a remote corner of the bar. *Great.* Just perfect.

Once I convinced Trish I was staying behind to ask some questions, and the last worker left, Sebastian made his way across the club in my direction. His walk was slow and deliberate, making me feel like prey.

I swallowed hard, trying my best to keep my eyes off his tall frame and orgasmic eyes. Yes... orgasmic fit him nicely. I knew the meaning of the word, but I'd never actually experienced it. Either way, he was the equivalent of the definition.

"You stayed," he commented after he sidled up to me. "Good girl."

He was too close again; Sebastian obviously didn't care about personal space. It made me uncomfortable and tingly at the same time.

"It's not like I had a choice," I oozed sarcasm.

I could hardly believe the way my words sounded. I was never rude to people and I'd never had such a tone in my voice before. Instead of getting angry, he just smirked down at me, like he enjoyed being snapped at.

"A little bit of fire in heaven, I see. I like that. However, everyone has a choice. You could have left, but you didn't."

His words were true, so I didn't respond.

He took the seat beside me and held out a glass. "Would you like a drink?"

"No, thank you. I'm not much of a drinker." I responded.

"Good to know."

Even the way his words rolled off of his tongue was sexual. He could be talking about politics or something equally as boring and still get your panties wet.

"You mentioned a proposition earlier?" I asked.

I hadn't even thought about the fact he might be asking me to stay behind so he could rape and kill me. Desperation erases your mind of all fear, apparently. Then again, was it considered rape, if the other party is willing and ready?

Shaking my train of thought, I tried to focus. *Willing and ready?* Did I really just think that?

"Yes." He turned toward me and the side of his mouth lifted, drawing my attention to his perfectly sculpted lips and the hint of a dimple that begged him to smile bigger. I wanted to finger it. I also wanted to run my fingers though his thick hair. "I'd like to buy you."

And just like that, my new found sexual fantasies went up in smoke. Surely I'd heard him wrong. I really needed to get out of my head and pay attention. I'd been around men before. What the heck was wrong with me?

"Excuse m-me?" I stuttered.

"I said, I'd like to buy you," he repeated.

I sat and gawked at him, positive he'd lost his marbles. For the life of me, I couldn't speak. Part of me was mad at Trish for not telling me her boss was a total head case.

"I've shocked you. Okay let me finish. I find you extremely attractive. If I was a man who enjoyed being in a relationship, I'd ask you to go on a date with me, but I'm not that kind of man.

"I don't like complications of any form, and I find that when emotions get involved, things become problematic. So, I'd prefer to have the sex, without the relationship. Your company, without the hassle."

I looked around the room to find a hidden camera somewhere. This wasn't actually happening to me for real. At any moment, a show host would pop out and the joke would be on me. But there were no cameras, and there was no host to relieve me from the awkward situation.

"Here's what I'm offering you." He reached into his pocket and pulled out a little black book. "I'll put your number in my book, and when I want you, I'll call you." He leaned in close and I could smell his cologne. It smelled like hot sex, and spice. At least, what I imagined hot sex smelled like. "And when I call you, you'll come, in more ways than one. I promise, beautiful girl, it will be mutually pleasurable for both of us."

My mouth dropped open and with a single finger to my chin, he closed it.

"I only have two rules." I stiffened when he ran that same finger down the top of my breast that I had foolishly exposed for him earlier tonight. "Don't ever deny me. And don't fall in love. As I said before, emotions are messy and I'd prefer not to get involved." He tucked his book back into his pocket. "If you break either of those rules, I'll remove you from my book and payment stops."

When I found my voice again, I spoke. "Payment? You want to *pay* me for sex?" I sounded as shocked as I felt.

"Not just for sex, your company as well, but that will be on my terms. And yes, at some point, I'm going to want to fuck you."

He lifted his drink to his lips, while keeping his eyes trained on mine. His throat worked up and down, swallowing the remnants of his glass. Then, there was his dimpled smile once more. "So what say you, Jessica? I can make it worth your while." A single brow lifted in emphasis.

Oh, I had no doubt in my mind he could "make it worth my while," but hell would freeze over and the devil himself would ice skate on it, before I sold my virginity to him. I mean, for the love of all that's holy, he *was* attractive... But I just couldn't. It wasn't in me to sell my body to some stranger, regardless of the amount of money.

I lifted my head, even though I wanted to hang it low and disappear. I knew for sure I was walking out of the club without a job, which meant things were about to get a lot worse.

"I'm sorry, *sir*, but I can't do that. I appreciate the offer, but I'm no one's whore."

As I stood to move away, he pulled me against his body. I looked up at him in shock, and to my dismay a little bit of excitement. My breasts crushed against his chest and he was very much aware as he bent over to whisper in my ear.

"My name's Sebastian, not sir."

I shook off the chills from his whispers, and walked away without looking back. As soon as I stepped into the cool morning air, I let the tears fall.

I'd just lost my job.

I made sure to wipe away my tears before I got back in the car with Kyle. He was asleep on the back seat with a smile on his face. I knew it would be gone the following day.

I DROPPED KYLE OFF AT school, and then slept for an hour on the back seat, before using almost all of my gas to job hunt. I didn't tell Kyle I'd lost our only source of income because it was clear he was starting to worry even more. He was old enough to know things couldn't get much worse. We were already living in a car. He didn't need to know that pretty soon our car would be out of gas and we'd really be screwed.

Once I picked him up, we got some fast food and ordered from the dollar menu again. It was all I could afford to buy without a kitchen to use for preparation. I had to make the tips I'd received stretch as far as possible.

I parked near his school, so I wouldn't have to drive back and waste gas, and we sat and did his homework together. When night came, he curled up in the back and I got as comfortable as possible in the front passenger's seat.

Kyle set the alarm on his watch, so I let myself fall into a deep sleep. It had been days since I'd actually gotten any sleep. I was in the middle of a decent dream, starring Sebastian Black, when I woke abruptly to the sound of thumping on the window above my head.

I jumped up and pulled the blanket closer to my body. Once my eyes adjusted to the early morning light, a police officer came into focus.

He looked down at me with furrowed brows, tapping on the glass again. "Miss, we need you to open the door."

Looking past him, I saw two other officers. One as round as he was tall, and one who looked like he'd just graduated from high school.

We'd overslept. I knew this because teachers were already starting to pull up and make their way into the school. All eyes were on my car, as it was surrounded by police cars. I didn't understand why they had to have their flashing blue lights on. We weren't criminals on the run. It didn't make any sense.

I reached out and popped the door open letting in the cold air. Kyle sat up at that exact minute with wide, shifty eyes.

"Roz?" he asked nervously.

"It's okay, Kyle. Just stay back there."

I crawled out of the car closing the door behind me and rubbed at my arms. It was freezing and I'd left my jacket inside the car.

TABATHA & MELISSA

"We had some reports about an abandoned car outside of the school. Some of the staff were worried." The police officer's expression changed and he shook his head. "Are you and this young man living in this car, miss?"

I didn't want to answer him, but I didn't have any other choice. "No. I accidently locked us out of the house last night and I didn't want him to be late for school this morning. I'm sorry, officer. I'll move the car right now. Thank you, but all is well." I started to move closer to the door.

I thought I was home free, until I felt a hot hand on my wrist. I looked up to see the round officer staring back at me with pinched lips and knowing eyes.

"I'm sorry, miss. We're going to need to take the young man into custody until it's verified that everything is indeed well."

I shook him from my wrist and turned to open the car door. I obviously wasn't thinking clearly since all I could think about was outrunning the cops. "No. That's not necessary. Like I said, we're fine and I'm taking him home right now."

No matter how many times I said those words, the police officer didn't listen. He pushed me to the side and pulled open the backdoor.

"*Roz!*" Kyle said in a full on panic. His tone tore at my heart and fear roared through my body.

He struggled in the officer's arms and reached out for me with tears on his cheeks, as they pulled him to the car with the blue lights on.

"Roz, please help!"

I pushed and fought against the other two, while my little brother was thrown into the back of the police car like a common criminal.

I lost it. Pulling free from the hands that held me, I ran to the car and pounded on the glass. Kyle's tear-stained face stared back at me.

"Miss, if you don't stop, we're going to have to take you into custody."

I heard the cop talking, but I wasn't processing it. I lost all track of reason. Reaching down, I picked up a rock and threw it at the window. The rock went through, leaving a gaping hole in its stead.

It was then reality hit home. I was thrown against the police car and my arms were pulled behind me. The cuffs were too tight, and when I was tossed in the backseat next to Kyle, I knew I'd sunk lower than I ever thought I would.

There was nothing I could do. I fought. I fought with all I had left, but it didn't matter. All that it got me was a one-way ticket to jail. Me—the virgin who'd never drank or done drugs.

I'd failed Kyle. I'd failed the last person left in my life and there was nothing I could do to make it right. Turning away from his sad eyes, I stared out the window and cried.

FIVE

SEBASTIAN

"**W**HAT DID YOU FIND OUT?" I asked the second Vick came into my office the following day.

"Not much. The young boy she's riding with is her little brother. They're living in their car outside of the middle school." She flopped into my favorite chair and put her feet up. "It's a damn shame she didn't take your deal. Looks to me like she could use it."

I was relieved to find out the boy wasn't her son. I would have continued to pursue her regardless, but a brother made things easier to deal with verses a kid. Either way, it was still an extra mouth for her to feed.

"I'm not worried. She'll be back. This is New York. The city will eat her alive if she doesn't take my deal." I went toward the door. I had a few business meetings to take care of and the walls were starting to close in on me. "Until then, keep an eye on her. Make sure nothing bad happens to her or her brother."

I spent the day going over deals and turning down offers to buy my club. Every greedy bastard in New York wanted to get their hands on what was mine. I wasn't having it. By the time I was getting in my car I was pissed, and annoyed that Vick hadn't called me with good news about Jessica.

I'd gone to my meetings, certain she would return to the club before I was done. I was on my way back when Vick sent me a text message that instantly changed my mood.

Vick: *Jessica's been taken into police custody.*
SB: *Meet me at the station in twenty minutes.*

I put my phone back in my pocket and grinned. Turning at the next light, I drove away from the club and toward the police station. I wanted her desperate, not desolate. The poor girl was totally innocent. Jail would break her down, which was the last thing I wanted. *I* wanted to break her in and I wanted to do it my way.

When I pulled up, Vick was already waiting outside.

"Are we rescuing the fair maiden?" she asked sarcastically.

"Not *we*, you. Post her bail, get her out. Do it without me learning her name."

I leaned against my car and looked down at my watch before crossing my arms. It distracted me from the tiny voice taunting me, saying I might not forget this whole thing even if I did learn her name.

Finding her wasn't something that happened every day. The best things in life are always more difficult to obtain. It was currently taking me a little longer than usual to get what I wanted, which made it that much more exciting. It had been a long time since one of my girls presented me with a challenge and it was exactly what I needed. In the end, I knew she would be mine. I always got what I wanted. Always.

I sat outside for what felt like an hour, and then Vick came out of the door, followed by Jessica. Her eyes connected with mine and her brows pulled down in confusion. Seeing she was safe, I turned away and got into my car. I waited until she climbed into Vick's car, and then pulled away.

I stopped for a quick dinner before going home. The club was closed on Sundays and Mondays, so being that it was Monday, it was deserted when I pulled up and parked. I slung my keys around my finger as I walked in, locked the door behind me, and went to my office.

Jessica was there waiting for me, like I'd hoped she would be. She stood from the couch in my office and our eyes locked as soon as I opened the door. Something about her was different. She looked as if she was seconds away from falling apart. Her shoulders were stiff and her flushed cheeks stood out from the rest of her pale face.

I closed the door behind me and ignored her as I walked past and sat behind my desk. I could sense her anxiousness.

"Sit," I firmly commanded.

When she was seated in front of me, I laced my fingers together and stared at her.

"Are you okay?"

I never asked such questions, but I needed to know she was mentally stable and able to make the decision I wanted her to make.

"Fine." Her voice broke. "Thank you for bailing me out," she said, as her eyes watered over.

I had to look away. I'd seen women cry... hell, I'd even made a few cry, but seeing her do it was different. It hurt in my stomach—made me feel empty. Tears never bothered me before, but her tears cut deep. Luckily, I had mastered the art of ignoring annoying emotions.

"Vick bailed you out." I didn't want her to think I was soft. I wasn't.

Bailing her out was how I got what I wanted. Nothing more, nothing less. Sitting back in my chair, I let my eyes devour her. "Was that all you came here for? A misplaced thank you?"

She looked as if she wanted to say something more, or possibly slap me, but apparently she lost her nerve because she nodded, and left the room. The strange part was, I wanted to go after her and ask her to stay.

SIX

ROSSLYN

JAIL WAS NOT FOR ME. The minute we got to the station, I was taken into a separate room from Kyle and told he was being transported to child services.

I cried when they took my fingerprints, and when it was time to take my mug shot, I almost threw up. What would my parents say if they could see me now? What would Gran think?

I sat in a cell with another girl who was there for prostitution. It was kind of comical since I was starting to believe that selling my body was the only way to fix everything. Maybe when I got out, I'd go to Sebastian and accept his offer. Sleeping with him didn't sound totally unappealing. It was really the part about getting paid that made it creepy.

An hour later, and a cop came to the cell calling my name.

"Your bail's been posted. You're free to go."

My confusion on how the hell my bail was posted overshadowed any relief I might have had in being free. I didn't have anyone to post bail other than Trish, and I hadn't had the chance to call her yet.

And then, there was the fact I was being set free, while my brother was being held God-knows-where. There was nothing for me to collect when I left. It was a sign of how my life was turning out. I needed to get used to having nothing.

I was shocked when I came out and found Vick looking back at me.

"I left my white horse outside," she said sarcastically. "Let's go."

I followed behind her and as soon as I walked through the station doors, my eyes found Sebastian's. In that moment, I knew who bailed me out.

How did he even know I'd been arrested? Should I be freaked out?

I climbed into Vick's black car and she pulled out with squealing tires, directly outside the police station. Like I wasn't already deathly afraid of going back.

"Sebastian bailed me out?" I asked when the silence in the car became too thick.

"Yep," she responded. "No offense, but I have better things to spend my money on."

I didn't bother responding.

"My brother, they took him into child services. Is there anyway..." I started.

"I'm taking you to Sebastian. Ask him."

I turned and stared out the window, as we drove entirely too fast toward Clive's. I had so much spinning in my head. First and foremost, I was seriously considering his deal.

I needed the money, and it wasn't like I wasn't attracted to him physically, despite his outrageous proposition. My body seemed to respond to him in ways I had never experienced with another man. It came alive whenever he was near.

LEAVING SEBASTIAN'S OFFICE, I MOVED through the darkness of the club, knowing that once I stepped through those doors, I'd be on the streets for the night. My car had been impounded and I had no money to get it out.

Vick took off after dropping me at the club, and I wasn't about to call and bother Trish because I knew she was using her Monday as a day to relax.

The door was cold against my palm when I reached out for it. The moment I began to push it open, the lights behind me came on. Turning around, I found Sebastian standing on the bottom step of the stairs.

"Do you have anywhere to go?"

I stared at him, debating how pathetic I wanted to appear. Finally, I moved past my pride. I felt the girl inside me crumble as the words left my mouth. "No."

His dark eyes moved from my head to my toes, and then he huffed in annoyance. "There's an extra room upstairs with a bed in it. You're welcome to crash here tonight." He turned and went back up the stairs without waiting for my response.

I followed behind him. I had no other option.

The room he gave me was huge—a large bed centered the room. I stepped through the door, closing it behind me and took in the space. To the right was a fully equipped bathroom. I wasted no time peeling my clothes off and getting into the shower.

I washed away the criminal grime and wrapped myself in a plush robe that was hanging on the back of the door.

Steam poured out when I stepped from the bathroom and made my way to bed.

I wasn't going to sleep, not without knowing where my brother was, but at least I could lie somewhere comfortable without worrying about someone breaking into my car and killing me. I didn't have anything to worry about here. At least I hoped I didn't.

I couldn't stop thinking about my brother and how I'd let him down. I'd never been away from him overnight. I didn't know if he was safe. I didn't know if he was warm, or if he was comfortable. These were just some of the things moving through my head.

I stared at the ceiling until the night sky turned pink. And then I finally fell asleep and slipped into one horrible nightmare after another.

I WOKE AT NOON WITH sounds coming from outside my door. Wrapping the robe tighter around my waist, I tip-toed down the hallway. A heavenly smell filled me and I followed it with my nose, like I was in one of those cheesy cartoons.

I hadn't eaten anything decent in forever and as soon as I stepped foot into the high-tech kitchen, my stomach growled loudly. It was then a half-naked Sebastian Black turned around from the stove and met my stare.

From the waist down he wore hip-hugging jeans that rode low, but from the waist up he was all muscle and dark skin. Muscles I didn't even know were possible rippled across his chest when he turned with a spatula in hand.

I felt my mouth hanging open and without realizing it, I gawked at every piece of his flesh my eyes could touch. His face split into a knowing grin.

"Like what you see?" he asked with a cocky smirk.

His hair was a sexy slept-on mess. I wanted to get my fingers stuck in its tangles. I averted my gaze and walked into the kitchen. Choosing a seat at a tiny table that was pushed up against a window, I looked out over the street in front of the club.

"By the sound of your stomach, I'm assuming you're starving. I've heard many noises from women's bodies in my time, but nothing quite like that."

I felt my face heat up as a blush took over.

Soon, a plate was set in front of me, full of bacon, eggs, and a side of fresh strawberries. My stomach growled again and he chuckled softly above me.

"Thank you," I whispered in humiliation.

He leaned down from behind, lips skimming the side of my neck, and the soft prickle of his stubble brushed against my skin. "For you, anything."

A shiver worked its way up my back and ran into my hair line. I was positive my hair grew an extra inch in that moment.

I dug into my eggs like the starved woman I was, not even realizing when he sat in front of me with a plate of his own.

He didn't waste any time and got straight to the questions. "Where's your brother?"

My fork full of eggs paused, suspended in the air. A fireball of guilt ignited in my stomach. I was in such a luxurious place, eating bacon and eggs, while he was stuck in some children's home. Swallowing hard, I answered. "They took him."

Throat clenching, tears rushed to my eyes.

"Who?" he asked.

I choked down my feelings. "Child protective services." I looked up just in time to see his tan face pale.

"Why didn't you say something sooner?" His chair scraped across the floor as he stood and went to his phone. Picking it up, he dialed a number and left the room.

I sat there confused, until finally he came back into the kitchen.

"Vick's on her way to pick up your brother." He sat back in his seat and began to eat again, acting as if he hadn't just turned my world right side up again, leaving me dizzy in the process.

I gawked at him. My eyes landed on his lips and I was taken aback by how full they looked. "What?" I asked breathlessly. No way did he fix everything for me with a single phone call.

He looked up from his food. "Your brother. Vick is getting him."

The muscles in his arms flexed as he bent over his plate. It was then a tattoo was revealed. It wrapped around his arm and moved up, out of sight. While I was never one to find such things attractive, it changed his look. He went from Sebastian, suit-wearing club owner, to Sebastian, tattooed Sex God, with muscles I wanted to touch.

Without a second thought, I stood and walked over to him. Completely against myself, I bent and wrapped my arms around his neck. He stiffened in my arms, and turned to look at me.

We were face to face. Nose to nose. Lips to lips. I could feel his breath against my mouth and the strange desire to kiss him took over.

Pulling away, I cleared my throat and looked away. "Thank you," I said.

"Don't thank me. Thank Vick," he said, before he dove back into his food with a pinched, angry brow.

I smiled to myself and sat back at the table.

He stood then and I looked up at him, but he wasn't paying me any attention.

Going to the sink he rinsed his plate and then turned to leave the room. I felt confused and disappointed all at once.

"I'll be in my office. When you're ready, find me there."

And then, he was gone.

I felt annoyed with him, and more with myself when I realized this was all a part of his plan. This was a game to him and he was currently winning.

When I was done, I rinsed my plate and went back to the room I'd stayed in the night before. I would *not* be looking for him like he expected. I couldn't be in the same room with him without wanting to slap him for being so smug and self-assured. Yet at the same time, I wanted kiss him because every time he looked at me I felt like I was seconds away from going up in flames.

I dressed in the only clothes I had and decided to get out of his apartment before I did something totally against who I was. Something like, drop my panties for him and beg for his touch. It could happen.

I felt a huge weight lifted off of my shoulders now that I knew Kyle was going to be okay, but at the same time, I knew I had to figure out my situation. And I had to figure it out *fast*.

I made it to the door of the club, and then stopped. It was insane, sure, but what if I took Sebastian's offer? I had already decided that having sex with him sounded... intriguing. And getting paid to do it? Well, hell. That was kind of a bonus in my current situation.

Sure, he was a little extreme and, for some odd reason, he refused to learn my name--insisting on calling me Jessica. And despite the fact he wanted me to think Vick was the one who was always fixing everything, I knew he was a good guy.

Lots of people didn't want to be in a relationship. Trish was one of them. I spent an entire night listening to the pros and cons of being single, and honestly it didn't sound terrible.

There was also the tiny fact I couldn't stop thinking about him. At first he'd seemed intense and somewhat odd, but now I'd been around him for a while, I was starting to feel different. I was a woman, and as Trish had once said, women have needs.

I never understood that statement, until Sebastian whispered in my ear. And also when I stepped into his kitchen this morning and saw him half-naked. The fact was, I wanted him. I could kill two birds with one stone. I could get money to set me and Kyle up, and I could spend some time with Sebastian. I'd be stupid to turn that down.

I turned on my heels and went back the way I came. I knew what I wanted—what I needed, and all of that was up those stairs in a pair of sexy jeans.

SEVEN

SEBASTIAN

I DIDN'T LIKE IT. HER staying at my place, us eating breakfast together—all of it felt right, which felt wrong. This shit was exactly why I had fucking rules. I was done making exceptions for her.

This girl was unknown to me, except her life seemed to be spiraling out of control... and I had the strongest desire to make everything better for her.

I was starting to think I should forget the whole deal and just learn her name. Take her under my wing, the way I did with Vick. But then she'd smile at me when I did something nice for her, and it would be better than sex with any of the women in my black book.

I was truly fucked.

If I'd learned anything in all my years, it was that you couldn't give a woman an inch without her expecting the whole fucking world.

I made my way up to my office and sat down behind my desk before turning the monitor on and clicking around my desktop. A little box popped up, awaiting my password, and I entered with swift taps on the keyboard.

Welcome, Mr. Black. A computerized voice buzzed through the speakers on my computer. The screen lit up showing four different pictures.

Each of the four screens was surveillance for the different rooms in my apartment. I even had surveillance for the club. I wasn't a very trusting person. In fact, I trusted no one. Therefore, there wasn't anything in my home or work that I couldn't see at all times.

I found Jessica still sitting in the kitchen as she ate alone. I was positive I knew what she was going to do, but it didn't hurt to insure my investments. Plus, I liked watching her.

After she finished her breakfast, she went to the room she'd stayed in for the night. Almost an hour later, she emerged dressed in clothes from the night before.

While I watched and waited, I made some necessary calls. One of which, included getting my driver here. Her car was a total piece of shit, at least what I'd seen of it the night I followed her outside. Plus, I liked the idea of her needing me for something else. It gave her more incentive to take my deal. Once she did, her car wouldn't matter anymore anyway since I'd have her use my driver or I'd get her a driver of her own.

I watched her walk to the entrance of the club and smiled to myself. I could appreciate her stubbornness. She wanted to feel like she was exercising all of her options, but the truth was, I was her only option. She was scared and feeling helpless, but I could sense other things stirring deep within her. She could deny it all she wanted, but she was excited by what I was offering her.

With a click, my monitor went black and then I waited. A few minutes later, when my office door opened, Jessica was staring back at me. She was stiff as she shut the door and made her way to the couch across from me.

"Can I help you?" I asked.

She trembled slightly, but it was enough for me to see it. And then she took a big cleansing breath.

"Yes, the proposition from the other night..." she stopped.

"What about it?" I asked.

"Does it still stand?"

I leaned back in my chair and stared at her. She licked her lips nervously and my cock started to grow. "It does."

"I'd like to take you up on your offer."

The words came from her lips too quickly. It was as if she was forcing herself to say them.

I couldn't help the grin that covered my face. "Are you sure?" *Seriously, Black.* What the hell was I doing? Why was I giving her an out?

I wanted her more than I'd wanted any other woman—maybe ever. This was my way of doing things, and I had the upper hand, as far as she was concerned. The last thing I needed to do was make her second guess her decision.

She nodded and her nostrils flared. "I'm sure."

I didn't like how her emotions were showing so clearly, but her words made me extremely happy. It was about time I had someone new. It wasn't normal for me to mold a woman into what I wanted, but for her, I'd make an exception.

Standing up, I made my way around the desk. Her eyes never left my face and her nerves were showing. My eyes dipped to her neck, just in time to see her swallow hard. I positioned myself in front of her and leaned against my desk. "Well if that's the case, stand up." I couldn't wait to run my fingertips across her perfect skin.

She stood on shaky legs, with her head down.

"Look at me, beautiful girl."

She lifted her face to mine with closed lids, and when she opened them, the rare green color caught me off guard. They were the color of moss—like the green of the Irish coastline. Beautiful. But then I looked harder and the fear lingering along the edges of her thick lashes cut me deep.

"I know you're afraid, but in time you'll learn to trust me." I reached out and fingered a strand of her hair.

It was red—the most luxurious shade of crimson I'd ever seen, and it felt like silk. I closed my eyes and imagined what her hair would feel like against my chest as she rode me.

She flinched when I let my fingers move against her cheek. "I trust you," she said.

Her words soothed a part of the ache that had lived in me for many years.

"You're quite possibly the most beautiful woman I've ever had the luxury to meet. Do you have any idea how attractive you are, Jessica?" I could feel myself getting lost in her already. She was the perfect aphrodisiac for a man like me.

"My name—" she started.

I ran my thumb across her lips. "Don't. If this is going to work, I never want to know your name. Your name is Jessica when you're with me, understand?"

She hesitated, but finally nodded and I continued to caress her lips with my thumb. They were soft—too soft for my rough fingers.

She was shaking. Her nerves were getting the best of her, and I was starting to realize something about Jessica that made me a bit nervous.

"Are you a virgin?" I asked, not one to beat around the bush. I was blunt and demanding, and if it was really going to work between us, she needed to understand that soon.

Her neck snapped when she looked up at me with wide, shocked eyes. "I…" she stopped suddenly. "That's a little personal don't you think?"

I couldn't help myself. I chuckled. "If you accept my proposal, I'll know you better than anyone ever has." I let my hands move lower and ran my palm across the side of her breast before I wrapped my hand around her waist and pulled her closer. "I'll know you inside and out. I'll taste you. I'll make you say and do things you never thought you would, and the best part is, you're going to love every second of it."

I felt her nipples stiffen against my chest and silently celebrated. "So I ask you again, has anyone ever been inside you? Has any other man ever tasted that sweet pussy?"

My dick pressed against the zipper of my pants and begged for release. I wanted to pull her hips close and press into her warmth, but I sensed it would scare her even more.

Her breathing changed and I let my eyes wander across her breasts as they lifted and fell with each breath.

Still, she didn't answer. Running a finger beneath her chin, I lifted her face to mine. I was close enough that her sweet breath rushed against my lips, prompting me to kiss her and taste her.

"I don't like to wait, sweetheart. Not even for someone as beautiful as you. Answer the question." I allowed my lips to brush against hers.

Her breathing accelerated and I was rewarded when her tongue peeked out of her mouth and ran across her lips.

"No," she whispered. "There's been no one."

A growl sounded from the back of my throat and again she swallowed hard.

The nice guy in me knew it was wrong to take something so special when I had nothing special to give in return. But then the devil in me spoke of how sweet and tight she would be.

What could I say? I was an asshole and the angel on my shoulder could suck my dick as far as I was concerned. I wanted her tight little pussy and I wanted it all to myself.

"So how exactly does this work?" she asked. Again, she licked her lips and took a deep breath.

Taking a step back, I sat down in my chair and leaned back. Folding my arms behind my head, I decided to take my time, after all, she had certainly taken hers. When I didn't respond right away, she licked her lips nervously and my cock twitched.

"Sorry, sweetheart, but I don't fuck virgins. They're too unpredictable, plus I'd have to put in all the work to get you exactly where I needed you." I let my chair go, sitting upright, and went back to flipping through my papers.

She hadn't expected my response and I left her feeling stunned and speechless.

"What?"

I was damned impressed with the lies I was able to spew without batting an eye. I wanted to fuck her all the more now that I knew she was a virgin. She was damn lucky a desk separated me from her untouched pussy.

"You made me go through all of that to tell me no?" She was outraged. I fucking loved it.

I sighed, faking annoyance and stood, pulling out a silver money clip, I pulled out a hundred. Making my way toward her, I held the bill between two fingers.

"Here's a hundred."

She looked down at the bill in my fingers and then back up at me. Her face had colored several shades of red. "Fuck you." She hissed and then turned on her heel.

Fortunately for her, I wasn't done with her yet. She pulled open my office door, but I was faster and I slammed it shut with my hand, blocking her between me and the door.

She didn't try to fight me and I knew I had her exactly where I wanted her. Flipping her around, I forced her to look at me.

"I'm a charitable man, ask anyone, but I only give one warning, so listen carefully. Nobody, and I mean nobody, talks to me like that." She didn't respond and really, I didn't need her to. "Because I'm such a generous guy, I'm going to give you a chance to prove to me that you'd be worth it. You know, despite the fact that you're a virgin."

"What makes you think I want to prove anything to you now?"

Leaning into the door on one arm, I held my finger up and made a *tsking* sound. "Want to or not, you owe me. But I have a feeling you want to."

"You're wrong," she challenged.

"Am I? Would you like me to find out?" She stiffened and I smiled. "Deny it all you want, sweetheart, the spark in your eyes tells me differently."

"You're delusional."

"And you're a fucking liar. A delusional asshole and a liar. What do you think about that?"

"I think this was a mistake."

"Maybe, but you still owe me."

"Owe you what?"

"You'll know soon enough." I turned around and walked toward my desk.

"I'm not going to sleep with you," she said confidently.

Making my way around my desk, I sat down, unaffected by her empty threat.

"If a little bit of truth is going to wound you so severely, then this arrangement would never work. If you think you can handle it and want to prove to me you'd be worth my time, then sit." I gestured to the chair in front of my desk. "I'll get you a room for the night."

I smiled inside when she took the seat, and then I made arrangements for her to get a room at a nice hotel close to the club.

"Your room's ready, and they know you're coming," I said. Putting the phone down, I stalked toward her once more. Placing my hands on either side of her chair, our faces were inches away from each other.

"Thank you," she whispered with her head down.

She had a serious problem with looking me in the eye. I wasn't sure I liked it very much.

Lifting her face to meet mine again, I grinned at her. "I gave you something. Now what are you going to give me?"

She visibly swallowed and her eyes widened. "What would you like?"

"You're nervous. I can see it in the stiffness of your shoulders, and the acceleration of your breathing." I drew circles on her knee with my fingertips. "I don't do slow and

I don't do soft and romantic, but for now, how about a kiss?"

"A kiss isn't soft or romantic?"

I smirked and wrapped my fingers around the strands at the base of her skull, pulling her head until she stood against me, her lips brushing mine. "If done right, not at all."

I pressed my lips to hers, ready to show her what a real kiss was, except, something different happened. She wasn't the only one affected. I was, too. I'd known from the first time I saw her that she was different, but my body could sense just how different she was.

Running my tongue along the seam of her lips, she released a tiny gasp and gave me entrance into her sweet mouth. She tasted like strawberries and cream. My mouth watered at the thought of tasting all of her.

Our tongues collided—mine more practiced than hers, but it didn't take away from the affect it had on my cock. If anything, her inexperience turned me on even more. I pressed my hardness against her stomach, letting her know what she was doing to me

She latched on to my shoulders and I let my hands dip lower to grab her hips. She was a handful. Her round hips fit perfectly in my grasp. Leaning back against my desk, I pulled her thighs against mine and she melted.

EIGHT

ROSSLYN

I DIDN'T KNOW WHAT I was doing. I had marched into his office totally sure of myself, knowing I needed to make money.

Sure, I'd kissed a boy before. Jeffery Middleton had practically shoved his tongue down my throat in eleventh grade; however it was nothing—*nothing*—like the kiss Sebastian was currently laying on me.

Once he pulled me up from the chair and devoured my mouth, I forgot all about my nerves. I wrapped my arms around his neck and he worked my hips against him in a way I'd never experienced.

And just like that, he pulled away, leaving me panting like some wild animal.

"That's enough for today." He grinned down at me.

His smile was heartbreaking. Smutty romance novels had nothing on those lips. I stepped back, knees jittery, and caught my breath as I pushed my hair behind my ear.

"A car is waiting for you downstairs and I'll have a phone sent to your hotel. Always answer it when I call. I'll see you soon, beautiful." He leaned down and gave me a soft kiss on the corner of my mouth.

"Okay," I whispered.

Kyle was waiting downstairs with Vick when I left Sebastian's office. I ran to him and held him so close, I was sure I was hurting him. Seeing him gave me a break from having to think about what the hell just happened upstairs.

"I'm so sorry. So, *so* sorry," I said through tears.

He pulled away and smiled up at me. "It's cool, Roz. It wasn't bad."

Vick cleared her throat, reminding me that my big display of emotion was seen by someone who'd probably never cried a day in her life.

"Who's car is this?" Kyle whispered, while giving Vick shifty eyes.

"It's my... boss's," I lied. "He was nice enough to let us borrow it."

I didn't want Kyle asking anymore questions, so I ushered him into the back of the sleek black car and avoided Vick's knowing eyes.

As soon as I shut the door, the driver pulled away from the club. I hadn't said a word to him, but he drove like he already knew our destination.

"Excuse me," I said loud enough to get his attention.

Warm brown eyes and a friendly smile found me in the review mirror. Silver hair peeked under his driver hat and soft lines surrounded his eyes and lips. "Yes, ma'am?"

"Where are you taking us?"

"To the Hilton, ma'am."

"The Hilton?"

"Yes, ma'am. Only the best for Mr. Black's..." his eyes quickly shifted toward Kyle and then back to me. "Employees."

I knew what he'd been about to say, but I didn't want to correct him. It was pointless to even tell him I wasn't Mr. Black's *anything* yet. Especially in front of Kyle.

"Thank you, Mister..."

"Martin. Just call me Mr. Martin," he smiled in the rear view mirror.

"Thank you, Mr. Martin." I leaned into my seat.

"Wow, the Hilton? You sure do have a nice boss, Roz."

Kyle was beyond excited about the whole experience. I wished I could match his enthusiasm, but I was less than thrilled.

When the driver pulled into the hotel, he told me to sit still. Seconds later, he was pulling our door open and holding it so we could step out. I flushed at the attention. I wasn't used to being treated like anyone special.

Kyle followed closely behind as we followed Mr. Martin into the front lobby and to the reception desk. When it was our turn, the woman behind the desk flashed a familiar smile for the older man.

"Hello, Martin. How are you today?"

"I'm doing well, Molly, and you?"

"Happy to see you as always. How can I help you?"

"I have two guests for Mr. Black. The suite, please."

The woman casted a knowing glance toward me. Her expression quickly changed to surprise, followed by confusion, when she spotted Kyle. I wrapped a protective arm around his shoulders and tried not to wonder what she was thinking.

"Of course," she nodded.

She signaled for someone behind me and then there was a bellhop there at our side.

"Please take these guests to Mr. Black's suite and don't forget their luggage," she ordered.

"Oh, we don't have..." I started to correct her.

I stopped when a cart was pulled up to the bellhop and I recognized our suitcases. *What the hell?*

I wondered how Sebastian had time to gather our things out of our car.

"Thank you," I said to both the desk clerk and bellhop.

"Right this way, Miss," the bellhop gestured.

Turning toward Mr. Martin, I smiled at him. "Thank you again."

"You're very welcome." He mirrored my smile and patted my hands.

Kyle and I spent the night in one of the nicest hotels I'd ever seen. The room was equipped with everything we needed, and had four separate areas. There were two huge bedrooms, and a deluxe bathroom with a massive tub. But the best part was the spacious living room, lined with a wall of windows, showcasing a stunning view of New York City.

Once Kyle was asleep for the night, I spent some time staring at the cars and the people bustling below. The surrounding buildings and streets were so beautiful from my vantage point. It was hard to wrap my head around our quick transition from sleeping in a shitty car... to this luxurious suite. *Un-frickin-believable.*

It wasn't until I yawned and fogged up the window that I realized how late it was. Padding across the mahogany wood floor on my bare feet, I entered the bathroom to get ready for bed. My stress level was nothing compared to the past few weeks, so instead of taking a shower, I filled the massive tub with hot, steaming water, and dropped in some lavender oil. I soaked my body until the water went cold.

Unfortunately, I couldn't hide from my conversation with Sebastian in his office.

I didn't know what I'd been thinking or doing for that matter. I had marched into his office, ready for anything. I had to make money and I was no longer going to deny what my body obviously wanted. But boy had I definitely paid a price.

When he'd so blatantly asked if I was a virgin I hadn't expected his reaction. In fact, if he had slapped me I couldn't have been more shocked. I felt like he *had* slapped me with his response. I thought he would've been pleased and turned on, not turned off.

I was humiliated and embarrassed, and I wanted nothing more than to never lay eyes on Sebastian Black again. But even now, as I laid in the tub, my forbidden thoughts betrayed me and the sight of him bare chested made my fingers wander over my body.

I could still wanted him, even if I pretended differently. He didn't want me and I should have been happy about it, or in the very least relieved. But something made me want to prove that despite the fact I was a virgin, I was still every bit as capable as the next girl.

I let my legs fall open and my fingers moved over my swollen lady bits, but before I could bring myself to orgasm, I stopped and closed my legs tightly. Covering my eyes with my hand, I exhaled loudly.

Who was I kidding? I couldn't even get myself off without worrying about embarrassing myself. How was I going to get a man like Sebastian off?

I expected a lot of things when I finally worked up the courage to take Sebastian's offer, but what was happening to me was completely unexpected. I was a woman, but it was clear I had no clue when it came to the opposite sex.

THE NEXT DAY, MR. MARTIN was outside waiting to take Kyle across town to school. I was wondering if I would ever be surprised at the things Sebastian knew without me ever telling him.

Kyle was more than happy to take the car and be chauffeured around in front of his friends, but I had a harder time being okay with it.

After making my way back up to the hotel suite, I laid around and waited for something—anything to happen. I hated sitting around, twiddling my thumbs.

Finally, when I thought I would explode from anticipation, someone knocked at the door. I opened it to find a young guy smiling back at me. He was boyish, with a lopsided ear-to-ear grin, and had an unfortunate case of teenage acne.

"Are you Jessica?" he asked.

I opened my mouth to say no, but then remembered when Sebastian insisted on calling me Jessica, which was the weirdest thing ever.

"Yep, that's me."

He held out a small pink box with a ribbon on top. "This is for you."

"Thank you."

He turned and left without saying goodbye.

Closing the door, I sat on the bed and pulled the lid off the box to find an expensive phone sitting inside. It was sleek, with a large touch screen. I ran my finger across it and it lit up with a picture of the Brooklyn Bridge.

As soon as I sat it on the bed, it chimed. The tiny symbol on the screen said I had a text message, but it took me a few minutes to figure out how to open it.

SB: *Meet me out front at 7. Wear something nice.*

I should have smashed his stupid phone and walked out of the hotel room, but I couldn't, and I kind of hated myself for it.

Like a true woman, I spent the rest of the afternoon obsessing over what I was going to do. If I'd had any flowers the hotel room would have been full of petals.

I was in the lobby twenty minutes before Kyle was even supposed to be out of school, but I couldn't stay in that room a second longer. I'd never been in a hotel as extravagant as this before and I was extremely curious.

I passed the five-star restaurant and walked through the different ballrooms, until I saw a sign labeled *Peterson Wedding*. Guests moved in and out of the beautiful double doors and after a quick peek around, I made my way toward them.

Pulling on the heavy handle, I slipped in and a wistful sigh escaped my lips. The room was breathtaking. It glittered and smelled like fresh flowers. I didn't stay long because I was obviously not dressed for the occasion, but for just a moment, I closed my eyes and I imagined having a life that included these kinds of luxuries.

An hour later, Mr. Martin dropped Kyle off, and we went back to the suite and did his homework together.

When we were done, I called for room service to bring some dinner. With our bellies stuffed, I left to get ready, and Kyle plopped down in front of the TV to watch some disgusting show about zombies.

I felt much better about leaving Kyle alone this time. There were plenty of locks on the hotel door, and I had a phone he could call if he needed something.

I dug through my suitcase for my nicest outfit, a light teal peasant top and a beige skirt that touched my ankles. I slipped on my sandals, ran a brush through my hair, and barely made it out front by seven.

A black car pulled up in front, and Sebastian climbed out of the back. His steps faltered as he looked me up and down. Then he surprised me with a grin and held his hand out to me.

Confused, I did the only thing that made sense, and placed my hand in his. Feeling a thumb close over the back of my fingers, he lifted them to his mouth.

His lips weren't soft or rough, there wasn't a word that described the way they felt or what they did to my insides.

"You look... sweet," he said with a dimpled grin.

It wasn't quite the compliment I was hoping for, but he was probably used to sexy vixens, with their short skirts and ample cleavage. Then again, maybe it wasn't a compliment at all. Maybe he was being an asshole.

"Well this was fun," I snapped and turned around.

His hand was firm as it circled my elbow and he pulled me around and toward the car.

"Untwist your virginal panties and let's go." He stopped in front of the car and opened the door, waiting for me to get in.

My gaze shifted between him and the open door and then I crossed my arms. "You act like you're doing me a favor."

"I am. Now get in the car. We have reservations."

"And if I refuse?"

"If you were going to refuse you would have done it already. You're curious, and you're going to get into the car."

As much as I wanted to prove him wrong, he was completely right. I was every one of those things, but I was starting to realize I wasn't the only one. Without a word, I got into the car and slid all the way over.

He followed me in, shutting the door. We were incased in darkness.

I didn't ask where we were going. Neither of us spoke, but as the city lights flowed across his face, I couldn't help but notice how nice he looked in his dark suit and tie. His hand rested on the door and my eyes went straight to his slender fingers. He really was magnificent.

"Like what you see?" he asked in a hushed whispered.

A heated blush rushed up my neck. I hadn't realized he was watching me, too. *My God.* He was so cocky, and while it should have been a turn off, it was the total opposite.

"Actually, I do. I've always thought New York was beautiful at night." I turned my head to look out my window and enjoyed his smirk.

"Don't let the pretty lights fool you. The most dangerous things in the world are beautiful."

When I looked back at him, he was staring out the window and looking completely lost in his own little world. I wanted to reach out to him, but he didn't seem like the type who'd want to be comforted.

The car slowed as we reached our destination and I was anxiously looking through the dark windows in anticipation. Seconds later, the door opened and Sebastian was getting out. He held his hand out for me and I took it upon my exit.

"Get ready," he said, before two older men opened the doors for us to the restaurant.

"Ready for what?"

He didn't answer as he ushered me through the set of double doors, keeping one hand on the small of my back.

"Right this way, Mr. Black," the host said. He grabbed two menus and started toward the back of the room.

I'd never been inside such a place. Crystal chandeliers hung above my head and mirrors were strategically placed around the room to reflect the candlelight, making the room look even larger than it already was.

Sebastian walked smoothly through the dining room, captivating his audience and demanding their attention. I watched in bewilderment as everyone stopped to gawk at him. He pulled my arm through his and that's when I realized they were also watching me, the girl on his arm.

"I hope you're hungry." He pulled me closer. "Because I'm starving."

His words brushed across the side of my neck and sent a wave of chills down my arms.

Everyone was staring at me. I self-consciously looked down at my outfit and knew right away I hadn't dressed nice enough. I looked like an uptight school teacher going on a field trip, while ladies around me were dressed in satin, lace, and diamonds.

My hand on his arm began to sweat and I closed my eyes and tried to breathe.

"Don't be nervous. You're the most beautiful woman in the room."

"Everyone's looking at me," I whispered.

"No. Everyone's looking at me. I always come here alone. These people have never seen me with a woman before."

"Then why did you bring me?" I asked as he helped me into my chair.

Leaning over me he whispered. "Because deal or no deal, you're my Jessica."

I had no idea what his obsession with calling me Jessica was, and again, I began to think that maybe Sebastian Black was certifiable.

When he sat down across from me, I worked up the nerve to finally ask something that had been bugging me since the first time we'd talked.

"Why do you refuse to know my name and why do you call me Jessica? Is that what you call all your girls?"

I tried not to fidget, or make uncomfortable eye contact, as I waited for him to answer my question.

When he finally did, I was thankful for the break of silence. "I most definitely *do not* call anyone else Jessica. Only you, and for a very special reason."

He didn't elaborate and I was left to question what exactly that meant.

"Would you care to explain why that is?"

"Actually, I don't. Not right now anyway."

He definitely made it clear I wasn't going to get anything else out of him. I guess I should've known. For the short time I knew him, it was obvious Sebastian Black could be very stubborn and determined.

Once the waiter came and filled our glasses with wine, we were left alone. He sipped his wine and stared at me, making me even more nervous than before.

"So you come here a lot?" I asked, trying to break the ice.

"Yes," he said simply. He wasn't going to make this dinner easy at all.

"You don't talk much."

He shrugged. "I'm not good with idle conversation."

"I thought you didn't... date?"

"I don't."

"Then what is this?"

"I told you what this is. You're proving you're worth the risk."

"And how am I supposed to do that?"

He stared at me for the longest time, then raised his eyebrows.

What the hell was that supposed to mean?

It was then the waiter came back to our table to take our order. When the waiter left, I continued with my questions. With every answer, I became even more curious about Sebastian Black.

"The others... they don't have any problems with your rules?"

"If they did, they wouldn't be one of my girls." He was so matter of fact. "You were ready to accept my offer, did you have a problem with my rules?"

My head snapped up. I didn't like having the situation thrown in my face. "I needed it."

"So you're saying you're different?"

"Yes."

"Because you need the money?"

"Yes," I insisted.

"And what makes you think any of the others didn't also need the money?"

I opened my mouth, but nothing came out. The truth was I didn't know, but I wanted badly to believe I was different, that under different circumstances, I wouldn't have sold myself to Sebastian Black for everything he could offer.

"The truth is, the money comes and goes, but they *don't*. They just keep coming, over and over again." He shrugged. "So maybe you are different."

I dropped my head to the side. "Has anyone left you before you could leave them?"

Jumping at the sound of his laughter, I looked around and saw that everyone was watching at us.

"What's so funny?" I demanded. "You're telling me no one has ever gotten tired of you before you could get tired of them?"

"Nobody." He was dead serious now.

"How do you know?"

"Because I have a cock that won't stop and enough money to buy all the company in the world."

"Don't you think someday you'll want more than an easy lay and women who only want your money?"

"Isn't that what a relationship is based around anyway? Sex and money. In my case, I get to have sex with a different girl every night and not have to worry about a jealous wife."

Suddenly I felt very sad for Sebastian. "Don't you want love?"

"Love doesn't exist, sweetheart. It's a pretty lie. Something women invented to tie a man down and destroy his manhood."

"You're wrong."

"You're wasting your breath, Jessica. Save your delusions about love and happily ever after for a sucker because I am far from fooled."

I wanted to argue that he was wrong. I had seen love—real love—between a man and a woman. My parents had loved each other completely and without reservation. I knew it existed and I fully planned on finding the same kind of love one day.

"I'm very different, Sebastian." I whispered, looking up to meet his frown. "I need the money right now, but I refuse to live a life without love and happiness. I won't come back when it's all said and done."

I didn't know if I had stunned him or angered him, maybe a bit of both, but he didn't respond right away. When he did, it was a complete change of topic.

"I certainly don't know a lot of virgins. How old are you?"

"Twenty-two," I said proudly, daring him to make fun of me.

"How is it that a twenty-two-year-old, with your looks, managed to stay a virgin?"

"If I have to explain the logistics to you, you're obviously not the sex god you claim to be."

I thought I'd gotten him with my witty remark, but he sat forward in his chair and showed me exactly what it felt like to have the breath knocked from you.

"I could fuck you senseless right here, right now, and give the women watching orgasms. That, sweetheart, is how good I am."

Thankfully, the waiter made a sudden appearance with our food. I looked at my plate and kept my head down for the remainder of the meal. I could feel Sebastian's hard gaze and it made me squirm.

I didn't know what to say and I was already worried I had said too much as it was. I couldn't afford for him to take back everything he had already offered... again. I was doing an awful job proving myself after my declaration.

After dinner, the car was out front, waiting for us. I climbed in and we rode in silence back to my hotel. He got out and held the door open for me. When I turned around to thank him for dinner, I found him standing there, with the car gone. He was coming to my room.

"Are you going to stand there all night, or are we going to go up?"

I twisted my fingers together. "Kyle..."

"Doesn't Kyle have his own room?"

"Well, yes, but..."

"But what? Have you given up? Are you no longer willing to prove yourself to me?"

"I think by now you've already made up your decision about me."

"Are you sure?"

I was until he said that. Why was I being such a prude? I could seduce Sebastian Black. I could.

My nerves went crazy and my legs started to shake as I turned and made my way to the elevator. I pressed the button for my floor and waited. My knees felt like Jell-O, and I silently hoped I didn't fall and face plant on the expensive tile floor.

He stood still beside me. He was too quiet, making my anxiety even worse. My hands shook when I pulled out my door key and tried to stick the card in the slot. Covering my hand with his, he took the card from my fingers.

"Allow me," he said as he opened the door.

And then, there I was, standing in a hotel room with a stranger who may or may not purchase me. Thankfully, Kyle was fast asleep in his room, I didn't want him asking questions I didn't know how to answer.

My back was to Sebastian, but I could see our reflection in the expansive glass view. I watched as he approached with the stride of a hungry tiger. A strut that relayed his confidence and security. Meanwhile, tension built inside me and threatened to break.

He ran warm fingers across the back of my neck as he moved my hair to the side. I jerked when he pressed his soft lips to the back of my neck.

"Exactly how far have you gone with a man, Jessica?"

I swallowed hard making my throat hurt. "Far enough."

My voice didn't sound like my own. It was deeper, darker... seductive. The girl who answered him wasn't me. Whatever he was doing, was affecting me.

I could feel his breath in my hair. "Has a man ever touched you? Have you touched a man before?"

"No," I whispered.

"Christ," he cursed. His hands moved from my shoulders and worked down my back, until his hands circled around my waist. He was hard and pressing into my back, which did nothing to help with my insecurities.

"You smell delicious," he said as he nibbled on my earlobe. "I shouldn't want you this much, but I can't seem to keep my hands off of you."

I leaned my head to the side, giving him more room to kiss. I wasn't a total idiot. I knew what men and women did together. I knew what foreplay was, and I definitely knew that Mr. Black was all about foreplay, as my nipples were pressing against my bra and the spot between my thighs was throbbing.

His hands moved up my waist and rested just beneath my bra. I was embarrassed by my erratic breathing because I was sure he could not only hear it, but feel it as well.

I looked down at this dark fingers and watched as they moved in and out with my breaths. Knotting his fingers in the front of my shirt, cool air kissed my belly button when he began to lift the fabric from my body.

"The skin on your neck is so soft. I can't help but wonder if you're this soft everywhere," he said, continuing to caress my skin with his warm lips.

And then he was sliding his fingers against my stomach, skin to skin. For a man with so much money, his fingertips were rough. I liked it. God forgive me, but I liked it so much.

He lifted my shirt further.

"Raise your arms, beautiful. I want to see your skin."

I did as he asked and he pulled my shirt over my head and up my arms. My skin pebbled when the air hit my naked flesh. I stood there with my back to him, in just a skirt and unattractive bra.

Working his fingers down my body, he turned me into putty on the spot.

"So perfect," he whispered in my hair.

I closed my eyes and let him have his way with me. I sucked in a breath when his fingers worked low and started to unzip my skirt. I wasn't ready, but there was no going back. I'd made a deal with the devil himself, and for my brother and for myself, I'd honor that deal.

My skirt fell to my ankles and I opened my eyes to look at myself in the glass. I was pale, which made his hands look even darker as they worked down my hips.

I watched his reflection as he moved to unbutton his jacket, pull it off his shoulders, and toss it to the side. He loosened his tie and slid it around his neck.

And then he was on his knees behind me, hands working up from the back of my calves to my thighs. I was shaking again, but I wasn't sure if it was my nerves or the sensations flying through my body at light speed. I was losing myself in him and it had only been a matter of minutes since we'd stepped into the room together.

He was good. Entirely too good.

He ran his nose along the inside of my leg and I closed my eyes and let my mouth open on a sigh.

"What are you doing to me?" I asked breathlessly.

Pressing his warm lips to the inside of my thigh he groaned his appreciation. "I want you desperate for me."

My head fell back when he continued the hot kisses on the insides of my legs. He was getting what he wanted. I could feel my heartbeat between my legs like it was begging and taunting already.

Reaching back, I dug my fingers into his hair and held him to me. And then he was turning me. I looked down into his eyes as he kneeled in front of me. It was awkward and amazing all at the same time to have such a demanding man on his knees in front of me.

A moan slipped from my lips when he began kissing my stomach, right above my panty line. I was so into it, I couldn't even think to be embarrassed by my plain-Jane cotton panties.

Oxygen no longer seemed important. All that mattered was the throb inside my panties and his mouth, which was now pressed against my inner thigh. He kissed everywhere, but the place I wanted it most. I was desperate.

I pulled the back of his head to me and tried to move him where I wanted him to be.

"Sebastian," I gasped.

Pulling away, he lowered his head and exhaled harshly before he stood and put his arms on my shoulders.

"Times up, sweetheart."

His words were a splash of cold water. "What?" I said frazzled.

"You did well—a very un-virgin like performance."

"But I didn't... that wasn't..."

He held a finger against my lips. "Be at the club tomorrow at noon. Don't be late." He placed a soft kiss on my cheek, his breath rustling the soft hair around my ear. "Goodnight, beautiful."

I wanted to stop him. I should have stopped him and made him listen to me, but it was too late and I'm not sure he would have listened to me anyway.

I turned around as he adjusted his tie and put his jacket back on. The door opened and shut a few seconds later, and the tension in the room lifted.

NINE

SEBASTIAN

"I HIRED A NEW WAITRESS. You'd know that if you were here last night," Vick said, filing papers in the cabinet in the corner of the room.

"I had business other than the club to attend to."

She turned, putting her hand on her hip and peering over at me with a pissed off expression. "Jessica Rabbit business?"

Setting my pen down on the desk, I sighed and met her stare. "Vick, what the fuck's your problem? "Seriously, what's with all the bitchiness lately?"

Slamming the cabinet, she shook her head and marched from the room.

Sighing, I picked up my pen and started going over numbers again. I'd lost track of the time, so when the door opened again I was expecting it to be Vick.

It wasn't. Jessica was standing there in a pair of cheap jeans and what was probably her second best shirt. She was too beautiful to wear such shitty clothes—something I planned to remedy as soon as things were in working order between us.

"Didn't your mother ever teach you to knock?"

Her sweet face clouded over before her eyes turned red with anger and her cheeks flushed.

"Don't ever talk about my mother," she bit off.

Her words were abrupt and to the point. Her anger evident in the tightness of her mouth. She was like a baby kitten ready to claw my face off.

There was more to my Jessica, yet nothing I needed to know about. But family was something I understood—something I'd longed for as a boy. For that reason alone, I'd never mention her family again.

"Noted," I said.

Her anger wasn't something that would garner an apology from me.

"Sit," I motioned to the chair in front of my desk.

Stepping forward, she moved around the chair and sat down crossing her arms. She still carried her resistance to me. I liked that. I appreciated the challenge she gave me.

"Ask me again," I simply stated.

She frowned, confused. "Ask you what again?"

"Ask me again," I repeated.

Leaning back in my chair, I let my eyes wander over her perky breasts in a very obvious manner. She licked her lips nervously and my cock started to grow.

"Does your offer still stand?" she asked hesitantly.

A grin tugged at the side of my mouth. "As a matter of fact, it does."

I loved having so much control over the things in my life. Jessica wasn't an exception.

Her eyes narrowed, and I waited to see whether or not she'd take the bait.

"So I guess I passed your little test then?"

I chuckled, "Oh no, sweetheart, that was just the beginning. I like my women a certain way, and you need to be..." I paused, thinking of the right words. "Tutored in the way I like my women."

She looked absolutely appalled. "Tutored for *your* pleasure?"

"Exactly," I grinned.

Standing from my chair, I walked over and hovered above her. She looked at me with hard green eyes.

"Do you ever do anything to please the women who learn to please you?" she snapped.

I grabbed her chin between my fingers and lifted it roughly. "While I thoroughly enjoy your smart mouth," I said, running my thumb across her bottom lip. "I won't tolerate it. And there will be consequences for misbehavior in the future."

"Consequences?" she challenged with a lifted brow.

I squeezed her chin. "However, I *do* enjoy admiring your mouth. Keep it up and I'll be forced to stuff something in it. Understood?"

Before she could respond, my mouth came down hard on hers. I pushed her lips apart with my tongue. I wasn't gentle, but it was both a punishment and a reward. She made noises in the back of her throat while I devoured her mouth.

When I lifted my head, her lips were red and swollen. She ran her tongue over the sensitive skin taunting me to kiss her again.

Stepping away from her, I walked back to my desk and resumed looking over my papers.

"I think I'd like to take you up on your offer."

I silently celebrated my win. "You think, or you are?"

She lifted her chin and with pinched lips she said, "I am."

I wanted her more than I'd wanted a woman in a long time. This was my way of doing things and she had to be all in before I'd proceed with her.

"Good. Let's start now."

I enjoyed the way her face lit up with surprise. Shocking her was insanely entertaining for me.

"Now?" she exclaimed. "But..."

"But what? I have a lot of work to do with you, so the sooner the better."

Before she could respond, I pulled out a small black gift bag from beneath my desk and pushed it toward her. She eyed it suspiciously and then took a step forward.

"What's this?"

I sighed. "Why don't you open it and find out?"

Slowly she hooked the edge of the bag with her finger and tried to peek around the hot pink tissue paper. I could have done without all the fuss, but the sales woman insisted it would be a nice touch.

Pulling it out, she lifted the first piece of clothing out and frowned. Looking at me, she pulled out the second piece and held them up so she could get a better look.

Her eyes found mind and I grinned.

"What the hell is this?"

"Mr. Black," I corrected her.

"What?"

"My name and what you're to address me as is Mr. Black."

"But why?"

Again, I sighed and rubbed the bridge of my nose. "Enough questioning everything I tell you to do. You're to call me Mr. Black and that my dear, Jessica, is an outfit. More importantly It's your outfit."

"This is *not* an outfit, *Mr. Black*." She was practically beside herself.

"It's whatever I fucking say it is and this is what pleases me. So put the damn thing on."

I'd startled her with my sharp words.

She looked at me abashed. "O-kay. I guess I'll put them on."

"It pleases you? That's your reasoning? Well, coconut cream pie *pleases* me, but you don't see me trying to wear it, do you?"

Standing, I stalked toward her. "First of all, I love coconut cream pie. Seeing you wear it would please me greatly since I could eat it off of you. Secondly, that smart mouth of yours has struck again. You have only yourself to blame for your next task."

"What next task?" she looked startled.

Good. Let her sweat.

Reaching around, I grabbed the bag and handed it to her. She hesitated and I shook it until she finally took it from me.

"The bathroom is through there." I leaned against my desk and folded my arms over my chest until she finally turned and walked toward the bathroom.

"Oh, and Jessica?"

She stopped, but didn't respond.

"Lose the bra and panties."

Her back stiffened, but she continued to the bathroom and shut the door. Seconds later, her voice drifted from the other room.

"Are you going to tell me why I have to wear this and what exactly I'll be doing?"

"I will as soon as you get your ass out here."

After a few minutes, the door opened slowly, but no Jessica appeared.

"I'm waiting... and I bet you could guess how much I fucking hate to wait."

I heard her sigh and then she was walking toward me. The outfit fit her exactly as I hoped it would. Actually, it was better than I imagined.

The black pin-striped skirt rode her thighs high and when she moved, I got a peek at the smooth pink folds between her legs. The jacket was tight over her breasts and with only one button, I could almost see her beautiful nipples.

The mere fucking sight of her nearly made me want to push her up against the wall and fuck five orgasms out of her.

"Come here," I commanded. She moved slowly to stand in front of me. "Turn around."

She opened her mouth to say something, but I flashed her a look and her mouth shut with a snap.

Telling her to turn around was a very fucking bad idea on my part. I had to control the urge to bend her over the chair.

"I'm here. Are you going to tell me what I need to do now?"

"For now, you're my assistant. You're going to caterer to my every want, my every... need." I ran the backs of my fingers over her exposed ass cheek and she let out a small gasp.

Taking a step forward, I slipped my hand between her silky thighs and she moaned.

"Sebastian."

Twisting my hands, I pinched her clit, and she cried out.

"Mr. Black," I corrected her. "When you're in this outfit... I'm Mr. Black."

I could see her shoulders tightening up.

"You made your choice, Jessica, and if you let yourself, you'll enjoy our arrangement quite nicely."

"Before or after you groom me?"

I flipped her around and leaned forward. "Before, during, and after. I promise you, sweetheart."

A flame of arousal danced inside of her eyes and I knew I had her.

"Follow me." I strode over to my chair and sat down.

She was hesitant, but she made her way around my desk until she was standing next to me. As much as her innocence was a turn on for me, I wanted to see the seductive side of her.

"In order to please me, you need to know what I like."

She swallowed. "What do you like?"

Grabbing her roughly by the hips, I pulled her directly in front of me and pushed her legs open, fitting my thighs between them. She gripped the edge of the desk.

"I like to look," I said, lifting my eyes toward her.

I knew the instant she understood what I meant. She almost looked ready to flee, but there was that spark again.

"Show me."

She slowly lifted herself onto my desk, keeping eye contact with me the entire time. I didn't look away from her as she opened her legs, putting a foot on either side of my chair.

"Do you like what you see, Mr. Black?" She asked tentatively.

My eyes dropped and I groaned to myself, I wanted nothing more than to bury my face in the softness between her legs.

"Yes, I do. Very much. Do you know what else I like?"

"What?"

Meeting her stare again, "My coffee. Black."

TEN

ROSSLYN

THE NEXT MORNING I WOKE with the sun. A coffee in hand, I stood at the massive set of windows and watched the world come alive. Memories from the night before and how I'd spent it filing papers and doing secretary work in the smallest clothes known to man, made me laugh. I should have been mad, but I couldn't help it. Sebastian really was a crazy freak, and I guess I was one, too, because I was kind of enjoying our little games.

An hour later, I walked Kyle to the lobby where we were met by Mr. Martin. When I got back to the room, I cried in the shower. It was the strangest thing to cry when things were sort of looking up, but I cried for Kyle, for Gran, for my parents—I sobbed loudly over life in general, which was so unbalanced. Things could change at the drop of a hat. Thanks to Sebastian, life was getting easier—more confusing, but easier.

Then again, Sebastian was just another thing in my life that wasn't permanent. Not to mention, he was all over the place. I wasn't sure I understood him, but I knew I'd gotten myself mixed into something crazy. After a life that was pretty boring and spent taking care of others, maybe crazy was what I needed.

When I was done, I turned off the shower, pulled back the curtain, only to find new clothes and a thick luxurious towel waiting in the bathroom for me.

Quickly, I dried my body and instead of dressing in the clothes, I threw the complimentary robe on. I didn't know who was in the room with me, but I wasn't going to sit around in the bathroom scared to find out.

I crept into the living space of the hotel and found Sebastian. He'd forgone his typical suit for a pair of jeans and a collar shirt that clung to his thick chest and arms. He was standing in the middle of the room, slinging a set of keys around his finger. Staring at the view of the city, his hair was messy and held a pair of sunglasses. He looked delicious.

Once he realized I was staring at him, he turned his gorgeous blue eyes on me.

The air left my body. "What are you doing here?" I asked.

The side of his mouth lifted, showing off his sexy set of dimples. "The room's in my name and I paid for it."

He stalked toward me and I was suddenly aware of how awful I must have looked. Maybe that was a good thing. Maybe he wouldn't want to have sex with me at that exact moment.

I reached up and touched a strand of soaking wet hair. "I know I must look..."

"Absolutely fucking sexy."

He ran his hand down my cheek and grinned down at me. "There are droplets of water covering the skin I can see. I'd like to lick them from your body."

I shivered and pulled the robe around me tighter.

"But first, I want to know why you're crying." He pinched my chin roughly like he had the day before, and exhilaration ran through me. "Sexy lips like these should never wear a frown."

I wanted him to kiss me hard, but he pulled away, releasing my chin.

He spoke and looked at me like we'd known each other for years. It wasn't terrible. It made me feel an odd sense of security that I hadn't felt since Gran was alive.

"It's nothing," I said.

"I think I know what's bothering you. Get dressed," he said sternly. "I want to show you something." He turned me toward the bathroom and patted my butt.

I picked out my nicest bra and panty set, and dressed quickly in the clothes he brought for me. The tags were still on them and I almost died when I saw that the pants alone were more than two hundred dollars. I quit looking from that point on. The shirt he bought fit perfectly and the green color of it looked nice with my red hair.

I brushed my teeth, ran a brush through my wet locks, and looked at myself in the stand-up mirror in the corner. Sebastian had really nice taste in clothing.

I went back into the living space and his eyes moved down my body like a seductive touch.

"You look amazing," he pulled his shades down over his eyes and started toward me.

"Thanks," I responded.

He held his hand out for me to proceed him onto the elevator, and then he got on, pushing the button to take us to the lobby.

His car was nice. No, it was beyond nice. It was a black Jaguar—sleek and sexy, just like him. He opened the door for me and I slid in. The rich leather hugged my bottom with love, and I melted into the comfort. He went around the car, took the keys from the valet, and slid in next to me.

He drove like a madman, flying past cars on one-way streets and running yellow lights as if they were green. My fingers dug into the door grip like it would keep me safe, and he chuckled at my side. He parked in front of a nice building. The brick outside was white and set with gold trimming.

There was a gorgeous archway that went into the front and glass doors with a doorman parked out front nodding nicely to the people that passed.

"Come on, beautiful," he said, tossing his keys to the valet.

I followed behind him to an elevator. We waited for the door to open and warmth moved up my spine when he placed a hand on the small of my back as we waited for the elevator.

The elevator opened into a room. It was furnished nicely with feminine décor and again had a wall of windows that showed New York City outside.

He grinned down at me before he stepped off of the elevator and pulled me along with him. I took the room in—a sleek condo with expensive furnishings that were definitely decorated by a professional. I tried to figure out where we were, and then I started to see familiar pieces placed around the room. Pictures from Gran's living room were on the wall and frames full of Kyle's smiles were sitting on a table to the side.

I gasped. "Is this..." I couldn't even finish the sentence.

"It's yours."

With a gapped mouth and eyes wide with shock, I made a circle in the room. I could hardly believe my eyes.

"But my things. How did you..." I felt the tears sting the back of my eyes.

"Vick. She took care of everything. Apparently, your friend that works at the club will tell anything for a few bucks."

I turned back to him with wide eyes. No one had ever done anything so amazing for me before. Everything that I'd stored in Trish's parents' garage was there.

There were so many things I wanted to say to him, but nothing felt good enough. Instead, I went to him and threw my arms around his neck. He tensed and stood there without hugging me back.

"Whoa," he chuckled, setting me away from him.

I pulled back and smiled up at him. "I have no words. Thank you, Sebastian. I'll pay you back. I'll..."

He held his hand up to silence me. "No worries. I'll collect payment very soon."

His eyes devoured my mouth and I swallowed hard.

"Let's take a look at the rest of the place," he said, turning his back to me and walking away.

The place was magnificent—no expense spared. It was huge, more than I knew what to do with, but I knew it wasn't permanent. This thing that was happening with Sebastian was just starting, but I wasn't stupid enough to think it would last forever. For Kyle, and secretly for me too, I'd do this. But I had to have a back-up plan.

Sebastian took me back to the hotel, and didn't stay. Business meetings were taking him away and the strange part was, I felt sad he was leaving. I was beginning to feel safe with him and that wasn't good. He was the opposite of safe. He was dangerous. Especially since he made me feel things physically I'd never felt before.

I packed all of our belongings, and went down to meet Kyle in the lobby after school.

"So we have a place now." My smile hurt my cheeks it was so big.

Pulling him into my side as we walked back to the elevator, I ruffled his hair.

"That's great. When do we move in?" he asked.

"Right now. Everything's already in place. All of our things are there. It's perfect, Kyle."

"But how?"

"A friend of mine is helping us out until I get on my feet."

"Pretty nice friend," he shrugged.

Thankfully, the subject was dropped and once we got to our place and he saw how fabulous it was, I didn't think he cared about the hows or whys.

That night I slept in my bed, in a secure place, surrounded by all my things. My hair was damp from soaking in a hot bath all night and my body felt more relaxed than it had in years.

ELEVEN

ROSSLYN

"**D**O THESE JEANS MAKE MY ass look fat?" Trish asked. She was turning in the mirror, trying to see her back.

"No," I said absently, staring out of the store into the rest of the Manhattan mall.

Women wrapped in expensive everything and carrying purses with pooches inside, chatted as they walked by.

A girl's day with Trish was exactly what I needed. Anything that got my mind off of the crazy mess my life was becoming.

"Fuck. I guess I'll get a smaller size then."

She stripped down not caring who saw her in just her panties. It was then I realized what she'd said.

"Wait. Are you saying you *want* a pair of jeans to make your ass look fat?" I asked confused.

"Yes. My ass is flat. I need something to perk it up." She reached down, grabbing her bottom and lifted it.

"Oh my God, Trish. You're so deranged."

Eleven pairs of jeans later, and she finally found a pair that she was happy with.

Next, we stopped at yet another clothing store, where I sat for another hour and watched her try on clothes.

Anything was better than sitting at the condo watching TV all day.

"Oh my God, you should try this on." Trish said from my side. "This would look amazing on your with your red hair."

I looked over to find her holding up green top. It was beautiful with a scoop neckline.

"I don't have the money to buy any new clothes right now," I giggled.

"Oh come on. You have to at least try it on." Shoving it into my arms, she pushed me into the dressing room.

I sighed loudly, before pulling my T-shirt over my head and slipping the green shirt on. The fabric felt like butter and it fit perfectly. I turned in the mirror admiring how nice it looked on me. Grabbing the tag that was dangling from the arm, I looked down at the expensive price tag.

"Come out. Let me see what it looks like," Trish called out on the other side of the door.

Opening the door, I stepped out and adjusted the shirt.

"See? I told you it would look amazing on you. Do you love it?"

I smiled and made a tiny turn. "I think I do."

After promising Trish I'd save and buy the shirt another day, we finally left the store and headed to the food court.

"So what exactly happened at Clive's?" she asked, sucking at her Starbucks cup.

The food court around us bustled with laughter and voices. I reached down and plucked at a fry on my tray.

"Nothing really," I shrugged.

Trish tilted her head to the side and looked at me like I was full of it, which I totally was.

"Don't give me that shit. Stacy, the pretty waitress with the nose ring, said she saw Sebastian talking to you personally. He never does that." She took another sip. "So what did he say?"

I debated whether or not telling her was a good idea. I'd known Trish a while and never had she been one to tell secrets. But then again, I'd never really had any juicy secrets to tell. She worked at Clive's and she was bound to let it slip at some point. The thought of it getting back to Sebastian that I was talking about him didn't scare me, but it wasn't something I wanted to happen.

"Really. Nothing happened. He just told me nicely that the job wasn't for me and sent me on my way." I was lying. I hated lying and it wasn't something I did often, but it was necessary.

Trish didn't know where I was staying. She was too caught up in her life to even ask, which was fine by me. Usually I'd be ticked off by her selfish ways, but this time, not so much.

"He's fucking sexy isn't he?"

"Who?" I asked.

"Sebastian, the owner of Clive's."

"Oh. Yeah I guess he's okay," I shrugged.

Another lie.

"You guess?" She reached out and playfully laid her hand on my forehead like she was checking my temperature. I laughed and smacked her hand away. "Seriously, Roz, you're either delirious from a burning fever, totally blind, or into sucking clit if you don't see how unbelievably hot that man is."

"Oh my God, you did not just say that?" I put my head down when I noticed the lady next to her looking at us with an appalled expression.

"Yes, I did. And just so you know, I'd love you if you were any of those." She stole a fry from my tray and tossed it into her mouth. "Sexy or not, he's a total knob slobber."

"What's a knob slobber?" I asked.

"Oh come on, Roz. As in, he slobs on knobs." She made the motion with her hand and mouth like she was going down on a guy.

At that point, the lady next to us got up and moved. Poor lady.

However, Trish's words did get my attention. "What makes you think he's gay?"

"He has to be. He works at this club full of hot bitches, including myself, and never once has he even batted an eyelash at any of them."

"That doesn't mean he's gay," I defended.

She looked at me like I was crazy, then grabbed her breasts and shook them. "Seriously, look at these. In two years, he would have at least flirted with me once."

I didn't say anything else after that. I could have knocked her off her high horse by telling her I knew for a fact Sebastian wasn't gay, but she was my friend and I'd rather she stay self-confident.

I waited until Trish was completely out of sight before I climbed into the back of the sleek black car that was waiting for me.

"Have a nice time shopping, Miss?" Mr. Martin asked, pulling away from the curb.

"I sure did." I plastered on a fake smile and turned to watch the city go by.

I rode to pick up Kyle from school, and then Mr. Martin drove us home. After a quick dinner of Sloppy Joes, Kyle showered and went to bed. I sat up and watched TV. The last thing I remembered was an episode of *Golden Girls*, before falling asleep on the couch.

I BRIEFLY REMEMBERED WAKING IN Sebastian's arms, as he carried me to my bedroom. I'd been too tired to try and talk to him, and my eyes had fluttered shut. Then I think he laid me in my bed, and pulled the covers up to my chest.

There'd been a soft warmth on my cheek that I was sure was a kiss, but I couldn't be bothered to open my eyes. I must have been dreaming though. Sebastian Black wasn't the kind of man to do anything soft and sweet.

I woke the next morning to Kyle making himself breakfast. I'd overslept, which was something I didn't do often. Climbing from the bed, I made my way to the bathroom and splashed cold water on my face to help wake myself up.

After brushing my hair and teeth, I went back into my room to get dressed for the day. I reached out to open my closet door when I saw the green shirt I'd admired the day before at the mall hanging on the door knob.

Picking it up, I saw that it was the perfect size and everything. It was then, the night before came rushing back to me. Sebastian had definitely been there. It hadn't been a dream like I'd thought it was.

TWELVE

SEBASTIAN

"SO WHAT'S THE DEAL WITH you and Jessica?" Vick stepped into my office with Starbucks and a forced smile.

Her grin alone was alarming because smiling was not her thing.

"What do you mean?"

"You have to admit things are different with her."

I couldn't put my finger on it, but Vick wasn't acting like herself.

"Our deal's no different than the rest of the girls in my book."

"Yeah fucking right," she snorted around her cup of coffee. "I don't recall you ever buying the other girls upscale condos."

"She needed a place. I'll make up the difference in her weekly payments. She'll get less." I was lying, but I didn't want Vick thinking Jessica was changing me. She wasn't.

"Don't bullshit me, Sebastian. I saw the account you opened for her. She has the same amount of starter money as the rest of the girls." She sat her hip against my desk and scowled down at me. "What's the deal? Is this bitch turning you soft?"

Anger struck me deep, in a place I hadn't visited since I was young and stupid, and fighting to survive on the streets of New York.

"Don't call her that," I barked, the side of my fist landed on my desk hard, shaking papers.

My voice was dark, daring her to say another word. Vick and I usually got along well, but her calling Jessica a bitch shook something loose.

She peered down at me with a look of pity. "No different, huh?" Shaking her head, she turned and walked out of my office.

My hands were shaking with rage. "You do not get to regard me in that manner!"

Without turning around, she called over her shoulder. "I'm sorry, *sir*. I thought it was my right to point out when the closest person to me was becoming a pussy-whipped dickwad."

The door slammed behind her, knocking a picture from my wall. I was going to have to take Vick down a fucking peg or two. She was definitely getting too comfortable trying to control me. I wasn't having it.

I didn't want to hear any more shit from fucking Laura Croft: Emasculator. Jessica was not changing me. I'd just met the girl and I'd barely had a taste of her yet. I wasn't changing for anyone, and I'd prove it.

I pulled out my book and flipped through the pages. Jessica wasn't ready for sex yet, but I was in need of some female attention. Picking out at random, I pulled out my phone and prepared to text one of my ladies, but a loud noise from the club below stopped me.

"Where the fuck is he?" a female voice bellowed.

Going to the window, the workers below parted as Bambi came bursting through the tables knocking chairs onto the floor. She wasn't as put together as she was every time we met. Her eyes were wide, but not the usual big doe eyes I was used to. She looked wild—feral, and on the hunt.

Taking the stairs as fast as I could, I went straight to her. She practically growled as I took her by the arm and pulled her into the VIP section. My employees didn't need to know my personal business and with her being an obnoxious bitch, it wouldn't be long before everyone knew everything.

"What seems to be the problem?" I asked calmly, hoping she'd follow my lead.

"I'm completely fucking *broke*. That's the problem. For months, your payments were getting me through. I lost my job since I left every time you called, and now you're completely cutting me off. That's bullshit and you know it, *Sebastian*." She put emphasis on my name since I'd never bothered to tell her.

I silently wondered how she found out who I was—how she found me.

"That sucks for you. However, the club isn't open right now. We open tonight at seven. Please return then."

"Excuse me?" she asked, appalled.

"I'm asking you to leave. If you don't, I'll have you forcefully removed from the premises."

"How could you treat me like this? I thought... I thought we had something special."

I pulled her close to me. So close, her tits pressed into my chest and I could taste her breath. She squirmed as if she was enjoying it.

"We had an arrangement. One that made you a lot of money and one that got me exactly what I wanted from you. I wasn't vague about our situation. You knew what you were walking into and you still did it. I got bored with you, which I tend to do, and now our arrangement is over. It's not my fault you don't know how to save money. Maybe if you hadn't blown it all on frivolous bullshit, you'd have a little something in your account. Now, I'm not asking, I'm telling. Get the fuck out of my establishment."

She stuttered over her unintelligible response, before she turned and fled from the club. I followed behind her, the employees turning away and working, as if they hadn't heard every bit of our argument. *Fuck it.* I was stressed beyond belief, and I hadn't had any pussy since I'd laid eyes on Jessica.

Jessica. She was beautiful and sexy—clueless to her seductiveness. She was the woman I'd been searching for, for years—the one type missing from my black book. And she was as good as mine.

I'd already bought her a condo and gave her an account full of money. Ready or not, it was time I started getting paid my part of the deal.

THE ELEVATOR DOOR OPENED INTO the clean, comfortable space of Jessica's condo. I'd been there the night before, but this time the place smelled like woman and fresh flowers. I inhaled her sweetness and closed my eyes to the rush of desire consuming me.

Stepping into the room, I was taken aback by how comfortable and at home I felt in the condo. The family pictures taken from Jessica's storage were littered across the wall and table in the living space. It was comforting.

A particular picture of Jessica and her little brother when they were younger, stuck out. I envied their relationship. Family—it's all I'd ever wanted. Yet at the same time, the fear of being left behind kept me from making any new relationships with anyone. It was an endless cycle.

It was then I noticed the music coming from the other room. My feet followed the tune, until I was standing in Jessica's bedroom doorway. She was there, with only a towel wrapped around her curvy frame. Her back was to me and she moved around the room, swinging her hips, singing badly into her brush.

Wet strands of red stuck to her back and beads of water rolled down her shoulders and into the towel. My mouth went dry thinking about sucking the water from her body.

Leaning my shoulder against the door frame, I watched silently with crossed arms. She was different— young and endearing, full of life. It was refreshing.

Jessica Rabbit, the cartoon character, had nothing on my Jessica. My Jessica wasn't a seductive siren on purpose, but it was the way she made me feel that prompted the name. From the moment I first saw her, I was always seconds away from wolf howling with bulging eyes.

Her towel rode up her thighs, exposing the bottom of her ass cheek and it was my undoing. Stepping into the room, I slipped up behind her and wrapped my hands around her hips. I was rock hard already, so I rubbed my hard cock into the back of her towel.

She screamed before turning in my arms. The towel was forgotten and it drifted to the floor between us. There she was, naked in my arms, and wet—so fucking wet everywhere. I could only hope soon the sweet spot between her legs would also be soaked for me.

Fingering a strand of her hair, my fingertips glistened from the moisture. She looked up at me with wide eyes. Her teeth sank into her bottom lip and when she released it, it was swollen and pink—begging me to bite it.

So I did.

I sucked her bottom lip into my mouth and bit down enough to make her go tense.

"You're driving me bat-shit crazy," I said, leaning in and slamming my mouth against hers.

She tasted amazing. Like fresh fruit in the rain. Like one of my favorite memories... like a home I never knew. And strangely, it angered me.

I pulled away, releasing her arms and her mouth all at once. She fell back, covering her breasts before I could see them. Bending down, she attempted to retrieve her towel, but I stopped her.

"Move your hands," I demanded. "I want to see your tits."

"Sebastian, this is..." she started.

I cut her off before she could finish. "What did I say?"

She stood there staring back at me. I could see the debate in her eyes. She wasn't sure if she should listen or tell me to go to hell. Finally, she dropped her hands from her body and stood in front of me, gloriously naked.

Heat radiated from my eyes as I let them dip and explore her balmy skin. Her dusty nipples hardened, taunting me to squeeze them. Reaching out, I pinched a nipple between my thumb and forefinger, eliciting a hissing sound from between her teeth.

"Does that hurt?" I asked.

"A little."

"But it still feels good, doesn't it?"

She'd be lying if she denied it. Her eyes were already sparkling with desire.

She didn't answer, prompting me to squeeze tighter.

"Yes!" she exclaimed.

"Yes, what?"

"It feels good."

I released her reddening nipple and relieved it with a nice lashing with my tongue. Her breathing hitched and then she moaned when I sucked the nipple into my mouth and nibbled sweetly. She'd earned that little bit for now.

When I pulled away and looked back at her, her eyes were glazed over with want. Already she was melting in my hands. It wouldn't be long before I'd have her tied to a bed, ass wiggling in the air, begging me to fuck her.

I ran a single finger from her collar bone, down over her moist nipple. I couldn't seem keep my hands off her. Her humid skin pebbled beneath my fingertip. I continued on my path, running it down her stomach to her navel. Her skin was like silk. It was wrong for her to cover it with cheap cotton.

Reaching into my pocket, I pulled out a card and placed it in her palm, closing her fingers around it.

"What's this?" she asked, opening her hand.

"It's for you to spend how you see fit. I only have one request, get rid of the cotton panties. Your body begs for silk and lace."

She shocked me by shoving the card back into my hand.

"No, Sebastian. You've done enough. I can't take this. The condo, the car, the shirt, all of it... by the way, thanks for the shirt. I don't even want to know how you knew I'd tried it on."

"I have my ways."

I didn't tell her that Martin had gotten out of the car for a walk and saw how happy she'd looked inside the store, shopping with her friend. He'd picked it up and turned it over to me. As I said before, he got paid the big bucks for a reason.

"Well, it's all too much. Not to mention, I haven't really done anything to earn any of this yet."

I grinned. She was so clueless and sweet. It was a wonder New York hadn't eaten her alive yet.

"Don't worry, you will."

Her face paled, shyness filling her expression, and I chuckled.

"Go shopping. Buy yourself something that will drive me crazy. I'll pick you up tonight at seven. Be ready and be dressed to kill."

I didn't wait for her to respond. I walked away. If I didn't get away from her soon I was going to do something stupid, and push her before she was ready—like laying her on the bed and sinking myself balls deep into her tight pussy.

I had full rights to do what I pleased with her, and I knew she'd go for it because she obviously felt indebted to me. But that was not my goal. I wanted her to want me the way I wanted her. I wanted her soaking wet and begging for my cock and anything else I had to offer. To have that, I'd wait—even if it killed me.

THIRTEEN

ROSSLYN

ONCE SEBASTIAN LEFT THE ROOM, I let myself relax. It wasn't that he scared me, but he made me physically aware of myself and of him. The way my body responded to him was something I wasn't accustomed to.

My nipple ached, stinging from his attention, and between my legs was soaked. Every part of me was hyper-sensitive. When I picked up my towel and rubbed it across my body, a tiny gasp escaped me.

I was alone. I'd listened carefully as the elevator opened and closed, assuring me Sebastian was gone. So I let my hands slowly drop down my body, my palms rubbing across my hard nipples and weaving sensation into my lower stomach.

It wasn't going to be long before I was begging him for everything he had to offer, but the whole being paid thing was really messing me up. Not to mention, I hated it that he called me Jessica.

Who the hell was this Jessica, anyway?

How could I get into anything sexual with him, knowing he didn't even want to know me? It all felt so wrong, but oh so right at the same time. It was confusing.

Not long after I dressed, Kyle stepped off the elevator. I could tell right away something was bothering him.

He tossed his bag onto the floor in the corner and went to the kitchen for the food that was there when we moved in. Teenage boys ate more than grown men.

Reaching down, I plucked his heavy bag from the floor and moved it to the table so he could start his homework once he was done with his after school snack. A white envelope fell out of the side pocket and landed at my feet.

"What's this?" I asked, sliding my finger into the envelope and popping it open.

"It's an invitation to an art program that's going on this summer," he shrugged. "It's not a big deal." His mouth was full of potato chips, and his voice was muffled.

My eyes scanned the letter. The art program was distinguished—as in, only thirty students in the entire state of New York were invited each year. And yet, my little brother managed to be one of them.

"Looks like a pretty big deal to me. Since when are you into art?" I asked, holding up the letter.

"Since always, I just kind of always kept it to myself. Then Mrs. Gelding, my art teacher, busted me drawing in my notebook. She's the one who sent my work off to the program coordinators."

I was flabbergasted. I thought I knew everything there was to know about my little brother... guess I was wrong. "Can I see your work?"

He pulled out a manila folder from his book bag and handed it over. Flipping through the art, drawings of New York City looked back at me. Lines drawn to perfection, and shadings in all the right places, formed an exact representation of the city. It was beautiful—more than beautiful.

As I flipped, I came across a picture which made my heart sink. There was Gran smiling back at me, wrinkles filling her face with happiness. It was a perfect likeness— exactly as I remembered her.

"There's one of you, too." Kyle mentioned at my side.

I hadn't known he was watching me and quickly swiped at the tear forming on my bottom lashes. I ran my fingers across the next drawing. It was me, and it was like looking in the mirror. Lines were etched into my frown, and my eyes were full of sadness.

Sliding the art back into the folder, I handed it over to him.

"These are amazing, Kyle. I can't... I don't know what to say. You're simply amazing. You have to go. No, you're going."

And I meant it. It would be a lonely summer, but it was honor to be invited to such a place and with his talent, he had to go. Not to mention, with everything I had going on around me with Sebastian and the new place, maybe Kyle being tucked away somewhere wasn't a bad idea.

"I can't," he said sternly, tucking his folder back into his bag.

"Why not? I think it's a great idea, Kyle. You could be the next big thing in the art world."

He laughed and shook his head, his floppy hair falling into his eyes. "I'd like to, but it's kind of expensive." He shrugged. "Like I said, it's no big deal."

And then, I knew. Kyle wanted to go—he wanted to go bad, but like he was always doing, he blew it off so I didn't get stressed out. Well, no more. It was time my little brother got something he wanted for once.

"How much?" I asked.

"It doesn't matter."

"How much, Kyle?"

He smiled sheepishly before giving in. "Five thousand for the summer," he answered.

I swallowed hard, trying to push down the lump stuck in my throat. It wasn't going to happen. It wasn't like five thousand dollars was just going to land at my feet, and as much as I loved my brother, there was no way in the world I was going to ask Sebastian for it.

I already hated the idea of him taking care of us, which is exactly what he was doing. I felt even worse knowing I'd done nothing so far to earn everything he'd given us. Then again, it was kind of scary. What would Sebastian consider adequate payment for everything?

"I'm sorry, Kyle." I said with a thick throat. "I'm so very sorry."

"No worries," he smiled, before going into his room.

I heard his music start to play softly from his old radio before his door clicked shut.

AN HOUR LATER, THE BANK card Sebastian had left behind, caught my attention. I'd forgotten all about it. I didn't want to spend the money on the card. I especially didn't want to spend it on myself like Sebastian had requested, but I wanted Kyle to be happy.

I called the number on the back of the card, only to find the account had five thousand dollars in it. My jaw dropped. It was fate. It was so much more than fate. I had the money to send Kyle to the art program. Even if it meant not having anything for myself for the entire summer, he was going.

I called his school and made the payment over the phone, telling the administrator I was an anonymous benefactor. Kyle already had questions about the condo. How would I explain suddenly having five grand for his program? It was easier to lie.

I could hardly wait to see the happy smile I was sure he'd be wearing when he came home from school the following day. I missed his smile—the special one he used to have before he began to understand the cruelty of the world. I planned on basking in his smile, and letting it fill me with happiness while secretly knowing I was the one that put it there.

Later, I dressed in my sexiest bra and panties—which of course were still cotton—and my nicest clothing, including the shirt Sebastian had bought me. He would know everything wasn't new, but I'd deal with that, if and when he brought it up.

I met him out front. He arrived in the black car Mr. Martin chauffeured. I liked it better when Sebastian drove because it was more comfortable. I didn't have to worry about what Mr. Martin could hear from the driver's seat.

Plus, all the drivers and expensive restaurants weren't for me. I wanted so badly for him to take me to a burger joint and a movie, but I kept quiet.

"Hi, Mr. Martin," I said when I slid into the car.

"Hello, Miss."

I turned to find Sebastian angrily staring at me.

"Why aren't you dressed to kill?"

I looked down at my outfit. Plucking at the front of my shirt, I acted seriously confused. "I thought I was dressed to kill."

He didn't find that comment as amusing as I did.

"Answer the question."

I sighed and gave in.

"I didn't have time to shop."

"You're lying," he said. "Let's try that again. Why aren't you—"

"I'm broke," I cut him off.

"How is that possible, Jessica? You had five thousand dollars in that account. I know this because I'm the one who opened it. Where did the money go?"

"I spent it."

"On what? I swear if I find out you're into some crazy shit, the deal's off."

"No. It's nothing like that."

"Then what?"

"Kyle. He got into this art program for the summer. Only thirty people were invited from around the state, and he made it in," I rushed. "I'll show you his work. He's really good. I just... I didn't want him to go without again."

"So now you're going to go without?"

"No. When he's happy, I'm happy. I'll do whatever it takes to make sure Kyle has a good life. If that means going without, then so be it."

"And what about your life? Don't you think you should have a good life, too?"

"My life is just fine."

"I disagree," he turned away, looking down at his expensive watch. "I'll put more money into the account."

"No!" I said too loudly. "I mean, please don't do that. I haven't done anything to earn it yet."

"Yet?" he lifted a brow and grinned.

A hot blush covered my cheeks. "You know what I mean. I just don't understand why you're doing this when I haven't... you know?"

"What would you say if I said *I'd* do whatever it took to make sure *you* had a good life?"

"I'd say you're nuts."

"Then I guess I'm nuts," he moved closer. "Very soon you'll pay me back, and I look forward to that kind of payment."

My blush heated. "Do you have to make it so obvious?" I asked quietly, motioning to Mr. Martin in the front seat.

He looked at me with confusion before his face cleared and he started to laugh. I sunk deeper into my embarrassment and into the seat.

"Were you under the assumption that Martin doesn't know what I do with my girls?" Again, he chuckled.

"Well, no. I mean..."

"Trust me. Martin gets paid the big bucks for a reason. He's paid to act with the upmost discretion." He reached forward and shook Mr. Martin's shoulder playfully. "Isn't that right, old man?"

My eyes met Mr. Martin's in the rear-view mirror and he nodded and smiled. "Absolutely, sir."

Sebastian grinned over at me, before looking out the window once more.

"Change of plans, Martin. Let's go to the other side of town and make a pit stop."

Instead of the expected expensive restaurant, Sebastian took me to a hole-in-the-wall burger joint called, The Pit

Stop. It was on the darker side of the city. The outside of the building looked sketchy, and the people who were coming from inside looked even worse.

"Are you that embarrassed by the way I dress?" I tried to control the edge in my voice and avoided all eye contact with him.

"What are you talking about?" He sounded genuinely confused.

Waving my arm, I said, "Didn't you bring me to this place so I wouldn't taint your reputation?"

"We really have to control your over-active emotions, Jessica. You're either hot or cold, and while that might sound appealing sexually, it's not when outside the bedroom. I didn't bring you here because I'm embarrassed by your choice of clothing. This is my favorite place to eat heart failing, artery clogging hamburgers."

I didn't respond to that. Instead, I contained my smiled and followed him in.

This time Sebastian was the one who stuck out like a sore thumb when we walked in. He held his head high as he moved confidently through the place in his expensive black suit. I covered my smile. The expressions on the faces of everyone around us were comical.

"What?" Sebastian asked when he noticed me staring and smiling.

"You look so out of place here," I giggled.

He tried hard not to smile, then his dimples deepened and the side of his mouth tilted upwards. "Trust me. I'm more comfortable in a place like this than you'd think."

His words made me wonder about him and where he'd come from. I knew next to nothing about Sebastian, but I suddenly had the desire to. He was an enigma—one who could wear expensive suits, but still feel comfortable in the ghettos of New York City.

We took the table in the back, tucked away from the rest of the people in the restaurant.

"Tell me something about you," I said, folding the napkin nervously in front of me.

When he didn't respond, I looked up to find him staring at me like I was his dinner. His eyes drifted from my face, down my neck, and landed on my chest.

"I don't talk about myself with my girls."

The strangest thing happened in that moment. I became jealous. It burned at my center, as if I had just eaten bad Mexican food. It made no sense because I didn't have a hold on Sebastian, whatsoever. I seriously doubted anyone in the world did.

"I apologize. I forgot I was just one of your *girls*. However many there are," I snapped, looking anywhere but at him. I was embarrassed by my reaction.

"Are you jealous of the other girls, Jessica?" he asked. His smile was cocky and smug.

"No."

There was no need to elaborate. I figured my lie would be more believable if I kept it short and sweet.

"Good. You have no reason to be. I haven't seen or spoken to any of them since the moment I first saw you."

The burn in my stomach dissolved and I found myself locked in a heated gaze. Then he turned away and tugged on his collar. He was finally the one uncomfortable, and I gathered he'd said more than he wanted to.

The waitress came and set our food on the table. Big, sloppy burgers, full of calories and goodness, with a side of fries and heart attack—it was exactly what I needed.

The burger was amazing and I couldn't help but groan in appreciation while I chewed.

"Good, right?" he asked around his bite.

"Oh my God, it's the best burger I've ever had."

And it was. I could totally see myself braving the city streets on occasion for the deliciousness that was my burger.

"This was my favorite place to eat when I was younger," he said, dipping his fry into the pile of ketchup on his burger wrapper.

I didn't want to say anything about the fact that he'd told me something personal, when I was supposedly just one of his *girls*. Instead, I smiled and said, "I think it might be my new favorite place. This is fantastic."

When we were done, and I was good and stuffed, Sebastian threw a hundred dollar bill on the table and stood. I followed him out into the night air, feeling completely satisfied with the food and Sebastian's company.

Mr. Martin pulled in front of the restaurant as we were walking out. Sebastian opened my door for me and I stepped up to get in.

"Give me your fucking wallet," a gruff voice said from behind us.

I turned to see Sebastian standing there with a gun stuck to his side. The man holding the gun looked as if he slept on the streets and was definitely on something. He was shaking and antsy, like he was dying for another hit of whatever it was he was strung out on. His bloodshot eyes stared at Sebastian as he waited.

"I mean it, motherfucker. Give me your goddamn wallet or I'll blow a hole in your side and take a little somethin' from that piece of hot ass with you, too."

TABATHA & MELISSA

Things were a blur from that point. When Sebastian went for the man, I barely saw him move before he had him on his stomach and the gun to his head.

"Be careful who you try to steal from, fuck face," he growled, pressing the gun deep into the man's temple. "I should kill you, but I'm going to let you go because I know this isn't your corner. Get your ass where you belong or I'll have Anthony blow your fucking head off. Got it?"

His voice was raw and angry. He spoke like the man who had tried to rob us. I could hardly believe how vicious he sounded. I didn't blame the man when he nodded his head and ran off.

The back of the car was holding me up. I was frozen in fear. Having a stranger threaten to kill you will do that I suppose.

"Are you okay?" Sebastian asked. He shook out his jacket like it was filthy and brushed off his pants.

I couldn't answer at first and just stared blankly in his direction.

"Jess—"

"Please don't call me that..." I pleaded on a shaky breath. I was sure my face had lost all color and I felt like I was going to be sick. "Not right now," I finally finished.

I knew he said I was the only one he called Jessica, but that didn't make it any easier to hear. If I was so special, why couldn't he know my name?

"Fine," he said tightly. He didn't like being told what to do and he disliked doing it even more. "Are you okay?" he asked.

"Me? Are *you* okay? You're the one who just had a gun pointed at you."

How could he seem so calm? After everything that had happened with my parents, I couldn't stomach the sight of guns. Some nights I was sure I could still hear the sounds of gun shots all around me. My fear kept me far away from them.

"This is New York, sweetheart. Everyone in this fucked up city has probably had a gun pointed at them in their lifetime."

I frowned. "If that was meant to reassure me, it didn't."

My stomach turned at the thought of having a gun pointed at me, and Kyle's face immediately popped into my head. I never wanted him to know that kind of fear. It was naïve to think I could shield him from all the bad and hate in this world, but I *had* to try. Before I could stop it, I was quickly hunted by a different time, a different image and I felt my body began to shake.

In a blink of an eye, Sebastian was at my side and his hands were moving over my arms and face. His fingers caressed the curve of my neck and he lifted my face to look at him.

He showed a combination of possessiveness, concern and... anger. I didn't understand the anger, but it made his blue eyes sparkle brilliantly.

"Why are you shaking?" His voice was rough.

"Why are you angry?"

"It's left over from the asshole who thought he could point a gun in my face."

I swallowed hard and prayed I didn't throw up on his expensive shoes.

"Now your turn. Why are you shaking?" he demanded.

I took a much need breath and exhaled my confession. "I hate guns. I can't stand them to the point that they make me physically ill."

He frowned. "Why?"

I felt confused by his question and I matched his frown. "Isn't it obvious? Guns kill people."

He smirked. "No, sweetheart, *people* kill people." He sounded dark and dangerous when he said it. "Guns are simply a means to an end."

"Again, if you're trying to comfort me, you're not doing a very good job."

"I don't do comfort, I do real and I'm as real as it gets."

"Noted," I snapped.

"Can you move? Are you able to get in the car?"

I nodded before sliding into the car. Sebastian waited until we were on the move before he spoke again.

"What's the real reason you're afraid of guns?"

I turned to look at him, but he was facing forward.

"Ever since I was a little girl I've always had a fear of them."

"That doesn't tell me *why*."

I didn't want to talk about my parents or their death, and I was sure Sebastian didn't want to hear the story either.

"I knew someone who was shot and killed." It wasn't a lie, but it wasn't the whole truth either.

A full minute passed before he said anything.

"So because of your fear, you leave yourself defenseless? What would have happened if I hadn't been here? What happens when the thing you're afraid of turns out to be the thing that can save your life? Except, you don't know how to use it."

"Then I'm screwed," I said simply.

"No." He finally turned to look at me and I controlled the urge to wiggle under his gaze. "Then you're dead."

I didn't know how to respond. Partly because I didn't have a rebuttal, and partly because deep down, I knew he was right. We lapsed into silence and it wasn't until we were close to my condo that I spoke.

"Who's Anthony?" I asked.

He continued to stare out the window as he answered. "Just a guy I used to know."

"I take it you're from that side of town?" I knew I was prying, but I couldn't help myself.

"Yes," he responded.

"Does your family still live there?"

Suddenly, he turned on me with angry eyes, like the ones he gave the man who tried to rob us.

"Did anyone ever tell you, you ask too many goddamn questions?" His tone was so abrupt, it caught me completely off guard.

"I'm sorry. I just thought—"

He cut me off. "You weren't thinking. We're here. Enjoy the rest of your evening."

He was dismissing me like I was a child. And unlike every other time, he wasn't going to walk me in, or even get out of the car for that matter.

By the time I made it to my floor, I felt awful. What if he didn't have a family? There I was, playing twenty questions and I hadn't even thought about whether or not I was asking something that might bother him.

He was being totally rude, but after thinking on it, I wasn't surprised. He'd told me from the start what our

agreement was and it didn't include personal questions—
at least when they came from me.

We were never going to veg out in front of the TV and
get to know each other. And even though I'd die before I
actually admitted it, I really wanted to get to know
Sebastian... in more ways than one.

FOURTEEN

SEBASTIAN

I WAS A FUCKING ASSHOLE. I'd known it all my life. I wasn't born that way, but the world around me had molded me into someone who could take shit and dish it out just as quickly. Being a cocky dick had never failed me so far, until today. The hurt look in her eyes when I'd yelled at her was like a stun gun.

She didn't know how fucked up I was. She didn't know asking about my family was the most hurtful thing she could do. I was wrong for snapping at her. There was a big difference between sexual authority and shouting at a woman. But I knew once I settled down, I was going to make it up to her.

Steaming water poured over my face and shoulders. The shower was the first place I went when I was back home. I'd walked through the crowded club, ignoring people who thought they were my friends, and went straight up the stairs. I'd have to go back down soon and play club owner, but all I wanted to do was stand under the heat and let it burn me.

"Who took a shit on your steak?" Vick asked when I went into the office.

She was sitting behind my desk with her feet up like she owned the place.

"Fuck you. Anything going on downstairs?" I asked, flipping through papers on my desk.

"Ouch. That burns a little. Good thing I'm into pain." She dropped her heavy boots to the floor and stood. "No one special, but you should still show your face."

Our relationship was strained—it had been ever since I'd laid eyes on Jessica. It was another hassle I didn't feel like dealing with, but at some point I was going to have to get to the bottom of Vick's problems.

She slammed the office door on her way out and I shook my head in aggravation. I was seconds away from turning around, going after her, and cursing her out. But then the door opened again, letting in the loud music from downstairs.

"What's wrong? You weren't done being a bitch?" I asked with my back to her.

"Actually, I came to apologize."

Jessica's soft voice filled the space behind me, prompting me to turn and face her. She had changed, and was now wearing a sexy black skirt and an off-the-shoulder pink top. Her typical blush covered her cheeks and neck. My cock grew hard in the seconds since she arrived.

"Apologize for what?" I asked.

She had no reason to be sorry. Me on the other hand, I should have apologized, but that wasn't something I ever did. Instead, I'd buy her something nice or give her an extra orgasm.

"I shouldn't have been nosey. I had no right to pry into your business or ask about your family."

I could have taken full advantage of her position, instead, I took her by the hand and pulled her to me. Burying my face in her hair, letting her fresh scent fill me.

"No. I was a total asshole. I shouldn't have snapped at you like that. Of course you'd want to know more about me. So, I'm sorry."

If Vick could hear me apologizing to one of the girls in my book, there is no doubt she'd cut my cock off and give it to someone more worthy. Honestly, it felt strange. I hadn't expected for the words to come out; they felt sticky on my tongue and I had to swallow hard to get the bitter taste out of my mouth.

"I say we both just forget it," she smiled.

Her smile was sweet. Way too sweet for a man like me, but I soaked it up anyway. She leaned in to hug me and I let her, even though I knew she'd feel how hard I was through my pants. She tensed against me and when she moved back her expression was different.

"Does that always happen to you?" she pointed.

I had to hold back the laugh bubbling up my chest. "Only every time I see you."

"Really? I do that to you?"

She was fucking clueless. How could she not know how delicious she looked in a skirt showcasing her fantastic legs? Not to mention a shirt that showed me some skin. It wasn't as indecent as most of my girls, but with her, it was ten times sexier.

"Yes." My voice was hoarse.

I hadn't gone this long without sex since I was seventeen. Just knowing she was looking at my dick was doing it for me. Hell, I felt like a fucking teenager all over again.

And then she made it worse.

"Can I touch it?"

Fuck me. Fuck all the sweet, tight pussies in the world. She was turning me on.

"You can do whatever you'd like." I was being calm and cool on the outside, but inside I was burning. My internal organs were on fire and ready for her touch.

I'd known when I first met Jessica that she would need time, and I think maybe that challenge made her more appealing. But now she was becoming curious—she wanted to touch me—and I wasn't sure I could hold back much longer.

With a shaking hand, she reached out and began to undo my belt. I almost came on the spot. There I was, thinking she'd palm me through my pants—get a feel for my length and girth—but oh no, my girl was going skin to skin.

I leaned my head back and closed my eyes, as she stuck her hand down my pants, her fingers feeling my shaft. Hot breath seeped between my teeth like a steaming pot and she yanked her hand away.

"Did I hurt you?"

"Fuck no," I said, taking her hand and putting it back where it belonged.

My pants began to fall around my hips and I pushed my boxers so they'd fall, too. I stood there with my stick pointing straight at her and let her touch and feel. It was the sweetest, most erotic thing I'd ever experienced.

Her fingers were cool and soft. They felt amazing. She got braver the longer she touched, letting her fingers wrap around me and squeeze. I couldn't take it anymore. I needed more. Reaching down, I covered her hand with mine and moved it up and down, showing her how I liked to be jacked off.

"Like that, sweetheart."

When I removed my hand, she kept going. Once she got the hang of it and her wrist starting working in circles, I was clutching the desk behind me. Her breathing sped up with mine and I watched as her tits moved up and down with her breaths. I was getting closer and closer. I knew it wouldn't be long before I came hard and fast into her hand.

"Stop, baby. I'm going come," I said, grabbing her hand to stop her movements.

"Isn't that the point?" she asked.

I considered letting her continue, but there was more fun to be had.

"Yeah, but when I do I want it to be in your mouth."

"You're so vulgar."

"That I am. Don't worry, you'll learn to love it."

She backed away from me, but I followed her step for step, until she ran into my desk.

"Will I?" she swallowed hard.

Her eyes were dilated and her heart was beating so hard I could see the slight pulse on the side of her neck.

"You definitely will." Reaching up, I ran a finger over that pulse and she tensed. "Are you afraid of me, Jessica?" I leaned in close.

"Should I be?" she asked.

Chuckling softly to myself, I moved so close my lips brushed along the rim of her ear. "Unequivocally."

"In that case, I am." Her deep breathing was hard in my ear.

Leaning back, I took in her flushed face, glazed over eyes, and moist lips. "Let's play a game," I said, running my fingers up her tense back.

"What kind of game?"

"It's called Sebastian says."

"That's not a real game," she rolled her eyes.

"Sebastian says be quiet," I said.

The side of her mouth lifted in a tiny smile.

Moving back, I took her in from head to toe. "Sebastian says take your top off."

She fidgeted. "Sebastian, I..."

I held up a hand. "Sebastian didn't say speak. So far, you're terrible at this game." I moved to the couch and took a seat. "Let's try this again. Sebastian says take off your top."

Closing her eyes, she lifted her shirt from the bottom and pulled it over her head. I wasn't surprised to see that her nipples were rock hard beneath her bra. As much as she hated to admit it, she was turned on. She was slowly beginning to thrive on being controlled, exactly like I'd hoped she would.

My eyes moved over her bra and down her flat stomach.

"Take off your bra," I said.

Without thinking, she moved her arms behind her and snapped her bra, letting it fall off her arms and to the floor.

"*Tsk, tsk,* naughty girl. I didn't say Sebastian says," I grinned.

"Dammit," she whispered.

Laughing, I continued. "I would leave you as is, but you need a punishment. Sebastian says take off your skirt."

Dipping her thumbs into the top of her skirt, she pulled it down, letting it pool around her feet. She stepped out of it, kicking it to the side.

Standing there in just her panties, she held her head high even though I could tell she was nervous. Already, she'd come a long way. I was strangely proud of her.

"Sebastian says touch yourself."

In that moment, I realized I'd been right about Jessica since the moment I'd met her. She *was* the seductive Jessica Rabbit. It just hadn't been nurtured and pulled out of her.

While most women would have went straight to touching their pussy, Jessica didn't. Without even realizing she was doing it, she seduced me. Starting at her neck, she ran her hands down the sides until they met in the front, just below her throat.

Her eyes remained on mine as she slowly worked her fingers down over her breasts, and running them over her nipples.

I swallowed hard as she pinched each peak before her hands continued their path down to her stomach. When she was beginning to enjoy it, she closed her eyes and put her head back. Her hands moved lower, hovering over her panty line in a teasing manner that made it hard to stay seated.

And then she was ever so carefully dipping her fingertips into the waist of her panties. I swallowed and leaned forward, waiting for the moment she touched herself for me.

Vick chose that moment to come busting into my office.

The sensual veil lifted and Jessica darted for her shirt to cover herself.

"Fuck!" I said, standing from the couch. I didn't even try to hide my raging hard on. "What is it?"

Vick stood there staring at us with a gapped mouth. "Was she stripping? Since when is that enough for you?"

Jessica's shoulders dropped and for the first time ever, I wanted to reach out and slap the shit out of Vick.

"Get the fuck out!" I bellowed.

"Whatever. You have a guest downstairs. When you're done playing with your toy, come down." She walked away, leaving the door open.

FIFTEEN

ROSSLYN

HIS *TOY.*

That's what she'd called me. The worst part, I couldn't even be mad at her words because that's exactly what I was. Bought and paid for.

And there I'd been, finally starting to play, and I liked it. Actually, I loved it. Having such a strong man in the palm of my hand—that's what you call power. And God help me, I wanted to feel powerful.

As soon as he walked over and slammed the door, I looked at him and saw the anger in his eyes.

"Ignore her," he said.

I was sick to death of people acting like I was seconds away from cracking. If I hadn't cracked yet, I sure wasn't going to now. I didn't want to ignore her. I wanted to use her words to make myself stronger. I wanted to use everything I'd learned so far to make myself tougher.

"She's right," I said. "I *am* your toy."

He attempted to smooth things over. "Don't think of it that way, Jess—"

I cut him off. "And I like it."

He stopped and stared back at me, as if I was a stranger who'd just entered the room. Finally, the side of his mouth lifted and his dimples sank into his cheeks.

TABATHA & MELISSA

"Then come here and let me play with you."

I went to him and when his fingers dug into my hips, I didn't pull away. I wanted this—I wanted him.

Using a finger, he tilted my face to his and ran his tongue across my lips.

"Do I really scare you?" he asked.

Again... treating me like I was about to crack. No more. I was done with that.

"No." To show him I was serious, I captured his bottom lips in my teeth and pulled. I'd once seen a woman do it in a movie, and it drove the man crazy. It did the same to Sebastian. His fingers dug into my arms as he moved me, pressing my ass into his desk. He stared down at me dangerously and I knew in that moment I was playing with fire. But, the last thing I felt was fear.

He was testing me, just as he had been since the moment I'd met him. It was an experiment to see how far I'd let him go when he slowly ran his palms up my thighs. It was a test when he stuck his finger in the side of my panties and began to softly run the back of his finger across me, every now and again letting his knuckle slide in and massage my clit. It was all a test and by the sounds of approval he made, I was passing.

My head fell back, letting the sensations his finger created move through me. I'd never felt anything so amazing.

Pulling his finger from my panties, he stuck his knuckle in his mouth and sucked. I almost exploded on the spot.

"Fuck. You taste amazing." He began to roll the cotton down my thighs until my panties were around my ankles. "You've earned a prize. You've been doing so well, I'm going to eat your pussy and you're going to let me. Do you understand?"

I bit into my bottom lip and nodded.

"I'm going to tongue your tight little slit until you beg me to stop. And then I'm going to stick my tongue deep in you and suck on your clit until you come. And when you do, I'm going to lap up your sweetness and swallow it."

My knees went weak with his words. I let him lift me onto the desk. Staring at the drop ceiling above me, I didn't fight him when he slowly spread my legs.

He wasted no time, and I was never more thankful. His tongue delved into my hole, then he ran it up and sucked on my clit with a loud smack. I lifted from the table and a sound I'd never made exploded from my mouth.

"Oh my God," the words rushed from my lips.

"Don't worship me yet, sweetheart. I'm just getting started."

And then his mouth was on me again, working me up and down. Sliding against my wet skin in ways I never knew were possible. His tongue curled, flicked, and touched every nerve I had, making me pant and pull at his hair. I'd never been so rough, but then again I'd never felt so amazing in my life.

"Tell me you want to come in my mouth. I want to hear your pretty mouth say dirty things."

His words sounded so far away, but they broke through my haze of wonder. When I didn't respond, he nipped at my lip making me hiss.

"Say it," he demanded.

I didn't care what it sounded like. I didn't care what I was saying as long as he didn't stop.

TABATHA & MELISSA

"Oh my God, Sebastian, I want to come in your mouth. Please make me come in your mouth."

And then the rise was there. He held me to the desk as I worked my pussy against his face. The wave of sensations washed against me. The music downstairs thumped against the glass wall in his office and matched the rhythm of my heartbeat. I screamed words I'd never said before in my life as my release hit me, and my juices poured into his mouth.

"Fuck. Yes, Sebastian. Yes."

He was true to his word as he began to lap up my sweetness like a thirsty man. He licked until my legs began to shake and every word I said came out in a loud stutter.

Leaning back, he wiped his mouth with the back of his arm. I laid there, bare and open to him as the room around me began to come back into focus.

"You're so fucking hot when you come."

He pushed his pants down and I knew what was about to happen. I didn't want to freak out, and I wasn't sure I was ready; I'd just never pictured my first time being on the desk in a nightclub, no matter how fancy it was.

He surprised me. Instead of pushing himself into me, he palmed his hardness and began to slowly jack off.

"I'm not going to fuck you here, but we can still have some fun."

I leaned up on my elbows and gasped when he played with the head of his shaft, running it over my clit. He pressed his hardness against my slit, and my muscles clenched. Holding the length of his cock against me with his thumbs, he pumped his hips and groaned. It felt good—his rhythm—his hotness pressing against me over and over again. I could feel the rise coming, with each stroke of his cock, his tip rubbed against my bundle of nerves.

"I'm going to come all over that pretty, pink pussy."

He grabbed my legs and pushed them together, cocooning his dick tightly in my slippery folds. Hugging my legs, he stared at me and began thrusting harder. The look in his eyes as he stared down at my naked flesh turned me on even more. I reached down and pushed his purple head against my clit as it poked through with each thrust, prompting him to move faster and faster, until I was sure I was going to break.

"Fuck, yes!" he threw his head back and I felt warmth seep onto my skin.

He continued to work himself, hips jerking, rubbing his hot release all over me. Watching him come undone pushed me over the edge. My body tensed and I screamed out a second orgasm.

When my legs fell open, he collapsed on top of me, head falling onto my stomach. Our breathing was loud and fast as I lost my fingers in his damp locks. My body hummed with the soft aftershocks of joy. I actually felt like purring.

SIXTEEN

SEBASTIAN

PRESSING MY LIPS TO THE warm skin beside her belly button, I kissed her and lifted myself from her body. Snuggling wasn't my thing, although, it was bit overwhelming how good it was to be with her—to feel her against me. It was better with her than any other woman, and we hadn't even fucked yet.

I'd known from the first moment I laid eyes on her, she was going to be perfection... and she didn't disappoint. The problem now was I couldn't get enough of her. I wanted to be around her and hear her voice, all the fucking time. I didn't know how to handle it. I didn't know what it meant. I just knew everything about her was addicting, and it was too much for me.

"Come on. I'll walk you to the car," I said once we adjusted our clothes.

It was the last thing I wanted to do. I didn't want her to leave. I wanted to take her to my apartment and spend the night between her legs, but that wasn't a possibility.

I wasn't going to break the rules, and having sex in my apartment was one of the rules. Vick was right. It was different with Jessica, but I had to stop it. I couldn't allow it to be different—at least any more than it already was.

"I'll see you soon," Jessica smiled up at me, before climbing into the back of the car.

I nodded, and contained the grin pulling at my lips.

Under no circumstances was I going to turn into a weak fuck. I would never become one of those pathetic pussy-whipped men. She was not going to change me.

I watched her go until I couldn't see the tail lights any more. Walking back inside, I headed over to the VIP section, where I spent the rest of the night getting fucked up with a few celebrity playboys.

For the next three days, I didn't text or visit Jessica, even though it killed me. I buried myself in paperwork and meetings, and tried not to think about her. I could have met with another one of my girls, but I wasn't feeling it. My balls were in a bunch, and my mind was a mess.

"You've been an asshole this week," Vick said, tossing a stack of papers on my desk. "This girl has your dick twisted, Sebastian. I think she's a bad idea."

"Tell me how you really feel," I responded without looking up.

"Whatever," she spat on her way out the door.

She was right. I was turning into a fucking head case. The club was always my number one priority, but since I'd met Jessica, it had become an afterthought. I spent less time downstairs, and more time with her. The mountain of paper on my desk that hadn't been done was proof of that.

Pushing the papers away, I stood and snatched my jacket from the back of the chair. The last few days had been hell, and it was time I had a little surprise visit.

The streets were slick with rain. The tires on my car slid when I took corners, going too fast for the weather.

The doorman outside of Jessica's building nodded to me as I passed. It was embarrassing to think, but I was actually getting excited to see her. An involuntary smile tugged at my mouth when I got on the elevator, but the minute the door opened to her top floor condo, the smile slipped from my face.

Jessica was sitting on the floor next to the elevator, crying. Her eyes were red and swollen as she swiped at her running noise with a tissue.

"What's wrong?" I asked.

She looked up at me and opened her mouth to speak. Instead, a sob exploded from her pouty lips and she covered her face with her hands. Leaning down, I slipped my arms beneath her and picked her up from the floor. She wrapped her arms around me and buried her face into my neck.

I wasn't one to stick around for tear-filled drama. Again, it was something different with her. Stepping into her room, I placed her on the edge of the bed. I plucked the pieces of wet hair from her face, as I kneeled in front of her.

"Tell me what it is."

She sniffed. "It's Kyle. He went to that program at the art institute an hour ago. He's going to be gone most of the summer."

"I thought that's what you wanted?" I asked confused.

"It is, but it doesn't mean I'm not going to miss him. I've taken care of him since he was practically a baby. I'm not sure how it's going to be with him gone. He's all I have."

The urge to tell her she had *me* was strong, but the forbidden words choked me when they got stuck in my throat.

Instead, I fingered a strand of her hair and tucked it behind her ear.

"Where's the art institute located? Is it very far?"

"It's about five hours away, but he's going to be staying there all summer instead of staying with me."

My smile returned. Even though she was crying and upset, I laughed. Her head popped up and she looked at me like I was nuts. I felt crazy. She was making me insane.

"Are you seriously laughing at me right now?" she asked angrily.

"Yes. You realize he's close enough for you to visit him, right?"

She sniffed and used her tissue to wipe. With her red eyes and ratty hair she should have looked a mess, but it was the total opposite. She looked soft, and full of emotions I'd never understand. She looked real—alive. I envied her ability to feel so deeply for someone, but felt sorry for her at the same time. Feeling things for people meant having the ability to feel pain as well.

"I know that. I'm just being dramatic. I'm a woman, I'm allowed."

She smiled through her tears and as cliché as it sounds, I lost my breath. It was like a punch to the lungs—an exhale of the man I thought I was and a rebirth of some new person who felt things for the woman in front of him.

Using my thumb, I captured a stray tear as it melted down her cheek.

"Thanks for being here, Sebastian," she whispered with her head down.

Lifting her face to meet mine again, I grinned at her. "I don't usually stick around for a woman's tears. I think I've earned something. What are you going to give me?"

She visibly swallowed and her eyes widened. "What do you want?"

Already I was thinking of the different positions I wanted to put her in. What position could get me deeper inside her perfect little pussy, but I knew I had to take it slow.

Tilting her head up higher, I took my time, skimming her lips with mine and feeling their warmth. I continued to do that until the moment I knew she wanted me to kiss her. She exhaled and closed her eyes and that was all the invite I needed.

I nibbled at her lips before pressing mine to hers tightly. A sweet noise rushed past her lips and vibrated my mouth. I kissed her deep, tasting her on my tongue and memorizing the moment for later days.

Her fingers worked their way into the hair at the back of my neck as she formed her body to mine. She fit as if she was made for me. It was the second time I'd ever kissed a woman without the intention of fucking her. Both times being with her.

She broke the kiss and smiled back at me. Capturing my cheek with her soft palm, I lost myself in her green orbs. "You're amazing, Sebastian," she whispered.

And then, I saw it. The thing which told me my time with one of my ladies was up—the thing that usually sent me running for the hills. It was in her eyes, the way she stared at me with an awestruck expression. She was falling for me. She'd broken one of my sacred rules.

The strangest things happened in that very moment. First, I had absolutely no desire to run from her. If anything, I wanted to bathe in her expression and celebrate her feelings for me. And second, I almost asked her what her real name was. I wanted to know her, who she was, what she liked. But worst of all, I wanted to keep her.

Instead, I pulled back, like her words were a slap to the face. Her brows pinched in confusion. I stood, smoothing the wrinkles from my pants.

"Our time here is up."

I wanted to say more—anything that would hurt her and change her opinion of me. I wasn't ready to let her go yet. I'd only had a taste of what she had to offer sexually, and now there were these forbidden feelings bouncing around that I didn't understand.

Instead of pushing and saying hurtful things, I turned and left her sitting on her bed with a confused expression.

I had some thinking to do. I needed to figure out what the hell was going on with me and I needed to fix it fast. Sebastian Black didn't get pussy-whipped, especially before he had the pussy.

Fuck me. Was that even possible?

AS SOON AS I GOT back to my office, I pulled my book out and flipped through the names. I knew exactly what I needed.

Wilma and Betty.

They were sure to take my mind off of the crazy bullshit currently taking over my life. I could already hear their moans and feel them wrapped around my hard cock.

I pulled out my phone and sent them a text, instructing them to meet in our usual room. As quickly as I stepped into my office, I stepped out.

The ride to the hotel was a blur. I drove on autopilot.

"Hello, Mr. Black," the front desk clerk said, smiling as he held out my room card.

I nodded. I didn't have time to chat with anyone. My cock was on a mission. I needed disconnected sex—no feelings, no bullshit.

When I stepped into the room, the girls had already started without me. Both were naked and making out on the bed. Peeling my jacket off, I undid my tie and stepped to the side of the bed. Wilma turned her attention to me, and began to unbutton my pants. She looked up at me with a seductive smile, pulling my pants and boxers down around my hips.

I was limp.

"What do we have here? This is unacceptable," she cooed.

Wrapping an experienced hand around my cock, she began to work it. I closed my eyes and tried to just be in the moment, but all I saw was fiery hair and green eyes. I shook my head, trying to get the image out of my mind. No matter how many times I pushed her away, she kept coming back.

"Come on, Sebastian. Give us what we want," Betty said, licking her lips as she leaned down and took Wilma's nipple in her mouth.

Absolutely nothing was happening downstairs. My balls were tight and ached for release. I wanted to fuck so bad I couldn't stand it, but I wasn't able to get hard.

I smacked Wilma's hand away and gripped myself. I began to stroke with a mission. I had a point to prove, and if that meant I had to pump my own dick until it chaffed I'd fucking do it.

Ten minutes later, even with an expert hand and a view of Wilma tongue-fucking Betty, there was nothing.

"I'm sorry girls. Today's not the day."

They continued as I dressed and left the room. I closed the door on Betty's moans.

There was no denying it. Jessica was changing me somehow. It was new, and I hated it, but there was nothing I could do. I was officially fucked.

She needed to go.

SEVENTEEN

ROSSLYN

I STOOD AND WATCHED THROUGH the wall of windows as the day turned into night. After my visit with Sebastian, things felt wrong. It'd been days, and he still hadn't contacted me. It wasn't like he was my boyfriend. I had no right to even think about him, unless he called.

I was already an emotional mess over Kyle leaving for a few weeks, but Sebastian Black was the most confusing man on earth. Every time I felt like I was seeing the real him, he would shut me out.

One thing was for sure, I really liked the real him—like really, really liked him. I'd never felt that way about anyone, and definitely not anyone who was like Sebastian. I wasn't sure how to respond to my feelings. I wasn't sure how to respond to anything involving him.

The one thing I did know, I didn't want to go another week without seeing him. Something told me he was on the verge of getting rid of me, and I wasn't sure I wanted that anymore. Not because of the money, but because I *wanted* him.

I spent day after day putting in applications and looking for places that were hiring. If Sebastian was done with me, I needed a back-up plan. I'd walk and fill out applications until my feet and fingers burned, and then I'd go back to the condo and soak until I was tired.

When I felt lonely, I'd touched myself and imagine it was him. I'd given myself orgasm after orgasm thinking about him, and I was done doing myself. I wanted Sebastian—around me, in me... in all ways possible.

I spent extra time in the shower, making sure to shave everything to perfection, and then I pulled out the only sexy bra and panties I owned. They were simple black lace, but anything was better than white cotton.

My body felt different beneath my fingers when I dressed myself in a black summer dress. It was short and I wasn't ever going to be able to bend over, but it was the only thing I owned that was even remotely sexy.

I felt fuller in my thighs—more womanly. Already I was turned on, just thinking about how brazen I was going to be. I wasn't the kind of woman who did crazy things, but I'd already decided I was going to do it. No one was going to hold me back anymore—not even me.

THE BARTENDERS SMILED AT ME when I walked by like they knew what I was there for. I was scared I'd run into Trish, so I moved quickly. My cheeks burned as I slid across the club and up the stairs to Sebastian's office. I held my hand up to tap on the door, but decided against it. I wanted to surprise him, or in the very least, act confident.

I grabbed the knob and pushed the door open, prepared to see him sitting at his desk, but he wasn't there. The office was dark, except for one light on his desk. Of course, it was my luck I'd get up the nerve to approach him for sex, and he wouldn't be there.

I stepped into his office, closing the door behind me, and went to his desk. Memories of how he'd licked and sucked me assailed my brain and I could feel myself getting wet for him again. Running my fingers over the smooth desktop, I leaned forward until I felt the hard wood against my chest.

I ran my hands down my body enjoying the feel of my palms through the thin cotton dress, and when I reached the apex of my thighs, I pushed in with my fingers.

It was insane to go into a man's office and masturbate to his memory, but I was feeling exceptionally crazy. I couldn't stop thinking about him or the way he'd made me feel. Plus, if he walked in, he'd definitely get a good view.

A sigh slipped from my lips when my fingers met my damp panties. I rubbed, enjoying the abrasive feel of the lace against my clit. I let my head lay on the desk and rolled my hips, grinding on my own hand. I'd become good at getting myself off. It wasn't going to take much and I'd be soaking my panties. Maybe I'd even do something really crazy and leave them on his desk when I was done.

"Oh yes," I moaned when I felt the liquid heat gather at my cusp.

"Do you always barge into offices to masturbate?" Sebastian's voice broke through my sexual haze.

I gasped, dropping my hands from my body, and spinning around to find him lounging on the couch in his office. He took a sip from his glass and ice clinked as he moved it.

"Should I call the police and report this incident?" he asked with a straight face, setting his glass on the side table.

Judging by the obvious bulge in his pants, he'd been watching me the whole time.

"I *have* been bad, sir. But maybe you should do the punishing yourself?"

His eyes lit up with a hint of a smile and I was happy I had pleased him.

"You'd like that wouldn't you?" he asked.

I nodded. "Yes."

"Sit on my desk and spread your legs," he demanded.

It was that very moment my nerves set in. A hot blush crept up my back and melted into my neck and cheeks. Instead of doing as he asked, I stood there and stared back at him like a lost puppy.

"I said... sit your plump ass on my fucking desk and spread those creamy thighs. Wide."

His blunt nature was shocking, but I liked it—I'd gotten used to it. I kept my eyes locked on his as I slowly sat on the edge of his desk and spread my legs. Knowing he was watching me somehow made the actions a turn-on.

"Your panties are so wet," he groaned. "You like touching yourself, don't you?"

I nodded and reached down, letting my fingers roam across my lace-covered, swollen bud. I laid back, enjoying my ministrations. My breathing became fast and short.

"I can't help but touch myself when I think of that tight, virgin pussy."

I could hear his hips rocking on the leather couch, and the sound of him rubbing his arousal through his pants.

"Pull your panties to the side, and fuck yourself with your finger."

Doing as he asked, I pressed my middle finger as deep as it would go. My channel begged for more, and I was sure only Sebastian could satisfy that part of me.

"Look at me."

I lifted my head off his desk and stared at him through half-lidded eyes. He unzipped his pants enough for his cock to pop out.

"Imagine you're using this..." he squeezed the head of his dick. "To get yourself off."

Pulling my finger out of my depths, I pressed against my sensitive nub and rubbed. I kept my eyes on the hand he was using to pull on his swollen cock, making sure to move my hand in the same rapid rhythm. My mouth hung open and my breaths rushed in and out, hard and fast.

"I love those sweet little smacking noises your fingers are making." He gripped his sac with his other hand and pulled.

I hadn't even realized my wetness was making noises. I didn't care. All I cared about was the way it felt.

I was rapidly approaching my release. I silently hoped he would come between my legs and press his body deep into mine. I wanted to come on him. I wanted to feel him penetrate me so hard, I didn't know where I ended and he began.

I opened my eyes a bit to see him still seated on the couch, pumping himself hard and fast. Just watching him was about to send me over the edge. I was so close to coming.

"Stop. Don't you dare come yet," he said.

I pulled my hand from my body and my insides clenched ready for a release that I wasn't giving it.

"What kind of punisher would I be, if I let you pleasure yourself?" he asked. "You need to learn to knock before you enter. You need to learn manners. Don't you, Jessica?"

Feeling rebellious and ready to push him as hard as he'd been pushing me, I stood my ground.

"No," I said sternly, hiding the smile that begged at my lips.

Standing up and slipping his belt from the loops, his pants fell to his hips, baring his long, thick shaft.

"What did you say?" he asked roughly.

My eyes flicked up to his—hot and angry, full of desire. "I said, *no*."

Sebastian hated the word no, but at the same time, I'd figured out that's what turned him on the most.

I could feel my body already seeping with lust, waiting for an orgasm that I knew would be epic. I wanted it all—everything that he could offer me.

"What did I tell you about saying no to me?" He folded the belt in half and smacked it against his palm.

"Never tell you no. Never refuse you." I bit the inside of my cheek as I waited for his punishment.

"And you did it anyway, didn't you?" He tried to cover his tiny smirk with a hard, unmoving stare.

"Yes."

"What happens to girls who are bad, Jessica?"

Again, the belt met his palm. I flinched at the noise it made. I could barely contain the excitement that filled me. I knew Sebastian was going to use the belt on me, and I couldn't wait to see how.

"They get punished."

"And you've been bad, haven't you?"

I nodded. "Very bad."

And then he was standing in front of me, belt in hand.

"Turn around and put your palms on the desk," he said sternly.

Turning, I laid my palms flat on the top as he had asked. Leaning over, I waited anxiously for his next move.

I didn't have to wait long before his belt landed hard against my bare ass cheek. I shouted out in shock and surprise.

Right after the belt smacked me, his hot hand ran over the spot, soothing the sting.

"One," he whispered in my ear.

I lifted my palms from the desk to turn around and face him, but his hand in the middle of my back stopped me as he pressed me harder into the desk.

"Don't not move," he said vehemently.

My face was now pressed into the desk as I waited for yet another sting from the belt. Again, he brought the belt down onto me, except this time it was the opposite ass cheek. It stung, and again I called out.

Leaning over me, he pressed his cheek against the sting before turning and pressing his lips to the burn.

"Two," he said hotly.

I was so turned on and I didn't understand it. He was hurting me, but it felt so good.

I waited with bated breath for more, but the belt never came down again. Instead, he moved the leather between my legs, running it over my swollen, lace-covered flesh and sending strong sensations through me. I moaned.

"Does that feel nice?" he asked.

I moaned my answer when he began moving the leather back and forth. And then he surprised me by smacking the belt against my wetness. It wasn't as hard as it had been against my ass, but still it stung a little.

I bit into my bottom lip to contain the sounds that rushed from the back of my throat. Again, he moved the leather against me, pressing it against my sensitive nub and bringing me close to orgasm.

"It's okay, baby. You've earned it. Feel it. It feels good, doesn't it?"

I nodded my answer.

"Please don't stop," the words leapt from my lips.

He stopped, and I looked back to see him pull the belt away from my body, It was glazed with my wetness and he licked it and moaned his approval before tossing his belt to the floor.

Turning away from me, he went back to the couch and took his seat again.

"You may continue," he said, as if he hadn't just spanked me with a belt.

I started toward him, but he held up his hand to stop me. "Keep touching yourself."

Again, I reached down and rubbed. It didn't take much and I could already feel myself rapidly approaching my release. And then it hit me like a ton of cement—hard and slow, it washed over me.

"That's it, baby. Come for me," he said through my orgasmic wave.

"Oh God," I shouted as hot liquid poured from my body. I felt the rush of it spill over my folds and down my thigh.

My legs shook beneath me, and I felt as if I was going to crumble to the floor in a hot, shaking mess. Once I rode the wave, I let my hands fall from my body. Breathing erratically, I was able to open my eyes again.

"Now come here."

He reached out for my hand. Bringing it to his mouth, he sucked my slick middle finger into his mouth. His tongue swirled around my fingertip sending a sharp sensation down my arm and in between my legs.

"You taste so sweet," he said, pulling my finger from his mouth with a pop.

I didn't know what the next step was. There I was standing there in front of him, juices flowing down my legs.

"Take your dress off." His heated stare turning even hotter. "I want to see your body."

Taking a deep breath, I reached down, grabbed the bottom of my dress, and lifted it. Cool air brushed my thighs, and then my stomach. My nipples tightening inside my bra, I tossed my dress to the floor.

My fingertips brushed across my lace panties, but before I could touch myself he stopped me again.

"I want those panties. Take them off and give them to me."

Hooking my thumbs into the top of my panties, I peeled them down. My eyes locked on his hard member, standing tall, begging for attention.

The warm moisture between my folds felt cool when the air touched it. I lifted my leg and pulled the lace from my foot. Trying to not be my usual awkward self, I held them out on one hooked finger.

He took the panties and held them to his nose, sniffing deeply.

"You smell amazing," he rasped. "They're fucking soaked, too. Open your legs some and let me see how wet you are."

I widened my stance.

"No. I still can't see. Stick two fingers inside and show me."

Doing as he asked, I dipped my middle finger and ring finger in deep, and moaned at the aching sensation.

Removing my fingers, I moved closer to where he sat on the couch. My panties draped across his shoulder.

This time, he took my drenched fingers and brought them down to his cock, using them to spread my juices around his glistening tip. He took his time, grinding his length, hard into my palm. His eyes locked on mine the entire time.

He brought my hand up to his face and licked between my fingers before letting go. When he pulled back, he grinned up at me.

"You're incredibly sexy," he said.

I was standing there in front of him in only my bra. My body was flushed, and still humming with satisfaction, but the ache deep inside of me needed to be rubbed.

"Sebastian..." I started.

"What is it, sweetheart? Anything you want, it's yours."

Without invitation, I moved forward and straddled his lap. When my wet sex rubbed against his hardness, his abs tightened and the muscles in his jaw popped.

"I want you." My words were deep and raspy.

"I'm all yours," he said, reaching up and pushing my hair over my shoulders.

My fingers went to work unbuttoning his shirt, as he reached over and drained the liquid in his glass.

Pushing the fabric to the side, I was met with bronzed, smooth skin and chiseled muscle. My fingers explored the dips and creases of his torso, and his muscles came alive beneath my fingertips.

Leaning over, I pressed my lips to his shoulder and kissed him from shoulder to chest. His hand moved to the back of my head, sweetly playing with the hair there. His salty flavor rushed across my tongue when I began to lick his nipple.

His head fell back against the couch and a deep sigh sounded. I used my teeth, nibbling on his pebbled nipple, as I continued to taste him.

His hands slid down my spine making me shiver, and then his skillful fingers unhooked my bra. It slipped from my body and he tossed it across the room. He grabbed onto my hips, pulling me harder against him.

"Tell me what you want, Jessica."

I knew what I wanted, but I didn't know how to say it. I whined as I circled my hips, spreading my wetness all over his exposed hardness.

"Say it, baby. Say you want me to fuck you. I love to hear that sweet mouth say dirty things." He moved his hips below me, his tip pressing against my opening.

"Fuck me, Sebastian. Please. I can't take it anymore."

I could hardly believe I'd said it. It sounded sexy and seductive, yet still full of need. And it worked because suddenly he flipped me on the couch and was perched above me.

His hand moved between us as he pushed at his pants, kicking them onto the floor beside us. He rubbed himself against me like the time before. Except this time, it wasn't enough. I wanted so much more.

Lifting my hips, I pressed up when he moved back, letting him know how badly I wanted him inside of me.

"Where do you want me?"

"Please, Sebastian. Put it in me."

"Put what in you, sweetheart?" He pressed again. "My cock? Tell me you want my cock inside of you."

I wiggled beneath him, trying hard to get him where I wanted him. "I want your big cock, deep inside of me."

He shifted his body, and I felt him against my entrance once again. "You're so fucking hot and wet."

And then he was pushing into me, filling me and stretching my body in a way it had never been stretched. I tensed beneath him, until he was as deep as he could go at the moment.

"Fuck. So hot, so tight." Pleasure filled his expression and his eyes closed. He pulled back, and pressed into me again, further this time. There was a tiny sting.

I hissed and my thighs tensed against his hips. His eyes popped open and softened.

"Are you okay?" he asked.

I bit my bottom lip and nodded. "Yes, don't stop." I reached around him and dug my nails into his ass. "More."

His lips brushed against my forehead and he began to move above me. His hips pressed into mine, his body filling me so completely I was sure I could feel him in my stomach. Sweat gathered between the two of us, making his body slide against mine.

He leaned on his forearms, which were planted firmly into the couch on each side of my head. His face hovered above mine and every now and again he'd lean down and kiss me, filling my mouth with his tongue and the flavor of him.

His movements sped up, and the ache deep inside of me intensified. It wasn't long before I was moving with him, lifting my hips to meet his thrust and digging my finger nails deep into the flesh on his back.

So close—I was so close. I started to make noises, silently begging him with my eyes for more. He shifted his hips, plowing into me with so much force it should have hurt, but it didn't—it felt so good. Better than anything I'd felt in my entire life.

"Come on my dick, Jessica. I want to feel that hot come all over the head of my cock."

It wasn't making love, it was fucking. At least that's what he called it. And while I probably should have been disgusted by his words and roughness, I loved it. It was pushing me closer and closer to the edge.

I wanted him to talk dirty to me. I wanted him to rough me up. I was tired of being treated like expensive china. I wasn't going to break.

He pushed me closer and higher, but no matter how hard he pushed, I wasn't going over the edge.

"Fuck it," he said, pulling out of my body.

Leaning back, he scooped up my hips and lifted my body from the couch and to his mouth. My shoulders dug into the couch, as my thighs and hips were thrust into the air. I was going to complain, but then he stuck two fingers deep inside of me and sucked my clit into his mouth.

He worked his fingers, rubbing against the ache, as he sucked a few times. I broke. He held my hips still as I bucked against his face, screaming out a release I was sure everyone downstairs could hear.

When I came down from my orgasm, he was above me again. He wasted no time plunging deep into me, igniting the spark once again. He didn't hold back, pounding into my body hard and fast.

Mumbling words I didn't even try to understand, he took over my body and I lay beneath him, watching his beautiful face morph in pleasure.

He was getting close. I knew because I was beginning to understand his expressions. His mouth fell open, his dark hair falling into his eyes. I pulled him closer, holding him to me.

"Fuck, I'm going to..."

And then he pulled from my body and grabbed himself, tugging and spilling his heat onto my stomach. He growled, as painful pleasure pulled his brows down and made him grit his teeth.

He fell to the couch beside me, our bodies pressed together in a sweaty glaze. Our breaths filled the room with panted heat, as we each tried to catch more oxygen.

Eventually, the room got quiet and the music downstairs pounded against the glass in a rhythm close to my heartbeat. I turned to face him, only to find him sleeping soundly.

Reaching out, I ran my fingers through his dark hair and leaned in for a kiss. There was absolutely no doubt in my mind anymore. I was falling in love with Sebastian, which was a really bad thing.

EIGHTEEN

SEBASTIAN

"SERIOUSLY, SEBASTIAN?" VICK YELLED FROM above me. "This is unacceptable, especially for you. Get your fucking clothes on and get your ass downstairs."

The side of my face was sticking to the leather on the couch and so was my soft cock. I didn't know how long I'd slept, but I woke up feeling like I'd spent time with every woman in my book. My body was relaxed and sated and I felt so completely exhausted, I could have rolled back over and went right back to sleep.

All I knew was Jessica had been there. She'd proved to me she was worth every dime and more—so much more. I also knew the minute I woke that Jessica was gone. Her warmth wasn't pressed against me the way it had been after I'd blown my load.

I was lying there, cold and naked on my leather couch, with Vick staring down at me with angry, beady eyes.

"What the fuck is happening to you? You never mixed business and pleasure before."

I'd definitely gone too far. I hadn't been planning to fuck her yet—in fact, I had been toying with the idea of letting her go. But the little mix wormed her way in. I wasn't able to hold back. Not with her touching herself and seducing the fuck out of me.

"Do you hear me?" Vick asked.

Her words cut into my memories of the night before, forcing my morning-after buzz to dissolve quickly.

"What are you talking about? I fired her. I'm not mixing anything." Standing from the couch, I stretched my naked body and cracked my neck.

"You're cocking her in your office, during club hours. This is the second time this has happened. You'd never bring your girls up here before. This shit has got to stop."

I reached down and slipped my pants on.

"This is my office, Vick. I'll *cock* every woman in my book, on my fucking desk, all night long, if I want to." I searched for my shirt and pushed my arms into it. "Since when do you give a shit about where and who I fuck?" I asked, buttoning my shirt.

"Since you started letting this bitch affect your job," she said, pulling the door open and letting the music from downstairs in. "I'm going down. There are people waiting to see you when you're done fucking around up here."

The door slammed behind her for the hundredth time this week. Even though I should have been royally pissed off at being spoken to like that, I wasn't. I couldn't think of anything, but the way Jessica felt against my skin. I could smell her all around me. It had never been that way with any other woman. Ever.

I'd been her first. Even though it was supposed to be a special moment for her, I couldn't help but feel like the moment had been special for me, too. Why me? Why had she so freely given herself to me the way she had? Money aside, I didn't have to push for it. *She* had come to *me*, and that made it feel totally different somehow. And what's worse, I didn't hate it.

I fucking loved it.

I spent the rest of the night getting drunker than a skunk in the VIP section. I downed shot after shot, hanging my arms around the shoulders of some of New York's hottest and richest. I was relaxed and actually enjoying myself in my own establishment, as if I wasn't at work.

Vick was nowhere to be found and for the first time, I was glad to not have her hovering over me. The waitresses kept the drinks flowing and it wasn't long before it was closing time. Somehow, I made it upstairs.

The next morning I woke up naked, with a raging hard on, and a headache that hurt too bad to even open my eyes. I could still smell her on my skin, and even though I knew it was a terrible idea, I needed to see her again.

"WHAT COLOR WOULD YOU LIKE?" the saleslady asked.

"Red."

The color of her hair—the color of lust, and sin, and all the other things I thought of when I thought of Jessica. No other color would do for her. Sure, she looked amazing in anything, but what she was doing to me was forbidden, and I wanted to remember that every time my eyes ran across her body.

I stood to the side and watched as the lady wrapped the red lingerie in a box full of tissue paper. I couldn't wait to see the lace thong tucked away in the sweet swells of her ass, or the sexy see-through bra, barely covering her perky tits. I was going to really enjoy peeling these expensive bits of lace from her body.

I had the packages delivered to her because I didn't feel right doing it myself. Delivering presents in person wasn't something I usually did. Hell, buying presents was something different altogether, but I didn't see Jessica spending money frivolously on herself. She wasn't that kind of girl. She was giving, and I couldn't wait until she was giving me what I wanted again.

As hard as it was, I stayed away from her. It was almost impossible, but necessary. I spent my nights in the club and my afternoons with business and paperwork. Whenever Vick came around, I pretended to be as normal as possible. I certainly didn't need her shit.

My standoff lasted two whole days. It was then I found myself driving over to Jessica's condo. I wanted to see her and I didn't give a shit what anyone else had to say about it. I was at a stoplight, in the middle of the city, when the familiar shade red hair caught my attention.

Jessica was walking down the sidewalk with a happy smile on her face. She had on a simple pair of jeans, a black T-shirt with a faded logo, and a pair of ballet flats. So simple, yet so glorious at the same time.

Not knowing she was being watching, I noticed how graceful, and unique she moved—she stuck out from the crowd. Her light was too bright to be just one of the crowd.

A homeless man was propped up against the side of a building, holey clothes hung from his frame, and his hand held out a cup waiting for change. Jessica smiled down at him, before digging into her pockets and dropping whatever change she had, in his cup.

There she was, not knowing I'd replenished her account, and she was giving a homeless man her last bit of change. It spoke a lot about the kind of person she was—the kind of person I could have loved when I was younger. But that was when my life was total chaos and I thought emotions were important.

The cars behind me began to honk and I took off toward her place. I knew I'd get there before her, but I kind of liked the element of surprise.

She stepped off the elevator and into her condo with a smile and a hand full of paperwork. She kicked her shoes off and sighed, reaching down to rub her feet. I liked the fact she seemed so comfortable in the home I'd given her. It made me feel accomplished, like I'd done more in my life than the club.

Without noticing me sitting on her couch, she went into the kitchen, placed the papers on the counter, and filled a glass with water. Her throat worked up and down as she gulped the entire glass down. Her shirt clung to her body, letting me see every dip and curve.

"Enjoy your walk?" I asked.

Her eyes went wide, and she covered her mouth to keep the water from spewing out.

"Sebastian, you scared me," she said, placing her empty glass on the counter.

"I can't help but wonder if you'd be so jumpy if you had a gun around here."

The memory of her pale face and the way she shook after we'd been held up, still sat in the front of my mind. I didn't like the idea of her walking the streets of New York without protection.

"I don't want to talk about guns again," she said, coming around the counter and into the living space where I'd been sitting.

"Why were you walking? You could have called Martin." I changed the subject.

"It's beautiful out today and I didn't have to go far. I needed the exercise anyway."

"What's with the papers?" I pointed to the stack on the counter.

"That's my five year plan." She stepped back to the counter and snatched up the papers.

I stood and moved closer to her. Taking the papers from her hand, I leaned in and did the one thing I'd been thinking about doing since I saw her walking down the sidewalk.

I kissed her.

It wasn't the usual hard, forceful kiss, but a quick one that satisfied me until I could get more.

When I pulled back, the surprise on her face was comical. I loved how I'd switched tables on her. Before, my aggressiveness had shocked her. And now, anytime I did anything normal or even remotely nice, she didn't know how to act. She was definitely fun to play with.

NINETEEN

ROSSLYN

HIS KISS FELT DIFFERENT. IT was soft, like a first kiss. It was nice. The one thing I could say about Sebastian, he was fantastic kisser—not that I had much to go on.

He pulled back and I felt his stare even with my eyes closed. I was still humming inside from his kiss when he spoke.

"What are these?" he asked.

"It's paperwork for a technical college. I was thinking of taking some online classes."

It was a quick decision when I'd gotten up that morning and had nothing to do. I'd always been obsessed with forensics and dreamed of a career in that field. Online classes would be something I could spend time on and it would be pushing me in a better direction financially. I was excited to do something for myself—something that could benefit my future.

"I didn't know you were interested in going to school."

"Well, yeah. I mean, it's a smart choice. I don't expect you to be my sexual benefactor forever. I need to be able to take care of myself. That means getting a degree and getting a job."

"You don't need to work. I'll take care of you."

"Come on, Sebastian. We both know this isn't going to last forever. You've already made it clear that you don't do *love,* and I've made it perfectly clear that I *do.* Plus, this isn't what I want. I don't want you to take care of me. I want to be able to take care of myself."

He looked down at the paperwork and made a face a few at the pictures from a crime scene.

"What the hell is this?" he asked.

"Those are the classes I'll look into once I do two years at the technical college. I want to get into forensics and help solve crimes."

He looked at me like I was crazy, and I couldn't help but giggle a little.

"What made you want to get into this?"

I didn't want to answer. Twelve years later and my parents' death was still a touchy subject. Probably because I never got closure. I wanted to make sure no other family had to go through that.

"The same thing that started my fear of guns," I answered.

"Someone you knew was shot?"

"Yes."

"Were you there?"

"No, but I'm the one that found her. They never caught her killer. I want to try to make a difference."

He didn't push anymore, which was one of the things I loved the most about Sebastian.

"If you think that's what you need to do. As long as it doesn't interfere with my time," his cocky smile made his dimples pop.

He was definitely being different since we'd slept together, but I didn't say anything about it. His smile was too sweet—I didn't want to ruin it. I'd probably never get over how sexy he was, and after giving myself over to him so completely I wasn't sure I wanted to.

"*Your* time? Seriously?"

"Yes, my time. When I want you, I want you. I don't like to wait."

I couldn't help myself. I giggled so hard my stomach hurt.

"Are you laughing at me?"

I liked how playful he was being. It made him seem like a normal everyday guy.

"Yes," I chuckled. "Sir, yes sir!" I playfully saluted him.

"Go ahead and laugh," he moved closer. "It doesn't matter because this belongs to me," he said, reaching down between my legs.

And just like that, the laughter stopped. I didn't like his tone, and hated that he was more right than he realized.

I smacked his hand away. "I belong to no one."

Pulling me to him, he leaned down and ran his nose up the side of my neck, before planting a soft kiss beneath my ear.

"That's where you're wrong, sweetheart. I licked it, so it's mine. "

And then, he was kissing me. I wanted to push him away, and I wanted to pull him closer. His hands made their way down my hips and grabbed me, lifting me up as he pressed his body into mine. He was promising me another night like the one before.

He broke away. "How about taking a tour of your bedroom?" His voice dropped before he leaned down and took my mouth again.

I didn't hold back, kissing him with all I had. With his hands cupping my face, he walked me backward, until my ass hit the door. He lifted me and I wrapped my legs around his waist. He pressed into me and I broke the kiss and moaned with closed eyes.

He pushed the door open and we stumbled into my room, surrounded by all of my things. I'd cried happy tears when I first saw how organized my personal items had been, and now the place was home. That was something I'd always be thankful for when it came to Sebastian. He was an asshole, but he'd given me a home when I didn't have one.

He pulled back and worked his way down the side of my neck. Stubble scratched against my skin and I lost my fingers in his hair, pulling him closer. I enjoyed the difference in him. He was like Jekyll and Hyde. It was amazing what sex could do to a man.

"It's going to be good. I promise I'll make it good for you," he said as he nipped at my chin.

I had no doubt about that. I'd learned a few days before, Sebastian knew exactly what he was doing. Laying me back on my bed, he followed me down, pressing me into my mattress.

Cool air brushed my stomach as he lifted my shirt. His heated touch scorched my skin and a hiss sounded from between my teeth.

Who was I?

I didn't feel like the old me at all anymore. I hadn't since he'd brought me to life on the couch in his office. It was like he was turning me into some carefree person, and I was all about everything he'd done so far. Lifting from the bed, he pulled my shirt off and smiled when my red bra was revealed.

"I like this," he said as he slid a finger in the cup, running his finger across my hardened nipple.

"Of course you do, you picked it out." I arched my back and whimpered.

"You're so responsive to my touch." He nuzzled in my cleavage. "I never want to stop touching you."

He bit my nipple through the bra and I was gone. I latched on to his shoulders and closed my eyes as his hand worked its way down my side, to the top of my jeans. My stomach sucked in from his touch, allowing him to slip his hand past my button and into my jeans. And then he was touching me through my panties.

It felt so good. I lifted my hips when he took his hand away. He pulled my zipper down and peeled my jeans from my hips. His fingertips felt rough against the skin inside my thighs. I opened wider once my jeans were on the floor.

"I can't wait another second to be inside you."

His lips brushed the inside of my leg and then he was rolling my panties down my legs.

He sucked the soft skin on the inside of my leg. His hot breath skimmed my wetness, warming me and making me ache even more. And then he was on top of me, staring down at me with his usual cocky grin. I could hardly wait to feel him.

I reached up, running my fingers through his hair and brushing the back of my fingertips down the back of his neck and kissing him softly on the corner of his mouth.

His expression changed and his body stiffened above me

"What are you doing?" he asked.

"What do you mean? I'm kissing you."

I was confused. I wasn't sure how to answer his question. It was obvious what we were doing, and if he didn't know, then I was obviously doing it wrong.

"This isn't *romance*, Jessica. Stop looking at me like that. Don't touch me sweetly. Be rough. This is fucking. That's all. It's not love. It'll never be love."

I stared at him. My heart tore in half, all of my feelings toward him spilling out, and pooling in a painful puddle in my stomach.

And then he leaned up, backing away from me. He grabbed my thighs roughly, flipping me onto my stomach.

Pulling my hips up to him, I instinctively followed and propped up on my hands. He pushed hard against me. "I'm going to fuck you so hard."

His words stung, and I didn't know how to react. I was still reeling from his other comments. Stunned into silence, I stared at the sheets below me.

Sebastian meant what he said, he was going to fuck me hard. My chest and the side of my head were suddenly pushed into the mattress, as he simultaneously pressed into me and pulled my arms tightly behind my back.

It was rough, and it actually felt good. However, I couldn't help but think that it would feel better if my heart wasn't dying a slow death. I just wished he would stop pushing me away. We obviously had a connection and I felt sorry for him and his inability to fully bond with another human being.

"You act sweet, but you're really a naughty girl aren't you, Jessica?" His body was leaning over me, allowing him to go deeper. "Tell me how dirty you are." His mouth brushed against my ear.

I couldn't answer. I wasn't emotionally present. It *did* feel amazing, his smooth arousal spreading me open, filling me. But I didn't want to reward his behavior from earlier, so I gave him nothing.

He realized I wasn't going to play along. Leaning back, he gripped my hips almost painfully, and started to move fast and hard. Out of nowhere, his palm landed hard against my ass. The loud smack rang throughout the room, and my ass stung badly before he rubbed it away with his warm palm.

"Fuck me," he rasped. "I can't get enough of your body."

His hands latched onto my breasts and he pulled me up, so that my back was pressed firmly against his front. His fingers plucked at my nipples before moving down over my stomach and between my legs. The pad of his finger rubbed sweet circles over my throbbing bud and it was all I could take.

Against my will, I called out. "Sebastian..."

My body shook against his, and I was coming, his hips continuing to work me. My body went limp and I fell forward. He held my hips in the air and continued on his mission for an orgasm.

Thrusting only a few more times, he pulled out, and came all over my ass. It was hot and dripping down my cheek. He spread the come around my ass with his tip, while milking his cock dry.

Letting his body fall next to mine with a huff, I quickly turned on my side, giving him my back. I couldn't process my feelings and didn't want to look at him for the moment.

My heart ached for what would obviously never be. And yet my body was in euphoria, coming down from a high like no other.

He'd been rough and aggressive, and if I was being honest with myself... I enjoyed it.

I felt his hot hand moving down my arm, but him touching me sweetly in any way felt like a lie. I didn't want to be lied to. Shaking his hand from my arm, I slid further away from him.

"Oh so now I can't touch you?" he asked.

"Not like that. Not with any softness. No romance remember, this is just fucking."

I was fucked, in more ways than one.

TWENTY

SEBASTIAN

SHE SLEPT NEXT TO ME, an occasional sound coming from her, as if she was dreaming and in distress. Her scarlet hair was covering most of her face, but I could still see the swollen swell of her pouty lips.

I was in a fucked up place, mentally. Worse than anything I'd gone through when I was younger, except for the night that continuously haunted my dreams. The experience hardened me and changed me into the man I was today. The only way I could make it through life after that night, was by not feeling anything at all. It was either that, or die from heartache.

Jessica had been breaking down the wall I built, and I reacted poorly because it scared me. I wasn't technically afraid of having feelings for *her*, I was afraid of feeling anything at all. I'd worked hard at blocking out everything to get through my days—to get myself through the one single moment that had defined the rest of my life.

And the worst part was, I hurt her. I could see it in her eyes when I lied to her face, saying it would never be about love.

Reaching out, I took a strand of her hair and rubbed it between two fingers. It was true, I had to admit it to myself. I was falling for her. Me—the man who didn't believe in the bullshit word everyone tossed around, the man who thought love was a woman's word. I'd always truly believed men weren't capable of love, especially a man like me. Yet there I was, staring down at this seemingly perfect creature, and trying to figure out exactly what I was feeling.

The whole thing felt suffocating, like the air around me was too thick, too humid. Whether I was thinking of my feelings or about not being near her, I constantly felt I couldn't breathe. A weight as heavy as New York City was pressing against my chest, and I couldn't lift it, no matter how angry or mean I was. It just wouldn't fucking budge.

And those eyes... those big, trusting, beautiful eyes. I couldn't fucking shake the moment when pain entered those eyes. They haunted me because I was the cause of that heartache.

Slipping from her bed, I dressed quietly, careful not to wake her. Staring down at her as she slept, I watched her breasts lift with each deep breath. I was mesmerized—caught effectively in a web I'd personally weaved. I had to get out of there. I had to free myself, before I couldn't.

The cool night air made me shiver as I stood outside and waited for the valet to bring my car around. The city lights blinked like the universe was trying to relay a secret message to only me—a visual Morse code of sorts for the crazy fucker. I closed my eyes to it and kept them closed, until I heard the purr of my Jaguar pulling up.

Once I was in the warmth of my car, I sat there and contemplated going back inside. The valet stood at the driver's side window, waiting for me to climb back out. I gripped the steering wheel and shook myself. Staying over wasn't my thing. Spending time after sex with a woman at all, was something I always avoided. Obviously, it was different with Jessica.

I decided against it and hit the road, driving slowly to give myself time to think, I passed the night-lifers and tried to pinpoint the exact moment the change in me had occurred.

When I got to the club, the place was alive—crawling with crowds of people I used to be like. I no longer felt like that man. Moving through the room, I bumped into dancers and nodded at those who knew my name, but didn't know me. Hell, I didn't know me—not really.

I didn't go to my office because I didn't want to deal with Vick. Instead, I went to my apartment. Trekking through my place, I headed straight to the bathroom for a shower. I peeled off my clothes, which smelled of Jessica, and stood under the hot spray in the silence of the tile-filled room. It seemed to be the only place I could think anymore. My office screamed Jessica, the club, the car, everything was tainted with a memory of her.

I stayed in longer than usual, letting the water dump directly onto my head—numbing my skin with the heat and hoping to numb my thoughts as well. When I stepped out, I grabbed a towel and found Vick leaning against the doorway with crossed arms.

"Ignoring me?" she asked with a lifted brow.

I ran the towel across my face and hair, before wrapping it around my body and exiting the shower.

"I needed a shower before I dealt with your shit."

Scooping up my toothbrush, I squeezed a layer of toothpaste on it and started brushing my teeth. She was pissing me off, standing over me with her arms crossed, like she controlled me. It was time I brought her back down to her level.

Rinsing my mouth, I pulled my towel from my waist and wiped my face. I walked beside her and into my bedroom. She followed. Pulling a pair of boxer briefs from the top drawer, I covered my ass and started toward my closet.

"What's going on with us, Sebastian? We used to be so close. It's like you don't even talk to me anymore. It's bullshit, and you know it."

I'd had enough. I turned on her quickly, getting close to her and making her take a step back. I would never hurt a woman, but this shit had to stop.

"Victoria, get off my sac already. For years I've covered your ass—turned the other cheek to some really fucked up shit, and this is how you repay me? I'm about this close," I held two fingers up, "to dropping your ass right where I found you. Now leave me the fuck alone!"

I watched as it happened, but I couldn't believe it. Her stoic face crumbled, and the dreaded expression I'd spent a good bit of time running from, spread across her face. Her eyes watered and her lip trembled... and it was then I knew—I just fucking knew. Vick stayed around to help me, out of loyalty and money, but there was something else I hadn't noticed. How had something so big slip past my radar? It was something I thought Vick incapable of. She showed emotion, and it was for me.

I looked at Vick like a sister, and now I could see she'd been harboring forbidden feelings for a man who, until recently, didn't know he was capable of feeling anything.

"No. Not you. This can't be happening," I begged under my breath.

"Sebastian…"

"Leave," I demanded.

"Sebastian, please listen…" she started.

"I said, get the *fuck* out of my apartment, now!"

She stared at me as if I was going to change my mind, and then turned and left without another word.

Instead of sticking around the club and socializing, I stayed in my office the rest of the night. I put myself so deep into paperwork, I tuned out the outside world.

That morning, I went to bed with thoughts of Jessica walking the streets alone. Suddenly the thought of something terrible happening to her consumed me. I thought about her fear of guns and wondered what could have happened to her to give her that fear. There were so many things I wanted to know, so many things I could've already known if I hadn't been such a selfish prick.

Instead of my usual nightmare, I dreamed of Jessica and her soft lips and trusting eyes. The dream turned into a nightmare and I found myself looking down at her as she died in my arms.

THE NEXT AFTERNOON, I FOUND myself somewhere I hadn't been in a while. Grady, the man behind the counter, nodded at me when I walked in. He was an older Italian with a thick Jersey accent.

His thick, black hair was dyed and oiled into a perfect wave, and his hairy arms and chest were visible through his button down shirt. The entire look was topped off with a collection of gold chains. He was old Italy.

Dabbling in a little bit everything, he was the man to see when you needed anything. I only used his services for one thing and one thing only. The rest of the illegal shit was in my past, where I meant it to stay.

"Long time no see, Black. What can I do for you?"

He lit the end of his cigar, filling the room with its thick pungent odor.

"I'm looking for something feminine, but still powerful enough to take a man down."

Eyeing me for a few brief seconds, he took another puff from his cigar and nodded. "I think I have just what you're looking for."

Turning around, he opened a cabinet and pulled out a pretty piece. It was small and tinted pink. I knew Jessica would definitely hate it, but a girl like her needed to know how to protect herself in case she was right and I didn't stick around. Which, let's face it, was bound to happen at some point.

I left Grady's with exactly what I came in for. Jessica might not like it, but I'd feel better about her being alone if she was packing. She'd have a lot to learn about how to use it. I'd be sure she understood what pulling the trigger meant, before she actually pulled it.

TWENTY-ONE

ROSSLYN

WHEN I WOKE THE NEXT morning, Sebastian was gone. I wasn't surprised. He wasn't the kind of guy who spent the night. Rolling over, I pressed my face into the pillow beside me and breathed him in.

There was a hole in my chest and my body ached sweetly. I stretched to wake it. Closing my eyes, I thought about how the last few days had gone. It was bad to be so caught up in a man like him, and I knew from the beginning he was going to crush my heart, but I hadn't cared at the time. I just didn't understand how bad it could hurt.

My cell on the bedside table chirped and I reached out to check it. The screen lit up with my touch, showing me a text notification. Since Kyle and Sebastian were the only two people who knew my number, I knew it was from Sebastian. I pressed my finger against the tiny pink envelope on the screen.

Sebastian: Be ready by ten and wear something comfortable. It's time to face your fears.

My stomach felt tight with fear already. I set the phone down and chewed on my bottom lip. I had no idea what the heck he was talking about, or what we would be doing come ten o'clock, but I got up and made my way toward the bathroom to shower.

The hot water soothed my sore muscles. I ran my fingers across my tight abs and aching thighs. I couldn't stop thinking about him. I didn't know how I was going to face him and keep my feelings hidden. My emotions had no place in this deal and I would just have to get over them.

Fifteen minutes later, I was wiping fresh steam from the mirror and wrapping a fluffy towel around my breasts. I stared at myself in the mirror and wondered what I'd gotten myself into with Sebastian.

I was caught up in him completely, but to him I was just another one of his girls. It hurt to even think about him spending nights like ours with other girls.

He'd made it abundantly clear he had no interest in me outside of sex or taking care of me financially; and even then, it was because he wanted something from me.

There would be no proposals of love, or vows of fidelity. He'd stated plainly what he wanted from day one, and that was my body only. My heart, or his for that matter, were not on the table and they never would be, no matter how badly I wanted to set mine up there for him.

I thought of Kyle, and how happy he was about the condo and the fact we weren't living in his school parking lot. No matter what, I had to do this for him. I couldn't lose him again, when he was all I had. At least that's what I'd keep telling myself. As bad as it stung, I refused to acknowledge that my reasons for being with Sebastian were becoming purely selfish.

Turning away from the mirror, I dried off and hung the towel up to comb through my wet hair. I got dressed, briefly wondering what a girl wore when she was facing her fears. I decided on jeans and a white button-up shirt.

The sound of the elevator made me stand from the couch. And then there he was, strutting into my apartment with his dark hair and shade-covered eyes, topped with that panty-soaking smile.

"Ready to go?" he asked.

"Where are we going?"

"You'll see."

He reached out and placed a hand on my lower back, ushering me onto the elevator. He didn't move his hand until he was opening the door to the car for me to climb in. I felt the loss of his warmth the minute he wasn't there. I reminded myself that he did such intimate gestures with all of his girls, he was just practiced at what he did.

I watched him move with purpose to the driver's side of the car. Once he was in and had his seatbelt on, I spoke.

"Can you tell me what this is about?"

"I have something for you. But first... I don't want you walking the streets alone anymore." His words had come from nowhere. "As long as we're doing this, you'll call Martin when you need to go somewhere. Understood?"

"It's not necessary. I have two feet and—"

He cut me off. "What did I say, Jessica?"

The way he was talking to me made me mad, even though I should've been used to it by that point. I crossed my arms over my chest and looked out the window, pretending to ignore his words.

"Don't go getting pissed at me. It's only because I don't want anything bad to happen to you."

I turned and looked at him shocked. His words were borderline sweet and I wasn't sure if I should enjoy them or check him for a fever.

"What?" I asked.

I had to be sure I wasn't hearing things.

Instead of answering me, he leaned across my lap, warming my legs. "It's also why I bought you..." he opened the glove compartment. "This."

I jerked when he set a pink gun on my lap. It was small. At first I thought it was a toy because of its color, but it was heavy—too heavy to be fake. Just having it close to me made me feel like having a panic attack.

"Sebastian..." I held my hands away from it, like it was going to bite me.

"Relax, Jessica. I'd never do anything to harm you. Do you trust that?" he asked, making a left turn.

"I don't trust guns."

"I understand. But do you trust me?"

I did. I trusted him with everything, except my heart, but neither had anything to do with the fact that guns scared the crap out of me.

"I need to know that when you're not with me, you're protected. It's either this, or I hire someone to follow you around." He kept his eyes on the road.

"I don't understand you. Why are you doing this?"

He avoided my confusion, steering clear of clarifying anything. It was like I wasn't even talking. He reached over and took the gun from my lap.

"It's a nine millimeter. Sixteen rounds in the clip. Right now the safety's on, but I'm taking you to learn how to shoot it."

At that exact moment, we pulled up to a large warehouse. The sign out front said *First Shot* and there was a picture of a gun beneath it.

"Sebastian?" I said in a panicked whisper. "What's going on? What are we doing here?"

"We're facing fear, Jessica. You can do this."

I was shaking my head before he finished. "No, I can't. I can't do this and I don't want to. Don't make me. Please, Sebastian."

I closed my eyes and I could hear the gunshots echoing through my memory. When the actual sound of gunshots rang out, I practically jumped into his lap.

"It's okay. You're okay." He rubbed my back and kissed my forehead. "Just do this for me."

I looked up into his eyes and they were different. It was like I was with a completely different man. Where was the asshole from before? Where was the guy who showed no concern for anyone but himself? Being with him could give a girl whiplash.

Sebastian, or at least the man beside me, was begging me. It was subtle, but he was definitely begging.

He'd done so much for me and Kyle already. Of course, I had to give in return, but giving to Sebastian was one of the best things I'd ever done in my life. I just wasn't sure I could give him this. It was so much deeper than my virginity.

It was fear—set deep in my core. I'd carried it around for twelve years, and it wasn't like I could just wave it away and pretend like that night never happened. It was a memory---a nightmare I'd relived every day since I was younger.

I closed my eyes and silently begged ten-year-old me to take a chance. I breathed deep, letting the warmth from his hand on my knee seep into me. *I can do this.*

Sebastian was one of the biggest assholes I'd ever met, but I liked making him happy. I didn't know what that said about me, and honestly, I didn't care.

"Okay, let's go. Just promise you'll stay with me."

"Of course I'll be there. There's nowhere else I'd rather be."

His words and the way he said them caught me off guard once again, and by the look on his face, they did the same to him. He turned away from me, unbuckled his seatbelt, and opened the door.

"Let's do this."

Gunshots. I didn't think I'd ever really get over the sound of them, and that's all you heard from the minute you got out of the car. Once you were inside, it was ten times worse. They echoed off of cement block walls and with every shot, I felt my fear rise.

I followed close behind him as he walked us to a room lined with partitions. A few people were in the room, each one with their own space, and each one aiming a gun at a paper with the black figure of a man on it.

Sebastian must have paid extra because our partition had a door to it. It was big enough for five people, and it had an extra counter to set things on the right. After entering the room, Sebastian pulled out my gun and set it on the counter.

Stepping close to me, he grinned and ran his hands down my arms. "Turn around."

He didn't give me much room to turn and my ass rubbed against his crotch in the process. A low groan slipped past his lips. Looking up, I shook my head and rolled my eyes.

He smirked.

"Focus," he picked up the gun and held it in front of me. "This is a gun. Like all guns, it's deadly, but it's not too heavy. Without this," he said holding up the clip of bullets, "it's just a piece of metal. Nothing to fear, right?"

He moved the end of the gun down the side of my neck and then throat. The cold metal chilled my skin and I gasped.

I needed a boost in confidence. With one of my biggest fears being rubbed against me, I needed to hear him say it was worth it.

"Tell me why you're doing this again." My voice squeaked.

"I told you. I need to know you're safe. I've seen some fucked up things in my life, Jess, and I don't want anything bad to happen to you. Okay?"

"Okay." Hearing his words, I would have agreed to anything.

And then he shocked me by saying, "Unbutton your shirt."

My eyes snapped toward his. "What?"

"Unbutton your shirt."

"Why?"

"Because I said so."

My eyes flashed to the door, but at his words, I was too turned on to really care if it was locked or not.

"Don't worry; no one's going to interrupt us."

"Did you have to pay extra for that?"

"Yes. And it's so going to be fucking worth it. Now, again, unbutton your shirt."

He watched me as my fingers found the first button and then the second until my shirt was completely undone.

"One of the best ways to get rid of a bad memory is to replace it with a good one. You fear guns, but I'm going to make you love this one."

His words made me shiver.

I was trembling, in a good way, before the cool end of the gun touched my stomach, moving my shirt to the side.

His eyes didn't release mine as I felt the tip move over one nipple and then the other. They hardened in a rush and Sebastian smiled his approval.

"See?" he said smugly. "Sometimes guns can be sexual."

"With you, everything is sexual."

"You're damn right, baby. Now take off your pants."

I didn't need him to tell me twice and I unbuttoned and let them fall down my hips and legs. He moved the gun down my stomach and used it to trace the line of my panties.

Once, twice, and then he was moving it between my things. I moaned when the hard tip caressed me through my panties, hitting the right spot. I could feel my body's response soaking through my panties and I surprised myself when I moved my hips over the blunt tip again.

"Sebastian..." I moaned and then my hips began to move in a steady motion.

"What, baby?"

"What are you doing to me?"

My breathing was hard, my hips moved faster as I built my release.

He chuckled. "It's all you, baby."

I gripped the edge of the table as I felt my orgasm take over my body. Shots were loud all around me masking my loud moans. Coming back to myself, I realized what I'd just done. I never thought I'd allow myself around a gun again, much less be given an orgasm by one.

Lifting the gun, he placed the clip in the bottom with a click and laid it back down.

"That was fucking hot, Jessica."

I looked up at him through my lashes and laughed. "That was... different."

"Ready to shoot now?"

A cold dose of fear laced my veins and I bit my lips, but nodded.

"Good."

Reaching beneath the counter, Sebastian pulled out a pair of ear muffs and placed them on my head. Once he placed the ear protection muffs on me, the sounds weren't so bad. But I could still feel their vibrations all around me every time a shot went off.

Leaning in, he pulled at the muffs uncovering my ear enough so I could hear him when he spoke.

Turning me around, his lips brushed the side of my face. "I'm going to shoot a few rounds and show you how to stand, and then you can shoot. Okay?"

With wide eyes I nodded my understanding. I was perfectly fine sitting tucked away in a corner, with my sound proof ear muffs.

I moved out of his way and he pulled out an even bigger black gun. He pressed a button and a paper with a man lined in black appeared in the distance.

Sebastian stood tall and straight, with his legs rooted firmly to the ground. Then he aimed his gun with his right hand, using his left to hold it steady. His hands kicked up every time he pulled the trigger, and I could hear the muffled sound of his shots.

Bang. Bang. Bang. Bang.

My heart was racing and if I pressed myself against the wall any harder, I would have been in the space next to us. As scared as I was, I couldn't help but take in his extraordinary form. His strong back—his lean arms. He wasn't in a suit, and had opted for a nice pair of thigh-hugging jeans and a loose shirt.

The platinum watch on his wrist shook with his shots, making my eyes move down his arms, to his broad shoulders. Everything about Sebastian was big and strong. It was then I realized, I really did feel safe with him. Whether he was in love or not, he was a good man who would never let anything bad happen to me or Kyle.

When he was done, he turned and faced me.

"Your turn," he mouthed.

I stepped up to him on shaky legs and when he held out the small pink gun, my fingers trembled around the coldness of it. I closed my eyes and adjusted it in my hand the way you should.

Sebastian pushed the button on the side wall, switching out the paper for a fresh one. Then he stood behind me, so close I could feel his heartbeat against my shoulder.

"Okay. Right before you're going to shoot, you'll want to take the safety off, here." He clicked a small button on the right side of my gun. "Then, open your legs a little and hold the gun straight." He ran his hands down my arms holding them out straight and helping me aim the gun. "There's going to be kickback when you pull the trigger, but nothing you can't handle. This gun is yours, which means it's perfect for you."

I took a deep breath, trying to calm my nerves before I set my finger on the trigger.

"When you shoot, imagine the person who made you afraid of guns is standing in front of that paper. Aim for their head."

I closed my eyes and the vision of the man came to me instantly. I couldn't see his face clearly, but I remembered his outline.

Opening my eyes, I aimed the gun and pulled the trigger. It felt good, so I pulled it again and again, until finally the gun was empty and the power of the bullet leaving the gun stopped pressing against my palm.

I stood there, with an empty clip, staring at the paper full of holes. I lowered my arms, but didn't let go of the gun. My body was shaking, but I wasn't entirely sure it was all from fear. Adrenaline was running wild through my system and I had to take a few deep breaths to contain myself.

My eyes dropped to my hands and the death grip on the gun between them. I never expected to feel so much power, so much courage, knowing I could protect myself and Kyle if anything bad every happened again.

It was exhilarating, and I was suddenly happy Sebastian had brought me here. He pushed me to better myself.

Putting the gun down, I turned around and threw my arms around his neck. Using my strength, I pulled myself up so we were face to face and my mouth found his.

I was fierce and hungry as my tongue pushed past his lips, pushing deeper into his mouth. He wasn't surprised by my reaction and he met my response with everything he had. Lifting my hips, I wrapped my legs around his waist and he turned, slamming us into the wall.

In one swift motion, he ripped my panties from my body and his pants were down around his ankles. He didn't waste any time as he thrust deep inside of me. He was right; it was so fucking worth it.

Slowly, and without him realizing it, Sebastian was changing my life.

TWENTY-TWO

ROSSLYN

AN HOUR LATER, WE WERE sitting in the back booth at the Pit Stop, the burger joint where we'd been held up outside. Leave it to Sebastian to take me back to the place where a bad memory existed. Except, I was glad he did. Their burgers were delicious and I felt stronger now that I knew how to protect myself.

I'd done it. I'd shot a gun, and I was good at it. When Sebastian showed me my paper full of holes, there were nine holes it. Not bad for a first timer.

"You did well," Sebastian stated.

"Thank you."

"I'm serious, Jessica. I'm proud of you. It takes a lot of guts to face a fear head on the way you did," he said, swirling his fry in a pile of ketchup.

"You know, I'm proud of me, too. I never thought I'd be able to touch a gun, much less shoot one. Thank you for taking me."

Something flashed in his eyes, resembling pleasure, although I wasn't positive because the only time I'd seen him look that way was when he was inside me.

"It was nothing. Plus, I enjoyed it. You looked fucking hot shooting that gun. I enjoyed fucking you in the middle of the shooting range."

I stopped before taking a bite of my burger and smiled at him.

"Do you ever think about anything besides sex?" I laughed.

A beautiful, real smile stretched his lips and he shook his head, "Not when I'm with you."

The next twenty minutes, I tried to eat while Sebastian found any way he could to touch me. Finally, he stood and slid into the booth next to me—his side warming mine.

Picking up one of my fries, he dipped it in the ketchup and held it up to me to take a bite.

I licked a drip of ketchup from the fry before taking a bite.

"You keep that shit up and I'll take you to the little bathroom in the back of this shit-hole for more."

"Sure you will," I teased.

"Don't bullshit, sweetheart. I can see it in your eyes, you're turned on. I bet you're already soaked for me." He leaned in, touching between my legs as he kissed me underneath my ear. "I'll tell you what, why don't you go to the ladies' room, put an extra layer of toilet paper in your panties, and come back here so I can take you home."

His words brushed my ear and made me shiver.

I ran my finger down the front of my shirt, before covering his hand and pressing it deeper into my jeans. I looked up at him and licked my lips. I knew what I was doing, and I knew it was working by the look in his eyes.

"What if I don't want to wait?"

His pupils dilated and he clenched his jaw. "You're playing with fire. If you're not careful, you'll get burnt."

I pressed his hand harder against me and a tiny moan escaped my throat.

"Fuck it. Come with me," he said, grabbing my hand and pulling me from the booth.

I held his hand as he dragged me to the back of the restaurant and then pulled me into the only bathroom in the place. It was small, almost too small for the two of us, and not completely clean. The toilet was tilted to the side and the sink looked like someone had colored it with a gray crayon on the inside, but it would have to do for a quickie.

"Remember, you asked for this," he said, locking the door behind us and stalking toward me.

He turned me and bent me over the small counter. Wasting no time, he went to work unbuttoning my jeans and pulling them down enough to expose little more than my ass.

"I can't open my legs this way." I said, pressing my bare bottom into him.

I heard his zipper come down and saw him lick his fingers, bringing them down to my wet opening. Then I felt the tip of his arousal pushing in.

"Good. It'll feel better for both of us."

He slid deep into me, pressing me harder against the counter. He felt bigger—filling me completely and rubbing my inner walls in a way that made me close my eyes in pleasure.

He moved fast and hard, without mercy, tugging on my hair to make me look up. His other hand grabbed my chin, forcing me to look into the mirror in front of us.

"I want you to watch while I fuck you."

I looked in the mirror and he glared back at me as he thrust his body into mine. The counter shook and a few times I was sure I heard someone knocking at the door, but I didn't care. All I cared about was the feeling moving through me as Sebastian took over my body.

He tugged my hair harder, making me call out and I met his dark, cocky smirk in the mirror. He was loving it as much as I was.

"Remember how much I adore that mouth of yours? I think I want to come in it this time," he stated.

Still, he continued to hammer me, balls slapping against slick, sweaty skin.

Pleasurable pain clouded my eyes, making my brows turn in as the ache where his body connected with mine spread into my thighs. The sounds of our bodies coming together echoed in the tile-filled bathroom and a bottle of hand soap went crashing to the floor.

The customers could hear us, I was sure of it. But, Sebastian continued. Looping his arms underneath mine, he latched on to my shoulders, leaning over me and working his hips faster than I knew possible. That's when I crashed.

Loud screams fell from my mouth, forcing Sebastian to cover it with his palm. I cried into his hand, before I bit its salty flesh. He cursed loudly, letting me know he was enjoying the sex as much as I was.

Finally he pulled out and turned me abruptly.

"Get on your fucking knees," he growled.

I dropped to my knees the best I could with my jeans around my thighs and as soon as I opened my mouth, the head of his penis pushed past my lips. I moved my tongue over him, tasting myself on his skin, sucking him deeper into my mouth. I had no idea what I was doing, but it didn't matter.

Sebastian threw his head back and pressed my mouth onto him harder as he exploded on the back of my tongue. Thick and hot, his come spewed all over, coating my mouth and throat with his personal flavor.

SEBASTIAN WAS QUIET IN THE car as he drove me back to my condo. I think he was realizing things were changing between us. Not good or bad, just different. We'd been spending so much time together, and that made me happy because I knew as long as he was with me, he wasn't with another girl.

I was done denying the fact I wanted Sebastian to myself. I tried not to think about what he did when he wasn't with me, and it was hard, but it was a part of the deal. I couldn't go changing things now. It was too late for that.

When we got to my building, he walked me inside and followed me into the elevator. Once he inserted his card and pressed the button for the top floor, he turned to me and pulled me to him.

"I'm angry with you," he stated.

His hands moved down my back and cupped my ass. He bit his lip as he stared at my chest.

"Well, I'm angry with you," I countered.

He smirked and chuckled. "What the hell did I do ?" he asked. "Besides fuck you senseless for an entire restaurant to hear?"

His smirk turned into another genuine smile. I loved his smile, but I'd never mention it for fear he'd never smile at me again.

"Oh, whatever. It wasn't that great," I joked and rolled my eyes.

His head fell back and he laughed. It was a deep hearty laugh that shook his chest.

"Is that so?" He reached up and fingered a strand of my hair. "I guess maybe I should give it another try then. I *did* promise only the best, didn't I?"

"Yep, you sure did." My smile hurt my face it was so big.

And then, just as quickly as it came, his happy expression cleared and he peered down at me in all seriousness.

"This wasn't supposed to happen," he said with his jaw muscles visibly clenching.

I didn't know how to reply. I was frightened I might turn him away somehow.

We stared at each other, until he moved quickly, smashing his mouth to mine and kissing me so hard it hurt.

I wasn't the same girl I was when we first met and so I didn't pull back. Instead, I kissed him just as hard, tugging at the back of his head and digging my nails into his shoulder to hold him closer.

We were still kissing like a couple of teenagers when the elevator opened to my place. He didn't let me go; instead he lifted me and slammed me against the wall opposite of the open elevator.

I'd expected that once we got to my floor, he would say goodbye and leave for the night, like usual. What I didn't expect was for him to stay with me and spend the night, giving me the best he'd promised from the beginning.

I WOKE IN THE MIDDLE of the night to Sebastian whining in his sleep as if he was in pain. The sheet clung to his wet, naked skin and his expression was full of agony.

He tossed and turned, trying to get away from something and I knew he was having a nightmare.

"Sebastian," I shook him.

Still he breathed hard and pulled at the sheet.

"Sebastian, wake up. You're having a nightmare," I said, shoving at his side and trying my hardest to wake him.

A howl exploded from his lips and he cried loudly with closed eyes. I didn't know what to do. This was Sebastian—cold, fearless Sebastian, and yet he was squirming around in my bed and practically bawling.

Laying my palm against his sweaty cheek, I tried once more to wake him.

"Sebastian, you have to wake up."

His eyes flew open and things moved quickly has he pushed me off of him and climbed on top of me.

"Murderer!" his voice cracked.

Thick fingers wrapped around my neck and squeezed.

I beat at his arms as my throat closed up and my ability to breathe was cut off.

"Sebastian," I croaked.

The sounds of my choking filled the room and my life flashed before my eyes. And then, as quickly as it started, his hold loosened and his angry expression cleared. He'd woken up and realized what he was doing.

Jumping away from me, his back slammed into the wall next to my bed. I sat up, coughing and trying to catch the breath that still didn't want to fill my lungs. When the black dots cleared my vision, I was able to reach out and turn on the lamp next to my bed. I could see Sebastian pressed tightly against the wall, staring at me—a look of absolute fear traced his dark features.

"I'm so... I can't believe," he whispered, his voice rough with sleep. "I don't know what... I... Are you okay?" he asked.

I wrapped my fingers around my aching throat and nodded my answer. I wasn't technically okay, but I could see by the devastated look on his face that he needed to know I was.

He crawled beside me and moved my hands from my neck to inspect it. I could feel the bruising and the ridges and welts from his fingers. By the look on his face, he could see them, too.

With a soft touch, he ran his fingers over my neck and shook his head with sadness in his eyes.

"I've never hurt a woman before. I know I'm rough in bed, but you have to believe I'd never..."

I stopped him. "I know. I believe you." I took his hand in mine and held it close to my chest. "What was your nightmare about?" I asked.

Looking down, his agonizing expression cleared and the old Sebastian slipped into his place. "It's nothing. I really am sorry I did that to you."

Apologizing had to sting, and I appreciated him for it. Sebastian never apologized, and for him to do so, meant he was really and honestly sorry.

"Lay back down and get some sleep. I'll stay until you do, but I have to get to the club and help close things up."

I didn't push. I'd dig deeper into all things Sebastian the next chance I got, but until then, I'd lay beside him and enjoy the moment of sweetness he was offering. His arms closed around me, pulling me into his chest and making me feel safe again, and then he rested his chin on my head. Within a matter of minutes, I fell back to sleep.

THE NEXT MORNING, EVEN THOUGH he'd said he was leaving, I woke with Sebastian watching me. With his head resting on his hand, he was drawing little patterns on my shoulder with the tip of his finger.

"I don't apologize often, but let me say it again. I'm sorry, Jessica. So sorry."

I nodded. I barely even noticed the name Jessica anymore. I was used to it, which wasn't necessarily a good thing.

"I forgive you."

And I did. I'd known Sebastian for a while and never once did I get the impression that he was someone who beat women. What was becoming obvious was he had some deep set problems—deeper than I'd initially thought.

Leaning up and hovering over me, he looked down at me with a soft expression.

"How can I feel this way about a woman if I don't even know her name?" His fingers sifted through my hair and down the side of my face.

"What do you mean?" I asked.

"There's no hidden message. I mean exactly what I said. These feelings I have, I don't understand how they're possible. I don't even know you're real name."

The night before was forgotten as I sat up and matched his stare.

"What are you saying, exactly?"

No way was Sebastian Black, asshole extraordinaire, saying what I thought he was saying.

"I'm saying I want to know you." Again, he captured a strand of my hair between his fingers. "The real you. Not Jessica... you."

His words struck deep in my chest and even though there were a million things I wanted to say to him, I kissed him instead.

For the first time since Gran died, I felt put together—like my life wasn't actually falling apart at the seams. I had Kyle, who was having the time of his life doing the thing he loved the most, and I had Sebastian, who was more than I ever dreamed I could have in a man. I'd almost forgotten what happiness felt like, but now that I had it, I never wanted to let it go.

He broke the kiss. Capturing my cheeks in his palms, he pressed his forehead to mine. "I'm almost there—so close it scares the shit out of me. I want to know your name, but I'm afraid I'll run when you tell me. And running from you is the last thing I want to do." His lips brushed mine and then he pulled back and looked me in my eyes. "Give me something to call you. Not Jessica, something that's yours."

Pulling away, I stared up at him. The way he was smiling down at me—the way he touched me, it was almost more than I could take.

"Are you sure?" I asked.

I wasn't going to tell him my whole name, but even giving him my nickname felt strange. I didn't want things to change and I felt like even giving him that little bit of myself would change the way he responded to me.

I didn't know whether things would change for the good or bad, and that's what scared me. Maybe he was confused about how he was feeling. Maybe once I told him my nickname, he'd leave and I'd never hear from again. I couldn't handle the thought of never seeing him again.

"I'm sure," he nodded.

Taking a deep breath, I swallowed. "Okay then, you can call me Roz."

His smile grew before he leaned in and kissed me again. His eyes sparkled mischievously, like we'd just broken the rules. In a way, I guess we had.

"Roz," my name rolled off his tongue. "It's perfect for you.

"Thank you," I whispered.

"No, thank you," he said, fingering a strand of my hair.

I fell asleep in his arms, and woke to him across the room from me, getting dressed. Leaning up on my side, I grinned at his bare ass as he slid his pants on. Turning around, he smiled when he caught me staring.

"Is it weird I don't want you to go?" I asked.

Coming over to the bed, he crawled over me and buried his face in the side of my neck, breathing me in.

"About as weird as me wanting to stay."

"Then stay."

He leaned up and grinned down at me. "Someone has to work the club. Why don't you come with me?"

"What would I tell everyone when they see us together?"

"You mean what do you tell your friend when she sees us together?"

"Yeah. I mean, I'm not sure she'd take our arrangement well."

He laughed, making the exciting twinkle in his eyes pop before his face went serious. "If she asks, just tell her I'm yours."

AFTER A NIGHT AT THE club, and lots of goofy stares from the employees at Clive's, I went back to Sebastian's apartment with him and spent the night. I woke to him watching me sleep.

"It's weird when you do that," I said into my pillow as I turned away.

"What is?" he asked.

"When you watch me sleep. What if I slobber in my sleep, or something equally as gross?"

He laughed, and I was happy he was opening up and laughing more. I was getting used to it.

"No slobbering, thankfully, but I can't help it. I envy the peace you get when you sleep." His smiling eyes turned sad.

Turning in his arms, I placed a hand on his cheek. "You don't sleep peacefully?"

"No," he said.

"Why?" I was hesitant to ask, but things between Sebastian and I were changing and I wanted to know more about him.

"My demons hunt my sleep. They make it impossible to know what peace is."

I stared at him, feeling my heart tug for Sebastian's obvious pain. "I wish I could take away your pain," I said, truthfully.

I leaned in and kissed him. He kissed me back, losing his fingers in my hair. When he broke the kiss, he looked down at me in confusion.

"I don't think that will ever go away, but you're changing me, Roz."

"Is that a bad thing?" I ran my fingers through his hair and pulled him closer to me.

"I don't know. It's unnerving," he said against my lips.

"Would it help if I told you you're changing me, too?" My lips moved along his jaw and he groaned deep in his throat, settling his weight on me.

"Let's spend the rest of the day in bed." His breath was hot against my nipple, making it harden instantly.

I sighed and arched my back, allowing his teeth to close around the nipple and then suck it into his mouth. I gasped, pushing myself closer to his heat. His hands circled my ribs holding me tight.

"I'm okay with that. Who says Sunday's can't be sinful?"

He chuckled against my fevered skin and I grabbed his head, lifting it.

"What's so funny, Mr. Black?"

He freed himself and went to work on my other nipple. I was losing all sense of reality, until he spoke again.

"Today's Monday, not Sunday, sweets."

Monday! I panicked and pushed at Sebastian. It took him a minute to realize what I was doing and he sat back confused. I jumped out of the bed with a sheet around my chest.

"What do you think you're doing?" he growled. Lunging for the sheet, he yanked it until I was no longer covered.

"Sebastian!" I squealed and dodged his hands as he tried to pull me back in bed. "I can't believe today's Monday. *Monday!*"

"What is so important about Monday?"

He sat on the end of the bed, as naked as he could be, and looked intently at me. I slipped into my lace panties and met his stare through wild, sex-mussed hair.

"I was supposed to turn in my college forms today. I can't believe I forgot," I scolded myself. "If I don't turn them in by four, I won't be able to get financial aid. I need to get back to the condo. Can you call Mr. Martin for me?"

I was in the process of pulling on my shirt when he laughed at me again.

"What exactly about my panic is funny to you, Sebastian?" I asked, frustrated because my head was stuck inside my shirt and would not come out.

"I have a computer here, baby. You can use it. Now, come here and let me help you," he chuckled.

I managed to slow my movements and step over to the bed. He shifted my shirt around and my head popped out of the correct hole.

"You do?"

He smiled and smoothed down my ratted hair. "I do."

I took a deep, calming breath. "Well, in that case, I could..." I looked at him from head to toe and settled on his manhood.

"What? What could you do to me right now?"

"Anything you want," I purred, straddling his lap and wrapping my arms around his neck.

An hour later, Sebastian let me into his office to use his computer. I was nearly swallowed by the big, black leather chair as I sat behind his desk. I ran my hands over the smooth wood.

"Well, I can see why you like sitting behind this desk all the time."

He smirked, and looked up at me. "Why's that?"

"I feel so powerful sitting here."

"Easy, tiger. Don't get too comfortable."

I laughed and turned on his monitor and a little box for his password popped up.

"I need your password."

"Here let me." He moved around his desk, leaning over me.

"Don't trust me with your secret evil plans?" I joked.

"Don't take it personally, baby. I don't trust anyone."

"Ouch." I knew he wasn't playing and I wasn't prepared for how much it would hurt to hear him admit that he didn't trust me.

I turned away from the keyboard and waited until I heard him typing away. Only the sound never came.

Instead, I felt his fingers along the side of my neck and he pushed away my hair and his lips moved over my skin.

"Harris," he whispered against my skin.

"What?" I asked, stunned. I didn't understand why he was whispering my last name in my ear.

"My password is Harris."

I calmed myself as I realized what he was talking about. "Harris."

"Yep."

"That's odd."

"What's odd?"

"Your password... that's my last name."

I felt Sebastian freeze the second the words left my mouth. Holding my breath, I realized what I'd done. Turning to look at him, I saw his expression had turned into horror.

He stepped away from me slowly, as if I were a snake ready to strike him. Neither of us said anything. Neither of us moved.

"Sebastian, I'm so sorry..."

A shield of ice fell over his face and he suddenly changed direction. Pulling me up from the chair, he dragged me across the room. "Do *not* say another word," he said venomously.

We were out of his office and going through the door of his apartment in seconds. I ripped my arm away from him and rubbed at the tender spot where his fingers had been.

His eyes followed my moment and settled on my reddening arm.

"You hurt me," I said in shock.

"I'm sorry," he said, before reaching up and tugging at his hair in aggravation. "I mean, I'm not sorry. I don't know what I am anymore. All I know is you need to get your things and get out."

My heart dropped. He couldn't be serious. Not after the way things had been going between us.

"Sebastian, just listen..."

"No. I need to be alone. Please, Roz. Just leave."

And just like that, the sound of my name from those lips, no longer brought me pleasure. I nodded, gathered my things, and left without so much as even a glance in his direction.

TWENTY-THREE

SEBASTIAN

THE SIMPLE SOUND OF HER gently closing my apartment door, slammed into my chest and knocked the air from my lungs.

Roz Harris. Rosslyn Harris. She hadn't said her first name, but I knew. I don't know how I knew, I just knew. Leaning against the wall, I swallowed hard and tried to take control of my brain before all the bad came rushing in.

Memories of a night many years before came crashing down, sending me into an instant hell. Every nightmare I'd had for the last twelve years featured her—her and her haunted young eyes. It couldn't be the same girl. There was no way this could be happening to me.

I went to the door, ready to pull it open and stop her, but I couldn't bring myself to do it. There wasn't enough strength in my body to even open a fucking door.

Walking away, I moved through my apartment like a madman. Bursting into my bedroom, I stopped when I was in front of my safe. Entering in the combination, I pulled it open.

The little box I kept small personal items in, was sitting there waiting for me. Flipping open the lid, I reached in and pulled out the locket. The broken chain was still attached.

Popping it open, my eyes moved over the baby's picture first, trying to see if he marked a resemblance at all to Kyle, but once my eyes landed on the girl's picture... I knew. Actually, as many times as I'd looked at her picture over the years, I couldn't believe I hadn't noticed sooner.

The red hair, the green eyes, and the smile on her sweet face—they were all an exact match. I sat back on the bed, clutching the locket in my hand and closed my eyes.

While Vick had moved on with her life, I'd searched and found out their names. It was sick, but I needed to know. Sitting here now, I wished I'd never done it.

What kind of sick fuck had I become? The type who fell in love with the daughter of the people I'd helped murder.

I could deny it all I wanted. I could push the feelings away until I couldn't push anymore, but I had to come to terms. I'd fallen in love with Roz. She was everything to me, had been from the moment I'd first laid eyes on her.

"You can call me Roz."

Her words swam through my mind, over and over again.

"That's my last name."

Harris. A name I knew well. A name which haunted me for the last twelve years of my life. And would continue to haunt me until the day I died.

What kind of cruel joke was this? Karma was ripping my ass a new one. The exact moment I knew I was in love for the first time in my life, was the exact moment I found out she could never be mine. Ever.

A WEEK. THAT'S HOW LONG it had been since I
realized I was in love. I hadn't seen her face—heard her
voice... nothing.

It was the right thing to do. So I blocked the world out
and let the club run itself while I got drunk and dwelled in
my self-loathing. I didn't answer the door. I didn't answer
any calls, and I didn't even think about looking at my text
messages.

Vick called and beat on my door constantly, but I
wasn't ready to see her face. I wasn't ready to find out
whether or not she knew I'd been fucking and dominating
a girl I owed the world to.

I was the reason her parents were gone. I didn't pull
the trigger, but I might as well have.

Finally, after a week of seclusion, I went to my office.
Within minutes Vick was bursting through the doors,
claws out, and frothing at the mouth.

"What the fuck, Sebastian?" Fire shot from her eyes.
"You just lock yourself in your apartment for a week? Fuck
the club? Fuck me? I'll have you know I busted my ass this
week picking up the slack for you."

Her words penetrated me and I flew off the handle.
Slamming my hands into the desk, I stood.

"I've picked up the slack for you for *years*," I yelled. "I
covered your ass a million times, including the time you
blew two people away. Don't you dare come in my office
with your shit or I swear to God..."

She stood there staring back at me, her face softening.
"I'm sorry. You're right."

I wanted to keep yelling at her. I wanted to scream and
throw things, but I couldn't. The truth was, I didn't trust

Vick since the night I watched her murder two innocent people.

I'd sat in my apartment for week thinking about all the shit I wanted to say to her when I saw her again, but now none of it felt good enough. Instead I stared at her, willing her to tell me everything she knew.

"Did you know?" I asked, my voice steady and hard as steel.

"Do I know what?" she asked.

"Don't fucking play games with me, Victoria." My voice echoed off the walls of my office. "Did. You. *Know?*"

It took a moment, as she gleaned my meaning, and then her face cleared of all confusion. Stunned surprise took its place, and I knew. I fucking knew my answer.

"And you let me fuck her? You knew who she was and you let me proposition her anyway?"

"How did you find out her name? She told you?"

"What the hell does it matter *how* I know her name? I fucking know her name."

She fell back a step and it was her turn to read the answer on my face.

"You asked her?" She couldn't control her shock and somewhere underneath was a little bit of anger. "You've never asked for a name."

"She's different," I growled and sighed, running my fingers through my hair. "Well, she *was* fucking different. You should have told me, Vick. You know very fucking well you should have told me."

"*You're* the one who went and got a conscious on me. You're the one who went digging for their names. I never asked you to tell me their names... never. This is your fault. You should've left well enough alone. You should've—"

TABATHA & MELISSA

I cut her off. "How long have you known? Since the police station? When did you find out who she was? Was it before or after I fucked her?"

Her face went hard, nostrils flaring, making her pretty face look unappealing.

"I knew who she was the minute she walked in the club, before I even hired her. I figured it wouldn't hurt if you spent some money on her—showed her a good time. We owed her that much."

Her words were like a punch to the gut. I couldn't believe the woman standing in front of me was someone I associated with—someone I'd taken under my wing. She was a figment of the girl I met in foster care. That little girl was gone, and in her stead was a monster. Someone I wasn't sure I could be around anymore.

"Did you tell her the truth, Sebastian? Does she know?"

She was only worried about herself.

"No."

Relief flooded her face, and she had the audacity to smile. "Good. You've always got my back."

"Get out," my words were quiet, but lethal.

"Sebastian, this is nothing. We'll get past it, like we've always done before."

"I said, get out."

She walked backward to the door, as if she was waiting for me to tell her to stay, and then turned and left.

TWENTY-FOUR

ROSSLYN

"**W**HAT THE HELL IS WRONG with you, Roz? You're like *Night of the Living Dead* over there." Trish said, licking banana frozen yogurt from her spoon.

I stared down at my cup and dug my spoon into it over and over again, turning my yogurt into mush, but never taking a bite. "I'm just tired."

Tired was an understatement. Since the moment Sebastian asked me to leave his apartment, I'd been a nervous wreck. There was no telling when I'd be kicked to the curb, but more than anything, I missed him. If I could go back and change the moment when things shifted between us, I would have never left his bed.

I could have stayed Jessica forever. I was willing to do that for him. I didn't care what that said about me. From the second I left the club, I knew I was in love with him.

After trying to have a semi-normal day at the mall with Trish, I called Mr. Martin and had him pick me up and take me back to my condo. Seeing as though he still answered my calls, things couldn't have been that bad, right? If Sebastian was really done with me, would his driver still be driving me around?

I moped around the condo for the past week, eating way too much junk food, and waiting for the sound of my phone to buzz or the elevator doors to beep. And still, there was nothing.

I talked on the phone with Kyle a few times, and he made me feel better. I was glad to know he was having a blast and making friends at the program. At least he was happy. I just wasn't sure his happiness would remain once Sebastian dropped me like a bad habit.

I was approved for financial aid and got signed up for some online classes, which was a good step in the right direction, but I needed to start job searching again.

I continued to put in applications to places within walking distance, as I waited to hear back from one them. If I had a job, maybe this whole situation wouldn't be so bad.

No matter how many times I told myself this, I knew that was a lie. Job or no job, I would still miss Sebastian. It was going to hurt badly when things were officially done between the two of us.

I was coming out of a jewelry store around the corner from my condo, when I spotted Mr. Martin sitting in the car across the street, waiting. Looking both ways, I ran across the street and was a few feet away from the car, when I saw Sebastian coming from a large unmarked building.

He was wearing a black suit, fit to perfection, and a pair of dark aviator glasses. He looked so sexy I almost fell to my knees and begged him not to leave me. I closed my eyes and thought about the way he'd touched me—the things he did to my body.

When I opened my eyes again, he was standing frozen next to the car, with his shades off and his hand holding onto the handle. He was staring at me, an angry expression on his face.

I held up my hand and sent him an awkward smile. It was a stupid thing to do, but I was so happy to see him, I didn't want to hide it. I was done hiding the way I felt.

He continued to stare for a while longer, until he slipped his shades back into place, and disappeared into the car.

I stood there in total shock as the car pulled away from the curb and disappeared into the traffic.

My heart ached. It was just too much. I barely held back the tears on the walk back to the condo, breaking down as soon as I stepped off the elevator.

Spending the night alone, I ate ice cream and watched old movies. There was a brief debate on whether or not to call Trish, but I didn't feel like explaining the condo or anything else. It was better if she stayed in the dark about my life, especially because it involved her boss.

I stared down at my cell phone, willing him to text or call, but there was nothing. I fell asleep on the couch with my phone in my hand, an empty ice cream carton on the table, puffy eyes, and the TV on.

The sound of gunshots woke me and I sat straight up in bed. It was a horrible sound. It hurt my ears and made a strange ache twist in my stomach. I gripped my sheets with sweaty palms and that's when I heard the firm footfalls on the hardwood outside my bedroom. Whoever it was, they were running. The sounds of them running down the stairs and out the back door, echoed in my room.

Kyle's loud crying sounded from his nursery and filled the deadly silence of the night. I was too afraid to get up, but once his cries got louder, I tiptoed to my bedroom door. Pulling the door open slowly so it didn't squeak, I tried to listen for any strange sounds.

The area outside my room was pitch-black. On silent feet, I ran across the hall to Kyle's nursery, but my eyes glanced into my parent's room and I froze. Terror was a punch to my chest, when lying there on the floor, in the light shining from their bathroom, was my father. He was in a puddle of blood, and his eyes were wide open, staring back at me. He wasn't moving, he wasn't breathing.

In shock, I turned away from Kyle's room and started toward my dad. It was then I saw my mother's body. I gasped when I saw her killer still standing above her.

My eyes dropped to my mother's lifeless body and I made an involuntary move toward her, but her killer jumped to his feet and I froze, not taking another step.

The intruder's breathing became louder, and mine seemed to stop completely. The stranger's eyes connected with mine. Time stopped as we stared at each other. Fear laced his expression and it confused me.

The harsh sound of his panting filled the room. It looked like he was debating his next move. His eyes moved to the door behind me. Shifting on his feet, the light caught something in his hand. It was my mother's locket, which had pictures of me and Kyle inside. It wasn't worth much, which made it strange that the guy was taking it, but then I looked around the room and saw their TV was missing.

The killer left my mother, necklace in hand, and ran toward me. I stopped breathing and dropped to my knees. Just when he got close to me and I was sure he was going to kill me too, he ran past me and down the stairs. The back door slammed. And then, even though I could hear Kyle crying, it was eerily silent.

I WOKE UP IN BED, with my pajamas on and a blanket draped over me. The sun from the windows blinded me when I opened my eyes.

A sound from inside the condo startled me and I reached over to my bedside table. Still in a sleep-induced haze, I pulled open the drawer, and grabbed the gun Sebastian bought me.

Walking toward the noise on quiet feet, I raised the gun, ready to shoot. Making it to the corner of the kitchen, I took a deep breath and tried to steel my nerves.

When I stepped around the corner, I came face to chest with a large man. Without thought, I pulled the trigger.

Nothing happened.

I looked up and Sebastian was standing before me, looking down with wild eyes. He reached out and took the gun from me.

"Holy shit. You could have killed me, Roz." He set the gun on the counter beside us. "Thank God you had the safety on. Speaking of which, you have to make sure the safety is off before you use it."

He turned and walked away from me, and back to the stove where he was cooking. I'm not sure how I missed the smell of bacon wafting all around.

"You're here," I stated the obvious.

"Yes I am," he grinned at me, as if I hadn't just tried to kill him. "A 'good morning' would be nice."

I was still in shock by the fact that I'd almost blown a hole in his chest.

"Good morning," I said slowly.

"Come sit down and eat some breakfast," he said, setting a plate on the counter full of bacon and eggs.

"You made me breakfast?"

"It was the least I could do."

I had a million questions I wanted to ask, but I didn't want to jinx the moment. Instead, I sat on the stool in front of my plate and started to pick at the bacon.

"Eat. We have a lot to talk about," he said, taking a big bite of bacon and chewing with a smile on his face.

I couldn't wait.

"I'm sorry, Sebastian. I didn't think. It just came out," I said.

"I didn't come here to talk about that."

"Oh." Maybe I had jumped the gun, thinking he was actually back.

"I came here today hoping you'd tell me your whole name."

"No," I said sternly. "I don't want you to push me away. I'll stay your Jessica."

There I'd said it. I showed my desperation and while I should have been completely embarrassed by it, I wasn't.

"So you're perfectly okay sleeping with a man who calls you by another woman's name forever?"

"Well maybe not forever, but..." I stopped. "What do you mean *forever?*"

LITTLE BLACK BOOK   221

Sebastian never said the word forever. I seriously doubted he even thought about the following week when it came to his girls.

"I mean, I went a week without you, and I'm not sure I ever want to go that long again."

He moved around the counter and stood next to me.

"Are you saying what I think you're saying, Mr. Black?" I asked playfully.

He looked down at me with a soft expression, before pressing his lips to mine. "Tell me your name," he said against my lips.

Pulling back, I let my eyes devour his face. If it was possibly going to be the last time I saw him, I wanted to take it all in.

"Rosslyn. My name's Rosslyn Harris."

He closed his eyes and swallowed hard before pulling me closer. "A beautiful name for a beautiful girl."

"You think I'm beautiful?" I asked as I batted my lashes at him.

"You know I do, smartass. And what makes it even better, you're all mine."

"Again, are you saying what I think you're saying, Mr. Black?"

"I don't know, Miss Rosslyn Harris. What is it you think I'm saying?"

It felt good to hear him say my name. After being called Jessica for so long, it was nice to finally be acknowledged as myself.

"It sounds to me like you're saying you're prepared to throw away you're little black book."

He threw his head back and laughed out loud before leaning down and kissing me softly. I lost my fingers in the soft hair that touched the back of his neck and he filled his hands with my hips. Pulling away, he smiled down at me before kissing the tip of my nose sweetly.

"What black book? I own no such thing," he grinned.

TWENTY-FIVE

SEBASTIAN

IT WAS OFFICIAL. I WAS the most stupid mother-fucker alive. I should have stayed away from her. I should have stayed off her register and cared for her from afar. It was the least I could do for her. But then I'd seen her and my resolve crumbled.

She had been standing there, across the street, looking at me with that fucking smile I loved so much. I wanted to go to her. I wanted to take her in my arms, put her in the back seat, and spend the rest of the day in bed with her. But I didn't. I blew her off, got in the car, and drove away.

I was in my office for the rest of the day and most of the night, doing everything but handcuffing myself to stay there. I hadn't seen Vick all day, even though I knew she was downstairs when the club opened for the night. She knew it was best to stay away from me.

It was about midnight when I broke. Grabbing my jacket, I left my office, marched down the stairs and through the busy club, and went straight to Rosslyn. I'd deal with the consequences later, if there even were any.

After thinking on it all night, I decided I could be with her. She'd never need to know anything about me and Vick. I could make her happy—give her back the life we'd taken away from her. I would give her anything she wanted.

When I got to condo, she was sleeping sweetly on the couch, clutching her phone. I sat beside her. Pushing the hair from her face, I watched her sleep for a bit, before taking her to bed. I spent the rest of the night staring out at the New York skyline and making plans.

"LET'S GO SOMEWHERE," I SAID.

She was lying beside me naked, her skin flush with mine.

"Where?"

"Some place tropical. I'm talking white sandy beaches, palm trees, and fruity drinks with umbrellas in them. I want to see you in a two piece with a big floppy hat."

She considered my offer and became serious. "There's one problem, though."

"Oh yeah? And what is that?"

"I don't *do* floppy," she said, grabbing my dick.

We broke down laughing and I kissed her nose. "You're right. Very poor choice of words."

"But you definitely had me at white sandy beaches. When do we leave?"

Two days later, we were on a plane leaving New York. The flight to Barbados wasn't terrible, at least for me it wasn't. I'd never seen Rosslyn drink, but she drank like a fish on the plane. She waited until it was time to board to let me know she'd never flown before.

By the time we landed, I still didn't have full circulation in my fingers, and she was slurring and leaning against me.

It was adorable to see her so carefree and giggly. Making our way outside, I let her use my body as wall.

A car picked us up at the airport and took us to our destination. It was a five-star hotel with all the amenities, and we had one of the large suites at the very top.

The elevator ride up to the room was the longest ride in the history of elevator rides. The only thing keeping me from fucking Rosslyn right there, was the elderly couple who smiled politely at us from the other side.

"Are you two on your honeymoon?" the lady asked.

Rosslyn smiled drunkenly up at me, waiting to see how I'd respond. A million smart-ass responses came to mind, but instead I smiled down at Rosslyn and pretended just a little while that a happily ever after existed between us.

"Yes," I whispered, never taking my eyes off of her. "She's definitely the one."

"How sweet," the lady said.

The elevator chimed and the doors opened to let the couple off on their floor. Reaching across the elevator, I pushed the button to the top floor rapidly before anyone else could get on. I was definitely not in the mood for anymore company.

"It's about time," Rosslyn chuckled, pushing me against the wall.

She rubbed against me, moving her lips over mine. I smiled and grabbed her ass, lifting her until she could wrap her legs around my waist.

"Our honeymoon, huh?" she taunted. "Sebastian Black *married*. That's kind of funny."

"Five more minutes." I nipped at her chin.

"Five more minutes?" she asked confused.

"Yes." I looked up as the red light lit up for our floor and the doors opened. "Now it's four, and then you can put that beautiful smart mouth to better use."

"Sebastian," she pushed playfully at my chest and giggled.

I didn't put her down when I walked out of the elevator, nor did I bat an eyelash at the couple who nearly jumped out of the way trying to get into the elevator after us.

"Excuse us," Rosslyn said as I pushed the key card into the door.

The night was a blur of crazy, out of control, wild sex. Everything was put to use, our hands, mouths, tongues and every body part possible. We invented new positions and enjoyed old ones. I didn't give her time to catch her breath, and in return, she didn't show me any mercy. It was fucking beautiful.

When we were both exhausted and couldn't keep our eyes open any longer, we fell asleep in the massive king-sized bed. Before I let my eyes close, I realized sleeping with Rosslyn in my arms was something I never wanted to give up. She could never find out my secret. I just wouldn't let it happen.

"CAN YOU RUB SOME OF this on me?" Rosslyn asked, holding out a bottle of sunblock.

"As if you'd have to ask me to rub your body," I teased. Taking the bottle, I squeezed a generous amount into my palm and rubbed it on her soft skin.

We were planning on spending a while on the beach because Rosslyn had never been to one before. And the last thing either of us wanted, was to ruin our mini vacation with a sunburn.

She looked amazing in a green and yellow bikini. Her long, shapely legs stretched out as she laid on her stomach, with her arms tucked under her face. I ran my fingers across the arch in her back, blending in the sunblock.

"This is heaven," she sighed, closing her eyes and breathing in deeply.

Leaning over her, I placed a soft kiss on her cheek. "The perfect place for my angel," I whispered in her ear.

A smile tugged at her plump lips and I had to control the urge to kiss her again and again. The heat from the sun, mixed with the heat I was feeling just looking at her, was too much.

"So I've been curious about something," she said, keeping her eyes closed.

"What?"

"What was the whole deal with the name Jessica? Where did it come from?"

The dreaded question. I didn't like to revisit my childhood very much, and I hated talking about it. But for Rosslyn, I'd do it.

"I didn't have a typical childhood, and was raised in multiple foster homes. Bad things happened around me, and to me, that I didn't want to think about. When I wanted to escape, I watched cartoons."

She opened her eyes and looked over at me.

I hated the look she was giving me—pity. "Please don't look at me like that. Going through hard times makes you who you are. Anyway, I named all the girls in my book after cartoon characters."

"The girls were your escape," she said.

She understood me like no other. It only made my heart swell more for her.

I let my fingers linger over her spine, as I looked away and explained. "Yes, but I reserved my favorite character, Jessica Rabbit, for the most special woman of all. When you walked into my club that first night, I knew you were my Jessica."

I could feel her eyes on me, but she didn't speak right away.

"Does that make you my rabbit? Can I call you Roger?"

A grin lifted my cheeks until they hurt. She was definitely the one. No pushing buttons or asking questions that made me uncomfortable. She let me come around in my own way, on my own time. Plus, she knew all about Roger Rabbit, my favorite cartoon character.

I was met with her sweet smile when I finally looked her in the face. She really was the most amazing woman. Leaning closer, I kissed her beneath her ear and inhaled her sweet scent, mixed with the coconut scented sunblock. She shivered and it gave me the satisfaction I'd been going after.

"You can call me anything you'd like. I'll be your rabbit all night long, baby."

"And keep going, and going, and going..."

I laid on top of her and tickled her sides. Laughing, I spoke in her ear. "Wrong rabbit, you minx."

She squirmed under me and I could already feel myself getting hard. Leaning back, I counted to ten. If this kept up, I'd walk around in a permanent state of arousal.

"I'm going for a swim," I said, standing from her chair.

"I'll be here," she said with a little wave.

The cold ocean water cooled my burning flesh as I waded out over my head and swam against the waves.

Turning around, I looked back at the beach. The white sand and blue umbrellas stretched as far as the eye could see. It was paradise, and I was happy to be able to share it with the woman who had captured my heart.

Later, we left the beach to go for some drinks at a tiki bar that wasn't far from where we'd been. Rosslyn walked with her sandals in hand, wearing a white bathing suit cover draping from her shoulder. Her red hair was disheveled and full of long loose curls from the ocean water drying in her hair. She was more than beautiful.

As promised, I order us two fruity drinks with umbrellas and we sat at the bar.

"What would you like to do next?" I asked, taking a pull from my straw.

"I don't care. This is paradise. I'm happy just sitting here," she smiled.

"I like making you happy."

I was turning into a mushy fucker, but I couldn't help it. It's what she did to me.

"Well, you're very good at it."

Leaning in, I kissed her. The taste of her strawberry flavored drink rolled across my tongue. She was delicious.

The following day, we moved from our hotel to a beach cottage I rented for the rest of the week. I was seriously considering buying a property while we were there, but I didn't want to spend any of my time with Rosslyn doing anything business related.

The cottage was all white, with massive floor to ceiling windows on all four sides. There were views of the beach and palm trees in every direction. I looked through one of the windows after my shower, to see Rosslyn standing on the upper deck looking out at the ocean. Her hair was pulled up in a knot, but stray flyway's swept across her face.

I watched as she closed her eyes and let the breeze move across her cheeks. She looked content, and I knew in that moment I'd spend the rest of my life making sure she always felt that way. There was no doubt about it, I was in love with her.

The beautiful woman I was looking at was mine, and I wanted her to know it. I needed her to know this was no longer a business arrangement for me. It was more and she was more. She was everything I ever wanted and all I would ever need. She was my happily ever after.

For a man who didn't understand emotions all that well, the feelings I experienced for Rosslyn were undeniable. She was the one, and it scared me and excited me at the same time.

Stepping out onto the deck, I went up behind her and pulled her body to mine. Resting my chin on her shoulder, I took in the sight in front of us.

"Thank you, Sebastian," she whispered.

"For what?"

"For this. For everything." She leaned back into me and rested her head on my shoulder. "I just wanted you to know you've made me the happiest I've ever been. I don't care if this lasts another week or another day, you're one of the best things that's ever happened to me."

Her words struck my heart like a bolt of lightning and I spun her in my arms and kissed her. The sound of the waves moved around us and she moaned sweetly into my mouth.

Pulling away, I pressed my forehead to hers and closed my eyes to take in the moment.

"I love you, Rosslyn."

The words exploded from my heart and slipped from my lips. I had no desire to take them back. If anything, I wanted to write them in the sky for the world to see. She needed to know because it was the truth, and as I'd always heard it would, the truth had definitely set me free when it came to her.

TWENTY-SIX

ROSSLYN

"*I LOVE YOU, ROSSLYN.*"

I looked up at him, his words filling me with so much joy, I was sure my heart would burst. He stared down at me with a straight face, his dark hair shifting in the ocean breeze. His blue eyes popped against the white cottage and fading sunset in the background.

"So I should be thanking you," he continued, smiling down at me. "I never thought I'd ever feel this way about anyone. For years I've been emotionally paralyzed, but you turned my fears against me and made them a thing of beauty."

I could hardly believe Sebastian Black was saying such pretty words. Reaching up, I captured his face in my palm and ran my thumb across the light stubble on his cheek. "I love you, too."

His expression changed into one of disbelief, as if someone could never love him. Then he leaned down and pressed his lips to mine. It was a kiss filled with promises of the future—a forever.

That night, we made love.

"There will be no fucking tonight," he whispered, lowering me onto the bed. "I want to do something I've never done. I want to make love to you." He kissed me tenderly, running lights touches down my body.

"Is this Sebastian Black doing soft and romantic?"

Parting my legs, his lips made a path down my stomach. "That's exactly what I'm doing."

It was slow and soft, and beautiful.

"I'm so in love with you," he whispered, plunging deep. Our bodies slowly rocked against one another.

His large shoulders blocked the dim light as he held his frame above me. I pressed the back of my head into the pillow, gasping and lifting my hips. Leaning up, I kissed him slow, his tongue moving against mine before he softly sucked on my bottom lip.

Running my hands down his back, I slipped them under the sheet tangled around us, and dug my nails into his round ass.

"I can't get enough of you, Rosslyn. I'll never get enough of you," he whispered against my lips before placing his forehead to mine and breathing hard.

Afterwards, I fell asleep wrapped in his arms. I'd never felt so high on life, and I was hoping I'd never have to come back down.

"I HAVE TAN LINES," I said, peeling off my bathing suit and getting ready to get in the shower.

"Tan lines are sexy."

I turned to see Sebastian relaxing on the bed, his arms tucked behind his head.

"You think everything is sexy."

"Everything that has to do with you."

The past week had been heaven. Lying on the beach, drinking margaritas, and having sex in the Jacuzzi.

Sebastian made me feel like a queen—a worshipped sex goddess he couldn't seem to get enough of. It was like he'd done a complete one-eighty.

He whispered words of love and affection, showing me how deeply he felt with everything he did. He touched me every chance he got and gave me kisses full of passion constantly. It was perfection, and I was starting to think that my life was finally falling into place.

After my shower, I dressed and Sebastian took me to dinner at a comfortable little restaurant on the beach. We ate seafood and drank too much.

Afterward, I kicked off my sandals and we walked on the beach holding hands. He looked incredible in a pair of rolled up khakis and a loose, white button down shirt. His hair was a wind-blown sexy mess and whenever he smiled, I knew his dimples were the cutest thing I'd ever see.

"Dance with me," he said, pulling me into his arms and dipping me.

I laughed and let my sandals fall to the ground. "There's no music."

"We'll make our own music."

He held my hand and my waist, humming softly in my ear. We danced under the stars, the waves in the background keeping up with his melody.

"You're such a romantic."

"Am not," he grinned.

"Then what would you call this?" I asked.

"I call this an excuse to feel your body against mine."

I giggled. "Sure it is."

And then he pushed his hardness against my thigh, and I couldn't help but giggle more.

"Pipe down, Pepe Le Pew," I joked.

This time he was the one laughing. He squeezed me tight. "I can't help it. You are ze corned beef to me, and I am ze cabbage to you," he said in his best French accent.

I didn't want our stay to come to an end, but unfortunately, reality was an evil bitch and Sebastian had to get back to his club. After packing, I had two extra suitcases, filled with stuff Sebastian had bought for me in Barbados.

The plane ride back was a lot smoother than it was coming, but Sebastian made the ride easier by holding my hand and whispering soothing words into my hair.

It was a late flight. There were only a few of us on the plane, so when Sebastian covered us with a blanket and I felt his hand slip between my thighs, I only put up a small fight.

His fingers worked their magic and before I knew it I was quietly panting and moaning into his shoulder. When we stepped off the plane, I was already looking forward to our next trip.

"STAY. SLEEP. I'M GOING TO make an appearance downstairs and I'll be right back."

He pulled away from me, pulling back the sheet and kissing any piece of bare skin he could find.

"Hurry back."

Thirty minutes passed and I figured I might as well get up and take a shower. Stepping into Sebastian's massive shower, I stood under the multiple shower heads and let the steaming water pour over me.

When I got out, the luxurious towel I wrapped around my body had been warmed by a towel warmer.

Going back into Sebastian's bedroom, I pulled off my robe and dressed in a pair of his boxers and one of his T-shirts. I had my own clothes, but I preferred wearing his.

I spent the next twenty minutes being nosey. There were pictures to look at and colognes on his dresser to smell. He was so organized, it was cute.

"Are you snooping?" I spun around to see Vick standing in the door way of Sebastian's room.

I flushed, twisting my hands together in front of me and smiled at her. She didn't smile back and there was something very odd about her behavior.

"Maybe just a little." I tried another small smile, but she wasn't having it.

"Sebastian doesn't like his girls being nosey, *Jessica*."

Her tone gave me pause. Not because it was angry, but because there was something else mixed in. She sounded... jealous.

"He doesn't call me that anymore. He knows my name."

She nodded condescendingly. "Oh, right. Do you think that makes you special, Rosslyn? Do you think Sebastian is going to marry you now and you'll ride off into the sunset together?"

My shoulders stiffened. "I don't know what to expect, but I know Sebastian is changing... and he likes it."

She scoffed, her face twisting angrily. "Are you shitting me with this? Men don't change, *especially* men like Sebastian."

I felt bad for Vick. She was in love with Sebastian and he was in love with someone else. I didn't know what that felt like, but it was easy to try and understand when I thought of Sebastian being with someone else.

"I'm sorry if this hurts you, Vick. I know it can't be easy to see Sebastian with me, but…"

She barked a laugh so loud it made me jump. "Wow, you really are fucking nuts." Her eyes narrowed and she glared at me like she was waiting for me to catch fire under her stare. "You have *no* idea what you're talking about and you have no idea who Sebastian really is, or what he's done in the past."

I shook my head. "I don't care what he's done in the past. What's done is done, and I'm sure there are things he regrets. But it doesn't change the way I feel about him now. I love him and I would do anything for him."

She stared at me long and hard. "So you're in love with him. You would do anything for him. Does that include keeping his secrets?"

"Yes."

"I bet if you knew, if you only knew, you'd hate him. You'd wish you never met him. You may even wish him dead."

I frowned, not understanding what she was trying to tell me. "What are you talking about?"

"Everyone has skeletons, *Rosslyn*. Some worse than others. You just have to know where to look."

She came toward me and I felt a rush of fear. But she walked past me and I turned, not trusting my back to her. Pulling on the corner of a picture of the Brooklyn Bridge, she revealed a safe tucked secretly behind it.

She didn't make a move to open it as she turned and walked back toward the door to leave the room. I didn't know what she expected me to do without the combination.

And then she began calling out numbers. "021201. If you want to know more about Sebastian, the things you have the right to know, then open the safe."

She didn't wait for me to respond as she walked from the room. I turned back to look at the safe and I felt nervous. My hands began to sweat and my heart was racing.

I rubbed my palms on my pants as I tried to tell myself there was nothing in that safe I needed to know about. But even as I told myself that, I was repeating the number Vick said back in my head over and over again. *021201, 021201, 021201.*

I could have left it alone and told Sebastian everything Vick said when he returned. I could have asked him what was in the safe, but I had the feeling he wouldn't tell me. I also had a feeling that whatever was in the safe would be long gone if I ever asked about it.

Taking a deep breath, I took a slow step toward the wall, and then another until I was close enough to enter the code. When I reached toward the buttons, my fingers shook. I ignored the trembling and placed my finger over the first number.

The safe made a sound that sounded louder than it actually was, and popped open. My head whipped toward the door, but it remained empty. My racing heart pounded in my ears as I pulled open the heavy door.

There was nothing out of the ordinary at first sight and I breathed a sigh of relief. I didn't know what I expected to find, but I was glad it wasn't any body parts. I shifted through the papers, they looked like old newspaper clippings, and a few stacks of money.

Then, I felt a small hand gun. It scared me at first and I snatched my hand back like it was a venomous snake. I scolded myself for acting like a scared idiot, and moved my fingers over the gun. It didn't look dangerous, but that didn't matter. It was older—not at all like something I pictured Sebastian using, but I figured it had sentimental value.

Next to the gun was a medium-sized, black box. I pulled it from the safe, opening the lid. There were pictures of Sebastian and Vick when they were younger, an old match box, and tiny trinkets that I'm sure meant something to Sebastian, but didn't stand out to me at all.

Shifting through the pictures, I smiled at each one. My eyes landed on the next item and all the happiness was sucked out of me. Lifting it, I looked down at the locket in the palm of my hand. It looked just like...but that was impossible. My mother's locket was stolen that night.

The chain was broken and slipped through the tiny clasp of the locket, making a tiny clinking noise when it hit the floor. Pressing on the side of the locket, it popped open and my heart shattered into a million pieces. My eyes took in the tiny picture of the infant I knew was Kyle before landing on my picture. I was nine in the picture and I was the happiest person in the world.

My tears blurred the picture, making the locket look as if it was floating in my palm. I was having a nightmare. No way was this happening. I was still sleeping and I needed to wake up.

TABATHA & MELISSA

I closed my eyes and tried to envision the boy from that night—the way he stood, the way he held his shoulders straight, and his walk... it all felt so familiar to me now.

Closing the locket, I clutched it tightly in my fist, the latch on the side digging into my palm. And then I remembered the gun.

I felt like I couldn't breathe as the realization of what that gun was, what it was used for, came to me. The truth of it was choking me and I couldn't do anything to stop it.

The newspaper clippings covered the gun, and I reached for them. A tear fell down my cheeks as I shifted through them, reading story after story about the death of my parents. The date caught my attention, February 12, 2001... 021201. Sebastian's safe code was the date my parents were killed.

"What are you doing?" Sebastian asked from behind me.

I turned on him with angry tear-filled eyes.

"What is this Sebastian?"

The color drained from his face. I watched as sadness and regret filled his features and I knew—I just knew.

Sebastian was a murderer.

TWENTY-SEVEN

SEBASTIAN

"**D**ID YOU HAVE A NICE little vacation?" Vick sneered from behind me.

I was looking down over my club. The place I once thought was the only thing I could love...until Rosslyn. I was in love with a women who trusted me when she had no right to.

I wasn't in the mood to fight with Vick. "We did."

Her stunned silence followed. She expected me to be harsh and rough with her, but I wasn't playing any games with her tonight.

"*We?* Now you're a couple?"

I sighed and dropped my head, pinching the bridge of my nose between two fingers. Obviously she was in the mood to push my buttons.

Turning around, I picked up my drink from corner of my desk and tossed back the remains. The glass made a deep sound when I set it back down. I'd lost count of how many drinks I'd had since I left Rosslyn sleeping, but the slight buzz was numbing the constant guilt I felt since I found out who she was.

"Yes, Vick, we're a couple. I told you she was different. I'm in love with her. I've never been in love with anyone the way I love her."

"You're in love with her. Are you insane Sebastian? We killed..."

I cut her off. "We? We didn't kill anyone. *You* did."

It was something that haunted my mind for years.

"Come the fuck on, Sebastian," Vick whispered as she disappeared over the side of the fence.

She was faster than me now that she was older, but still clumsy, which was why I never let her do jobs by herself. She wasn't ready, even if she thought she was.

I lifted myself up over the fence and fell to my feet beside her.

"You're getting slow," she grinned over at me.

"Fuck you," I said, standing up and dusting off the knees of my pants. "Let's get this shit over with. I told Anthony we'd be back in two hours.

We moved across the perfectly manicured backyard toward the house Vick had her eyes on for the last year. She said it was the house of her dreams. She wanted a home and family like the one inside.

We all had our dreams and envisioned the kind of life we'd have if we hadn't been given away, so I understood her obsession with the house. Even though I'd told her, over and over again, I picked the houses, I knew her birthday was coming. So like a dumbass, I promised her we'd do the house she wanted.

"Okay, are you sure the people are out of town? I asked.

"Yes. Now quit worrying. We'll be in and out before you know it."

I trusted Vick with my life. I had no reason to believe she would lie to me about anything.

"Fine, but still no lights. The neighbors around neighborhoods like this, watch each other's backs. Let's just get in, get the shit, and get the fuck out."

"I'm not an idiot, Sebastian. I've done this more than you."

The stolen credit card I used on the back door, bent as I pressed it into the lock. Pulling on the knob, the door popped open.

"Like a pro," Vick whispered with a smile.

She bumped her shoulder into mine playfully. That was the problem. She played too much in serious situations like the one we were in.

I gave her the evil eye, telling her to shut the fuck up, and then moved stealthily through the house. Vick was on my heels as we moved through the place, looking for valuables. The bottom floor was spotless and we didn't find much of anything.

"Come on," Vick whispered, taking the stairs to the second floor.

I followed behind her and into the master bedroom.

"Jackpot," Vick whispered, tugging on my arm. "Help me get the TV."

Nodding my head, I moved toward the wall with the TV and we both lifted it from the stand and onto the floor. It was at that moment, the bathroom door flew open and a man in a pair of silk pajama pants stepped out. He was yawning with his eyes closed and scratching his head. Once his eyes opened, they landed on us. Vick and I both froze in the light coming from the bathroom.

"What are you doing in my house?"

He moved toward the side of the bed toward the phone. It was then I saw a lady sleeping on the other side.

I held up my hands. "No need for that. We'll just leave."

I moved toward the door hoping Vick would follow. Neither of us needed to be arrested.

I was standing in the doorway when I looked back. Vick wasn't there. Instead, she was standing in front of the man and she was holding a gun up at him.

"What are you doing?" I said, making my way back toward her. "No. This is not how this is going down."

I broke into houses to survive, but carrying a gun around and pulling it on people was not okay with me.

"He's going to call the cops, Sebastian," she said in a hushed tone. "Fuck, now he knows your name. I'm sorry. Shit, I'm so sorry."

Her eyes were wild. She was freaking out.

"Vick, just give me the gun. We'll get the hell out of here, and no one will know anything. Let's just go." I said calmly as I reached out for the gun.

Her hand was shaking, which meant her trigger finger was shaking, too.

And then everything moved in slow motion. The husband stood there with his hands up, fear in his eyes, while the wife started to stir. And then she sat straight up in bed and screamed.

The gunshots rang out, deafening me as I watched the man fall to the floor. Blood oozed from his neck and he choked as he tried to breathe. I moved quickly toward Vick, but it was too late. The wife was running toward the door and Vick was shooting over and over again.

Everything went silent, except for the sounds of the husband taking his last breath, and the wife beginning to choke and gasp for life. And then, the screams of a baby in the room next door.

Vick dropped the gun, and took off running as if I wasn't even in the room with her. Her loud footsteps on the wooden stairs echoed throughout the house. I stood there in shock, sure that I was dreaming, but the woman started moaning. I should have ran, but I didn't. Instead, I dropped to my knees next to the woman dying on the floor and I grabbed her hand.

"I'm so sorry," I whispered to her. "I'm so sorry."

Her wide eyes were trained on me as her body started to shake. Blood splattered from her mouth and landed on her lips. She was trying to say something, but I couldn't understand. Leaning down closer to her, I turned my head so that she could speak in my ear.

"Please," she struggled to say.

And then I felt her shaking fingers on mine as she placed something hard and cold in my palm. She closed my hand around the object and pleaded to me with her eyes. I didn't know what she was asking me for, but I couldn't help her.

I should have called the police or the ambulance, but I wasn't thinking straight and I was scared. I'd never seen anyone die before and my stomach was twisting with fear. All I did was lean over her and watch as a tiny tear fell from her eye and she took her last breath.

I opened my hand and looked down at the locket in my palm. What was she trying to tell me?

And then a sound at my left made me jump and I looked up to see a young girl standing in the doorway looking back at me. She was no more than ten. Her tiny feet peeked out from under her nightgown as her fear-filled eyes took in the scene around her.

The woman obviously wanted me to have the locket. I didn't know what else to do, so I popped the chain from around her neck. I stood holding her locket in my hand. My eyes clashed with the little girl's once more, and then I took off, running past her and down the stairs. Once I lifted myself over the fence, I puked all over the ground, before running off into the darkness.

As badly as I wanted to turn myself in, it meant turning Vick in, too, and that was something I wasn't willing to do. She was the only family I had—my baby sister. What she had done was wrong, but I couldn't let her go to jail. I couldn't.

That night, I changed. I lay in bed and blocked out all the memories of the night, cutting off my emotions completely, so that I didn't feel the guilt or the hurt tearing me apart.

Popping open the locket the woman had given me, I saw two pictures inside. One of the little girl, and another of the baby I'd heard screaming. I'd witnessed two people die—parents. I'd left two children, mother and fatherless. I'd sentenced them to a life like mine. It was something I'd never get over for the rest of my life... never.

"What the hell are you talking about, Sebastian? We were both there."

Her words pulled me from my memories. "You're right. I never should have let you..." I didn't finish.

"Are you thinking of ratting me out? The least you can do is tell me before you do."

My gaze snapped in her direction. "You know me better than that. I'm not a fucking rat. I'd never do that to you and I'd never do that to Rosslyn. She can never find out what happened that night."

"Oh, screw the bitch, Sebastian. *I'm* the one you should be loyal to. Me, not her."

"I said, I wasn't going to tell her. I can't lose her, and if she finds out, she'll leave me. I need her, Vick. She's *it* for me."

Vick's face crumbled and she fell back a step. "But I thought..."

Even through my drunken haze, I didn't miss the total devastation on her face. I'd suspected Vick's feelings for me a couple of weeks ago, but tonight confirmed it. It was like a punch in the gut. She was in love with me.

How could I have not seen it all these years? She was like a sister to me, so it never occurred to me her feelings ran deeper than mine. She watched me screw anyone and everyone, and never batted an eyelash. But with Rosslyn things were different, and now all of Vick's issues over the past few weeks made sense.

"Vick..." I raised my hands in the air feeling helpless. How was I supposed to tell her I didn't feel the same for her?

Tears fell down her cheeks and she swiped at them angrily and then wrapped her arms around her middle. I hadn't seen this side of her in a very long time, and I was reminded of the girl she used to be. She was vulnerable and I was watching it in slow motion as I was breaking her heart.

As much as things had changed between me and Vick in the past weeks, a part of me clung to the old her. I couldn't just turn away from her pain. Holding my arms out toward her, I waited, hoping she'd accept my comfort.

Within a second, she was across the room and throwing her arms around my waist.

Her tears soaked the front of my suit, but I didn't care. She needed comfort. Guilt thickened in my gut as I realized things were going to be different from that point on. The moment felt like it was marking the end of our friendship.

"I love you, Sebastian. I've been with you since the beginning. No one else."

"Shhh," I whispered, smoothing the side of her head.

"She'll never be good enough for you. She'll never know you like I do. I accept you for who you are and what you've done. Would she say the same if she found out about your, our, past?"

"Vick..." I started to explain to her, but she cut me off.

"Tell me you don't love me, Sebastian. Tell me you've never loved me." She begged, looking up at me with tear-filled eyes.

"I'm sorry, but I don't feel the same way. You've always been like a sister to me."

"That's not true." She shook her head furiously. "Kiss me."

Before I could stop her, her fingers were gripping my jacket and she was pulling me forward. She caught me by surprise and was able to press her lips against mine.

Desperation was a bitter taste. I felt her tongue move along my lips and I wrapped my fingers around her elbows roughly, and tried to pull her from me.

"I love it when you're rough," she growled. "I know how you like to fuck. Fuck me, Sebastian. Fuck me hard." She bit my lip, freeing her arms and started attacking the buttons on her shirt.

"Stop it, Vick." I pushed her away and she fell back a few steps.

She blinked at me and then glared. "She's going to break your heart. She's not like us. She'll never be like us. You and I are the same. We don't get happily ever after."

"Maybe I won't get a happy ending, but even after all the shit I've done, you and I are nothing alike."

She smirked, fixed her shirt, and turned around. Without another word, she left the room, slamming my door behind her. If I had been smart, I would have followed her to make sure she left the club, but I wasn't smart.

"What is this, Sebastian? Tell me what it is." Roz screamed at me.

Tears ran down her cheeks, taking pieces of my heart with them.

The inevitable had happened and now I was going to lose everything I loved.

"Rosslyn, sweetheart. I can explain. Just let me ex—"

"Don't you *dare* call me sweetheart. Tell me what it is. I just want to hear you say the words. I need to know this is real."

"Rosslyn, please..."

"Stop! Just say the words."

She was breaking in front of me—crackling from the inside out, and there was nothing I could do to stop it. Taking a deep cleansing breath, I closed my eyes and prepared for the end of everything.

"It's your mother's locket."

The words cut into my throat like large shards of glass. I could practically taste the blood in the back of my mouth.

"And how did you get it?"

Her shoulders were stiff and the hand holding out the locket was shaking so bad I thought she might drop it.

"Please, baby. Let me explain."

I just needed her to listen for just a few minutes. I wanted her to know the truth. She needed to know that while I was there, I didn't pull the trigger. I didn't technically kill her parents.

"Don't call me baby! I'm not your fucking *baby!*"

I flinched at her words.

"It was you. You were the boy leaning over my mother, weren't you?"

She wasn't asking the right questions. I needed her to ask me if I'd killed them.

"Yes, it was me," tears came unbidden to my eyes. "But I *swear*, Rosslyn. I swear I didn't kill your parents."

"Then who did?"

The name sat on the tip of my tongue waiting to lunge into the air around me, and instead of holding it back like I always had, I let it jump.

"Vick."

She ran her hands down her face, before tugging at her hair. "I can't..." She closed her eyes and shook her head. "This isn't happening."

"I was there, Rosslyn, but I didn't kill them. I need you to hear me, I need to know that you understand."

"Do you think it makes it better that you were just *there*, Sebastian? You *never* should have been in my house. You may not have pulled the trigger, but you took away everything with just your presence."

"Ross—" I took a step closer to her, but she jerked away.

"Don't. Don't you dare. You don't get to touch me. I don't want to look at you, you make me sick."

"I'm sorry, I should've told you."

"Wait..." she lifted her accusing gaze, really looking at me for the first time. "How long have you known about me? From the beginning, Sebastian? Is that why you did all this? Was this some sick fucking game to you?"

"No. I didn't find out until—"

"The password," she interrupted. "That's why you flipped out when I told you it was my last name."

"I swear I was going to leave you alone. I was. But I loved you, Rosslyn. I still love you. I *need* you." Tears fell down my cheeks, for the first time since I was a little boy.

"You've been fucking me this whole time... knowing who killed my parents?"

I wanted to tell her so many things, but nothing I could say was going to make it okay. I knew I was going to lose her and as I watched her stare back at me with hate-filled eyes, I understood she was no longer mine. I had no right to try and dissuade her from leaving me.

"I need to get out of here. I need to get away from you."

And then she started to walk past, to leave the room. Panic ripped through me. Not because I was afraid she was going to the police, but because I knew once she left, I'd never see her again.

Reaching out, I pulled her to me when she came near, and she lashed out. Slapping at my face and chest, she screamed. I held her close to protect herself and me.

"Please don't do this. I just found you. I can't lose you now." The lump in my chest moved into my throat and threatened to choke me.

"I was never yours, Sebastian. The minute you stepped into my house twelve years ago, I've wanted you dead."

"Don't say that. You love me, Rosslyn. I know you do."

She wasn't hearing me as she continued to shake free of me. Finally, with a burst of strength I didn't know she had, she kicked at my foot and shin, before pushing me away with a growl.

I slammed into the wall, and lost my footing. She ran. I was just getting into the living space as she slung open the front door and dashed down the stairs. I chased her, taking the stairs as quickly as I could, but once she hit the floor full of dancers, she disappeared into the crowd.

I searched for her like a crazed man. Pushing through dancers and knocking over drinks. People looked at me like I was nuts, and maybe I was. I darted toward the door, sure I'd cut her off, but she was nowhere to be found.

Leaving the club, I stood on the wet asphalt and let me eyes take in the area. The love of my life was out there somewhere, alone on the streets. If something happened to her, I'd never forgive myself.

Turning, I ran back upstairs to my apartment to get my keys. She'd have to either go home or find a place to stay. I'd find her and make sure she was safe. No matter where she was, I'd find her and make this better.

TWENTY-EIGHT

ROSSLYN

"**A**RE YOU SURE IT'S OKAY if I stay here a while?" I asked, blowing my nose in a tissue that was starting to fall apart. "I don't want to be a bother."

"Girl, please. You're welcome to stay here," Trish said, handing me a new tissue. "I just really wish you'd tell me what the hell is going on."

She seemed genuinely concerned, but I wasn't ready to talk. Not to mention, I still didn't know what to do. I didn't know if I should call the police, or what. I just needed a place to hide out until I got my head on straight.

I had a week before Kyle came home, and there was no way in the world I was going back to that condo. I wasn't going to let the man who killed my parents take care of me.

"I can't," I said through my tears. "I wish I could, but I just can't."

She reached out and smoothed the hair on the side of my head. "When you're ready to talk, I'm here."

Trish attempted to call off the date she'd been talking about for the last two weeks, but I refused to let her do that. I was an emotional mess and I wanted to spend the

254   TABATHA & MELISSA

night alone. I was more than happy to watch Trish walk out the door an hour later.

I laid on the couch and cried for most of the night. At some point, I fell into a fitful sleep. Memories of the night I'd kept under lock and key were released and I had no choice but to relive it all over again. Except my nightmare was different this time. This time I was the victim.

The sound of gunshots rang out and Kyle's screams broke my heart all over again. And then there was the intruder's face—Sebastian's icy eyes cut through me, leaving me feeling cold and afraid.

He turned away from my mother's lifeless body and made his way toward me.

"You're next you little bitch," he growled in my face.

His fingers dug into my arms, pinning me to the door of my parents' room, and then he leaned in and kissed me.

I was tossing on the couch, when I heard a strange noise. My eyes opened, my senses on alert, and I sat up in the darkness of the room. I gasped when a shadow shifted against the wall across from me.

When the face was no longer shielded by the obscurities of the night, I wasn't flooded with any sort of relief. She stood across from me, a gun in her hand, and there was no tremble as she took a step forward and pointed it at me.

"What are you doing here, Vick?" I asked, standing from the couch and praying my knees held me up.

"Don't play stupid, Rosslyn, you know why I'm here," she hissed.

The moonlight peeking through the curtains reflected against the metal in her grasp, and I watched her eyes shift toward the gun briefly before turning hate-filled eyes on me.

"Ironic, isn't it?" she asked.

"What?" I tried to keep the shudder from my voice.

"That I'm going kill you with the gun I killed your parents with. I know you don't want to hear this," she shrugged, "but it was a fucking rush like no other."

My stomach lurched, but I didn't give her the satisfaction of reacting to her words.

"You're lying. That gun's in Sebastian's safe."

She scoffed, "I took it, you little twit. After you ran out and Sebastian followed, it wasn't hard to grab."

"Why are you doing this?"

"Because you're a bitch who took something that didn't belong to you. Sebastian's mine—always has been. I should've been the one he fell in love with. We're the same, him and I."

"You're wrong," I said calmly. "He's not a killer."

"Even after everything he told you, you're still in love with him, aren't you?"

I knew answering her was only going to piss her off even more, but if I was going to die, I needed to say it out loud.

"Yes. I still love him."

I closed my eyes and envisioned Sebastian's face—his smile. He was such a loving person—broken, but loving. I suddenly had a clear head, which was weird, considering there was a gun pointed at me.

The clarity of the situation hit me. Seeing how sick and twisted Vick really was, there was no way Sebastian was anything like her. Sure, he had no business being in my house the night of my parent's murder, but Sebastian could never kill someone—he couldn't.

"You forgive him?"

"I'm not so sure there's anything to forgive. He didn't pull the trigger, *you* did. He was just in the wrong place at the wrong time."

"You're a stupid bitch. I'll be doing the world a favor by taking you out," she said, leveling the gun at my face.

My heart was beating so hard, it was beginning to hurt. "If being in love means being stupid, then yeah, I guess I'm a stupid bitch."

"Well, the world's about to be one stupid bitch short. He's mine, and I don't share."

"I'm not going to tell anyone, Vick."

"And I should believe you, why?"

"Because, if I was going to turn you in I would have gone straight to the police station after I left Sebastian."

"Maybe you won't tell, but I'm not taking any chances."

"Sebastian won't want you just because I'm dead. And when he finds out you're the one who..." I couldn't get the words past my lips.

"Killed you? Pulled the trigger? Ended your sorry life? Don't worry, Sebastian will realize I did this for him. I'm the one who stuck with him over the years. I watched from the side as he fucked everything with a pussy, but I never had to worry because Sebastian didn't fall in love. At least he didn't, until you."

"I'll leave." I grasped for straws. "I'll go far away from here and then you can have Sebastian all to yourself. He doesn't have to know and he won't be upset if I'm still alive."

She looked as if she was actually thinking about it, and for a moment, I felt some sort of hope.

"Nah, killing you sounds better. Sebastian won't just let you leave. He'll search until he finds you. I'm sorry, *Jessica*, but this is the only way."

"No, it's not, Victoria." Sebastian's voice sounded from beside us.

I nearly cried out in relief at the sound of his voice and Vick spun around, just as stunned as I was.

He stood tall in the doorway. The darkness of the night covering half of his face. He stepped into the room, making it feel smaller. I wanted to run to him. I wanted to hold him in my arms and tell him I forgave him. If I was going to die, he needed to know he could go on with my forgiveness.

"What are you doing here?" Vick hissed. "You just had to come to her rescue, didn't you?"

"I'm not going to let you kill her," Sebastian's deep voice brought me an ounce of relief.

"Well, since I'm the only one with a gun here, it looks like you're fucked out of a choice."

"Don't do this. Even if Rosslyn wasn't in the picture, you and I would've never happened. You were different after killing her parents and I never looked at you the same."

I listened to Sebastian try and talk Vick down, all the while trying to think of a plan. He wasn't going to be able to distract her forever. I reached back toward the table next to the couch, my fingers barely touching the edge of the bag I'd brought with me.

I breathed a silent sigh of relief when my fingers brushed against the cold metal tucked beneath my wallet.

Wrapping my fingers around it, I stood up and held the gun behind my back.

"After everything we've been through, I can't believe you're saying this to me," Vick sniffled. Raising the gun again, she began to silently cry. Except this time, the gun wasn't pointed at me, it was pointed at Sebastian.

"I guess this isn't going to end in anyone's favor because if I can't have you, than neither can she."

I froze, her words destroying my whole world. The dreaded sound of a gunshot filled the apartment, echoing off the walls and slamming into my chest.

"No!" I screamed.

Sebastian fell back against the wall. His eyes locked on mine in anguish, as he began to slide down to the floor. His body went limp when he fell to the carpet and his eyes closed.

Vick turned toward me, black mascara-filled tears streaming down her face. She raised her gun at me again. "You did this, you bitch. You made me kill him."

My grip tightened around the gun in my hand as my thumb went over the safety, unlocking it. "You were wrong about one thing, Vick. You're not the only one..."

Her eyes filled with confusion and then panic when I pulled the gun from behind my back and shot once.

Vick's eyes went blank as she blinked and stumbled backwards. She looked down and touched her chest, blood tainting the tips of her fingers. She fell to the floor with a heavy thud and the gun fell from her hand sliding on the floor.

I moved across the room toward Sebastian, and fell to my knees next to his still frame. Snatching my cell from my pocket, I dialed 9-1-1 and screamed into the phone that I needed help.

I didn't listen to the dispatcher, instead, I pulled Sebastian's head into my lap and pressed my cheek to his.

"Sebastian," I sobbed, shaking him. "Don't you dare die. You can't leave me, you can't. We just found each other, remember? Please, I just found you," I cried into his neck.

He didn't move. I held him close and waited until I heard the sirens from afar. I remained there, holding him in my arms, begging him not to leave, while the cops burst through the door.

Everything happened in a blur and I felt like I was no longer a part of my body as I watched them cover Vick's body. When they finally got me to let go of Sebastian, I was pulled over to the couch and questioned. I nodded my answers and cried.

"So then she pulled the gun on you?" the officer asked. "Can you tell me what happened then?"

I was talking, but it didn't sound like me. I explained to them everything that happened, and how Vick had been the one who killed my parents twelve years before. I didn't tell them about Sebastian, I didn't want his name linked to their murder. He was there, but I knew in my heart that he was just as much a victim as they were.

I was outside, standing on the sidewalk, when they brought Vick's lifeless body down and wheeled her past me. I wrapped my arms tightly around myself and cried when Sebastian's followed.

"I want to ride with him." I told the paramedic as they put Sebastian in the ambulance.

The paramedic looked at me funny, but nodded and helped me into the back. Another paramedic got in behind me and closed the doors.

I didn't know if they were scared of my catatonic like state or what, but they didn't protest when I crawled onto the gurney with Sebastian and wrapped my arms around him. He was still warm, and his pulse was slow, but at least it was still there.

EPILOGUE

ROSSLYN

"Some people come into our lives and quickly go. Some stay for a while, leave footprints on our hearts, and we are never, ever the same."
—*FLAVIA WEEDN*

I STOOD THERE STARING DOWN at the flawlessly chiseled headstone. I hadn't been to the grave since the day we put the coffin in the ground. I hadn't been brave enough and the guilt only made it worse. Guilt for loving the man who'd altered my life so completely in so many ways.

I'd like to think my parents would have forgiven Sebastian, too. He was so young the night they were murdered—only seventeen. And although he'd broken into our house, he never expected for anyone to get killed. Vick was the killer, and now she was dead, too.

Kneeling down, I placed a white rose on the grave and ran my fingers over the rough engraving.

"Roz?" Kyle whispered, coming to stand beside me. He gave me a small smile and then wrapped his arm around my shoulders.

I wiped at the single tear that slid down my cheek. "Hey, kiddo,"

"Are you okay?"

"Yeah. Just sad."

I hadn't told Kyle about Sebastian's role in our parent's murder. I didn't know if he'd understand why I'd forgiven so easily. All he knew was the person responsible for our parent's death was finally found and closure was ours.

"I think it's okay to be sad, as long as you know it's okay to be happy, too."

I smiled up at him. "When did you become so smart, kid?"

"I had some help from my big sister."

"Hey, what about me?"

Kyle pretended to be annoyed as a big hand ruffled his hair, before pulling him into a playful head lock.

"Sebastian," he groaned. "You messed up my hair."

Sebastian's deep laugh was like a soft caress as it wrapped around me. Moving my arm under his, I wrapped it around his waist and pulled him close. He gave me a gentle squeeze and we moved back to give Kyle a little privacy with our parents.

I watched as he put a white rose down next to mine and then whispered something, before getting up and putting his hands in his pockets. There were no tears as he looked up at me, but his eyes glistened.

"I'm going to go wait with Mr. Martin," Kyle said and then ran toward the car.

"Are you okay?" Sebastian asked into my hair, planting a soft kiss in the strands.

"It's always hard visiting them, but I needed to do this for Kyle."

"You both needed this."

"Thank you for coming," I said, looking up at him.

"I owe you this, Rosslyn." He was silent for a second. "I've been here before."

I pulled back. "You have? When?"

"About a year after it happened. I needed to apologize for taking them away from you and Kyle. I visited them once a week, until Vick found out and freaked."

I didn't want to talk about Vick, or anything to do with her, so I didn't respond. We were together. We were both alive. That's all that mattered.

Sebastian pulled away and took a step forward, kneeling so he could place his rose next to Kyle's and mine.

"I'm so sorry, Mr. and Mrs. Harris. I plan to take care of Rosslyn and Kyle for the rest of my life."

His declaration brought tears to my eyes. I took his hand as he stood and held it out to me. Pulling me into his arms, I laid my head against his chest, feeling soothed by the sound of his heartbeat.

I moved my fingers along the buttons of his shirt, until I found bare skin, and then the scar of his bullet wound. I squeezed my eyes shut and tried to forget what it felt like to almost lose him, focusing on the fact he was still here with me.

"We're going to be late," he whispered.

I nodded, letting him pull me toward Mr. Martin and Kyle.

"JONATHON HALE," THE DEAN CALLED over the microphone.

The closer he got to the name Harris, the more nervous I became.

Looking up into the stands, I smiled at Sebastian, Kyle and Trish—flashing our secret wave. I'd done it. I'd gone to school and I'd finished the first two years at tech. After that, I'd be moving onto Cornell University for my master's degree.

"Rosslyn Harris."

I moved toward the stage. When I took my diploma and shook hands with the dean, I could hear Sebastian's cheer above the applause.

After the ceremony, the crowd was clearing out and we made our way to the car.

"I'm so proud of you, Roz." Kyle threw his arm around my shoulder.

His was taller than me now, had been for the last year. He was turning out to be such a good kid, and did well in school. Not to mention his art, which was already being sold in a few select galleries New York City. Kyle was amazing—strong for such a young age, and I couldn't help but feel pride over playing a major part in raising him.

"Yes. We need to celebrate," Sebastian said.

"I don't know. I kind of just want to go home, pop some popcorn, and watch a movie," I replied.

We all walked to the car in conversation, and when I started to get in, Sebastian pulled me to the side.

I tugged at my black dress and smiled up at him. His eyes devoured me and memories of all the times he'd loved me came rushing back.

"You look beautiful," he said, running a single finger down my bare arm.

"Thank you."

"I'm so proud of you, Rosslyn," he grinned.

"Well, thank you, sir. It makes me happy to please you," I said, as I playfully flirted.

"Is that so?" he flirted back.

"Yes."

"So you'd do *anything* to make me happy then?"

I loved how frisky he was being. It was never boring with Sebastian. He kept me on my toes and made each day an adventure.

"Absolutely."

"Then in that case, I have a new proposal for you." His smile was so big, his adorable dimples were making an appearance.

I couldn't help myself, I giggled. "Oh really? What kind of proposal?

He moved in, his unique scent swarming all around me. Pulling me closer, he cupped my face with his hands and stared into my eyes. "My name's Sebastian Black, and I'd like to spend the rest of my life with you..."

THE FUCKING END...

KEEP READING FOR MORE FROM TABATHA AND MELISSA!

THE Wrath OF SIN

A mortal sin NOVEL

I CAN'T DECIDE WHAT I want to do more...*kill her or fuck her.*

Wrath is everywhere, even in the deepest recesses of the innocent. It alters the souls of the desperate and depressed. Changing you, consuming you until all that's left is the sick desire to destroy everything in your path.

SIN

I'm not a murderer, but hate will make you do crazy things. I hate the man who stole my life from me, and it's only fair that I steal something precious from him. But revenge is bittersweet when passion overpowers your reason, and the girl that's precious to him becomes the voice of reason for me. Pushing me to feel human again, she threatens to change everything.

She calls me Sin, and she will feel my WRATH.

EMILY

Excitement, passion, desire – those were all foreign to me. I needed something more in my life, but when I meet him, I get more than I bargained for. I'm sickened with desire for my keeper. He's a mystery, an enigma, but he's hurting. I want to be the one to save him, but I have to save myself first.

I call him Sin, and he's the epitome of LUST.

Prologue

THE SOFT SCENT OF HER swarmed around me. It had been so long since I'd been that close to a woman—like really close, not just physically speaking. It was a reminder of all the things I'd missed over the last six years.

She pressed against me and I could feel the contour of her soft breasts through her thin silk top. I pulled her closer to me and latched my arms behind her back. Her thick, russet hair stuck to my sweat-covered cheeks and instinctively I breathed in the brief hint of her strawberry shampoo. She smelled amazing, and she felt even better pressed tightly to the front of my body.

Parts of me that I hadn't used in years sprang to life and made me forget all about the reason I was there with her in the first place. Again, she moved and I pulled her closer to me. I wasn't going to let her go. I was finally going to get what I wanted.

Her sharp teeth cut into my bicep and I hissed loudly at the sting of her teeth puncturing my skin. I tugged on her ponytail and she released my flesh. Bringing her face to face with me, I smiled down at her. She was as good as mine. There was no escaping me.

"What are you going to do?" she asked.

Her voice was thick and husky—that of a passionate woman in the midst of release.

I brought my nose to her neck and breathed her in once more. It was going to be a long while before I was this close to a woman again. Her femininity moved me beyond distraction, but I had to stay the course.

Looking down into her fevered eyes, I took a deep breath.

"What do you think I'm going to do? A life for a life— it's only fair. She was taken from me, now I'm taking you from him."

ACKNOWLEDGEMENTS

FROM TABATHA & MELISSA

To Cover It Designs, thank you for knocking this cover out of the park. It was a joy working with you again and we look forward to working with you again in the future.

Victoria Schmitz, our sweet and wonderful editor, you're the most patient person alive. No seriously, we want to be you when we grow up. Had we been you, we would have climbed through the computer and knocked us the hell out, but you didn't. You sent smiley faces, even when I knew you were cussing me. Thank you for picking through Little Black Book and finding the gold that lies beneath. You rock, chick!

Thank you to Holly Malgeri, Cheree Crump, Annie Gabor, Sarah Davey, and Jennifer Wedmore for giving Sebastian a beta spin. You girls are speed reading divas and we freaking adore you.

FROM TABATHA VARGO

THANK YOU! THANK YOU! Yes, you! If you're reading this, then you're awesome. No, you're freaking amazing. I have the most incredible readers. You guys pick up my books, you read them, and you love them, and that to me is just the most wonderful feeling ever. So to you, the reader, you kick way more ass than I could ever dream of kicking. Thank you from the depths of my heart and beyond.

Secondly, thank you to the amazing Melissa Andrea for becoming a part of my work and helping me make it all it can be. You've been there for me like no other and I no longer look at you as a co-worker, but as a best friend and a sister. I can't wait to spend an amazing summer with you and your family.

I want to thank my husband Matthew. He has taught me everything I know about love and romance. He's my biggest supporter and always has been. Thank you, baby. I love you.

Melissa Burek, we've known each other for years, but just this past year we've gotten super close. Thank you for coming into my crazy author world and loving it as much as I do. I appreciate you having my back in this. You're amazing and I thank you.

To best freaking street team on the planet, you girls are die hard. I love each of your faces and I'm so thankful to have such kick ass chicks on my side. Thank you for every share, idea, comment… just thank you for everything. The support you give me blows my mind and I'm so thankful for each and every one of you. If I could, I'd give you all great big squeezing hugs.

To every blogger/page administrator who has posted or shared anything for me since I've started publishing, thank you. I can't stress enough how much you guys mean to me. You guys supported me from day one and that's more valuable to me than gold. I send you all bear hugs and love.

To all my friends and family who have been supportive of my writing throughout the years. Thank you. I love you.

And finally to my daughter, Ashlynn, who's my inspiration for everything I do. You're my life. I love you more than love, baby girl. LOVE. LOVE.

STALK TABATHA VARGO:

www.tabathavargo.blogspot.com
www.facebook.com/tabathadvargo
www.twitter.com/tabathavargo
Represented by Jane Dystel of Dystel & Goderich Literary Management

FROM MELISSA ANDREA

I couldn't start this without saying how much I love and appreciate all of you amazing readers!! You may think authors are the stars, but we only shine because of you!! Thank you for giving me your time, praise, and love. I cherish all of those things as much as I cherish you!!

I am so in love with this book and I'm so beyond please to help Tabatha with Little Black Book. We make an amazing power team and I am happy to call her my bestie, my twin, my go-to-girl!! You are my other half in this crazy, crazy world, and I am so happy we got to do this again, sweets!! Love you lots.

A big shout out to my hubs for making sure life goes on even if I'm not always there to take part in it. For making sure I eat when I've been glued to my computer all day. For making sure we don't live like cave people, and for doing all of that on top of having a full-time job. Nobody is perfect, but you're perfect for me!

As always, to my girls, you're the gravity that keeps me here. You're the reason I breathe and live and have the courage to do what I want in life. I hope you realize dreams can come true and because of you beautiful ladies, I know that too. Never grow up, babies!!

And last, but never least, to my family for always being there to support me and cheer me on. Thank you for being proud of me, Mom, but you should be proud of yourself because I'm this amazing because of you!! Ha-ha, but no, really! LOVE YOU!!

STALK MELISSA ANDREA:

www.facebook.com/m.andrea.author
www.melissaandrea.com